FLIPPING

BOXCARS

A Novel

AMISTAD
An Imprint of HarperCollinsPublishers

CEDRIC KYLES

FLIPPING BOXCARS

with ALAN EISENSTOCK

FLIPPING BOXCARS. Copyright © 2023 by Cedric Antonio Kyles. All rights reserved. Printed in the United States of America. No part of this book may be used or reproduced in any manner whatsoever without written permission except in the case of brief quotations embodied in critical articles and reviews. For information, address HarperCollins Publishers, 195 Broadway, New York, NY 10007.

HarperCollins books may be purchased for educational, business, or sales promotional use. For information, please email the Special Markets Department at SPsales@harpercollins.com.

FIRST EDITION

Designed by Janet Evans-Scanlon
Photograph on p. 320 of Floyd "Babe" Boyce courtesy of the author.

Library of Congress Cataloging-in-Publication Data is available upon request.

ISBN 978-0-06-325899-0

23 24 25 26 27 LBC 5 4 3 2 1

FLIPPING BOXCARS

SQUARE PAIR

◆

TWO FOURS, ALSO CALLED "HARD EIGHT"

SATURDAY, JULY 3, 1948
11:58 P.M.

Babe Boyce couldn't lose.

Bet after bet went his way. Pass line bets, backup bets, come bets, the field, the hard ways—the ten, four, six, and especially the hard eight—they all came in. Babe stacked his growing piles of chips in front of him, so many chips that the croupier, whom Babe called Stick Man, handed him his own tray. And when Babe filled that up with his winnings, the chips spilling onto the felt like a small black river, Stick Man handed him a second tray, and Babe started slamming chips into that one, too.

The dice came to Babe again.

"Let's do the hard eight one more time! Two fours. Square pair. Eight. Eight's my lucky number. August eight. My birthday. And the day I got engaged. Eight, eight. Come on, eight!"

He tossed the dice and—

"Eight again! And he made it the hard way," Stick Man shouted. The crowd around the table roared. Babe ducked his head, gave the room a *What can you do?* shrug, and allowed a grin to snake across his face as Stick Man slid thirty more black chips—worth a hundred dollars apiece—across the felt toward Babe. Babe snatched them away as fast as a magic trick and slid them into his tray with a clack.

"Guess tonight's my night," Babe said.

A cheer went up.

At midnight, the bell from the church at the end of Main Street clanged twelve mournful times, like a dirge, and Babe felt the energy in the casino shift. He actually saw it coming first, a shadow creeping across the craps table like a dark mist, hanging there for a moment as the entire room went dark.

Then the new day started—July Fourth—and Babe couldn't win.

PRESS IT UP

◆

RAISE THE BET

1

THURSDAY, JULY 1, 1948

Karter set up the meet.

Midnight. Outside of town. Two miles down a dirt road.

Karter drove Babe's silver 1948 Studebaker Commander, new that year. Karter poked through the intersection, stopped the car, left the lights on, and kept the engine running. The big man with the glimmering gold grille and the ever-present wooden matchstick tucked into the side of his mouth, red tip out, adjusted himself behind the wheel. He grunted.

"What are you doing?" Babe said.

"Trying to get comfortable."

"You're never comfortable."

"I was once. I had to be. Because I remember the feeling."

"When? Wasn't in the army."

"Hell no."

"Oh, now I remember. When you were inside your mama's womb."

"Probably was that long ago. Babe, seriously, I've been meaning to talk to you. I'm moving back to Chicago. I can't take this town. It's too small. Too peaceful. Too quiet. It's so quiet I can't sleep at night."

"You've been saying this for years."

"Haven't slept in years."

Karter lifted his butt, smoothed his pants, shook his shoulders.

"This *suit*," he said.

"You need a dresser. You need me to come with you to buy your clothes."

Karter wriggled at the waist. "Damn thing's too tight."

"It's like a cheap hotel. No ballroom."

Karter grunted again and loosened a notch on his belt. The big man exhaled loudly, dramatically, as if he'd just finished running a hundred-yard dash.

"Woo," Karter said.

"You got your gun?"

Karter rolled his eyes.

"Good," Babe said.

"Got two," Karter said.

"Should be sufficient."

"He's late," Karter said.

"We're early."

Then, abruptly, a car approached, coming at them, the snowy light from its headlamps washing over them. A Cadillac. Moving quickly at first, then slowing to a crawl. The Caddy stopped just short of the intersection, and the two cars faced each other like two steel bulls about to charge. The Cadillac's doors swung open and three figures began walking toward Babe and Karter, their footsteps crunching on the dirt road.

"Let's go," Karter said, starting to exit the car.

Babe placed his hand on Karter's massive forearm.

"Me first."

Babe opened his door, ducked into a blind spot, and caressed Honey, his gun, inherited from his father, who fought in World War I. It was a single-action, semiautomatic Colt 1911 with a lacquered honey-colored handle he polished religiously. He eased Honey from the holster inside his breast pocket and stepped forward, barely out of the frosty haze of the Cadillac's headlights. He kept the gun hidden, behind the sway of his suit jacket. He walked toward the three men, then moved aside into another dark spot on the road.

"Mr. Wojak," he said.

"That's me," the man in the middle said.

The two men flanking Wojak kept coming.

"That's far enough," Babe said.

Wojak nodded and the two men halted.

"Mr. Boyce," Wojak said. "Your reputation precedes you."

"*Merci*," Babe said.

"Step out where I can see you."

"I'm good here. And please, call me Babe. All my friends do."

"All right, Babe. And please call me Tommy."

"*Tomas*," Babe said. "In Polish."

"I go by Tommy," Wojak said.

Tommy Wojak.

A new name to Babe. But the name didn't matter. Wojak repped the Polish arm of The Outfit crime syndicate in Chicago. The Poles were run by the shadowy Hymie Weiss, whose second-in-command, Jake Guzik, was the public face of the organization. Babe tilted his head and took a long look at this guy, this Tommy Wojak, this up-and-comer, assessing him. Babe knew how to read cards, dice, and especially people. Babe saw *gravity* in Wojak. Presence. Something about Tommy Wojak's posture in the moonlight told Babe that Tommy was a person to take seriously.

"My contact in Chicago informs me that I'll be dealing with you from now on," Babe said.

"Is that a problem?"

"Not at all. I'm curious. What happened to Stanley?"

"He took another position," Wojak said.

Babe nearly laughed.

Another position. Yeah. A position in the ground. Put there, no doubt, by Wojak.

"No problem at all," Babe said. "My contact also told me that you have a special shipment arriving by train this weekend."

"July fifth," Wojak said. "Pick up at the old train station in Cuba, Missouri. Midnight. A boxcar full. Thirty pallets. Three thousand cases. If you want it."

"That's a big haul," Babe said. "More brown liquor than I've ever moved at one time, by a lot."

"Could be a new opportunity. A windfall. Of course, if you don't want it, I understand. I'll find a new partner. Somebody closer to the Windy City. Less of an inconvenience. I'll tell Hymie you passed. But, hey, we had a good run."

What balls, Babe thought. *Tommy Wojak's threatening me. Right here, on my home turf. Calling my hand.*

"Gotta tell you, this is primo stuff," Wojak said. "Top of the line."

A threat disguised as an invitation. Take it or leave it. Or else.

"The only stuff worth drinking," Babe said. "Or selling."

Wojak grinned, flashing teeth white as piano keys. "Liquid gold."

"I heard that," Babe said. "So, for clarification, Monday night, you got your man on the train, escorting those cases up from Kentucky. Which distillery?"

Trick question. Babe tossed it off as casually as flicking lint from his lapel.

"Fucking guy. You're testing me, right?"

Even in the dark you could slice Wojak's annoyance with a cleaver.

"Nobody's distilling good brown whiskey out of Kentucky since the war. You know that. We're coming out of Canada."

"That's preferable right now. Though things are changing."

"Let's cut the bullshit. You want this shipment or not?"

Babe paused for effect, pretending to consider the proposition.

"I'll have to consult with my business manager. He's in the car."

The Commander's door swung open. Karter unfolded himself from behind the steering wheel and, with surprising speed and athleticism, stepped out of the car. At his first step, the entire road seemed to tremor and sag. Karter kept his guns hidden as he walked toward the three men. Karter stopped suddenly, standing military straight, announcing himself without a word, all six feet ten inches and three hundred fifty pounds of him.

Wojak and his two bodyguards froze at the sight of him.

"This is your business manager?" Wojak said.

"You heard of J. P. Morgan?"

"Yeah."

"This is F. U. Morgan."

Karter stared straight at Wojak and his men, training his eyes on them like high beams. He had already devised his plan. He would take out Wojak and the one to his right. Babe, whose hand dangled at his side, his fingers sliding down the crease in his pants next to his gun, would take out the one on Wojak's left. If this went bad.

"I'll take half the shipment," Babe said.

Wojak seemed to relax. He snapped his starched white cuffs an extra inch through the arms of his suit jacket.

"Half," Wojak said. "Yeah. I can't do that."

"I'm offering to take fifteen hundred cases."

"You have to take all of it. The whole lot."

"All three thousand cases."

A statement. Not a question.

In that mere second, that blip of time, Babe looked into his future. He saw the farmland Rosie had purchased, and he saw his four kids running free, no longer confined inside the tiny alley house off Main Street. He saw the new house he would build. A porch in front. An open kitchen stocked with every food type imaginable. A living room with floor-to-ceiling bookcases filled with books. Three bedrooms for the kids, not one for all of them, a master bedroom for him and Rosie. Bathrooms *inside*.

And he envisioned the culmination of his dream—not a mile away from his dream house, a sagging, crumpling, currently dilapidated mansion in disrepair that he would buy, retain the bones and the style, and remodel into his own entertainment complex, his own Sportsman Hall, with restaurants and a bar, all legit—a Black-owned business catering to the folks on his side of town. His business. All his. A brand-new beginning at forty. He would start over as his own man. All he needed was money, enough money to buy the mansion, finance the remodel, and pay off the politicians for the permits.

"I presume you'll take those thirty-six thousand bottles on consignment," Babe said, allowing his grin to twist across his face.

Wojak laughed, a sudden high-pitched keen that caused Karter to wrap his fingers around the handle of his gun. After a hesitation, Wojak's bodyguards laughed with him. Babe joined in. Karter kept stock-still except for sliding the matchstick to the other side of his mouth.

Then Wojak went savagely serious. He sniffed and studied his glossy gold cufflinks. "Consignment. Good one, Babe. Funny. Yeah. No. Cash only. For the *lot*."

Now came the fun part. The deal making. The gambling.

"We've been doing business a long time, Tommy—"

"We just met," Tommy said.

"I meant with The Outfit."

"I know what you meant."

"What's my cost?"

"Per case?"

"Per bottle."

"I can tell you have a price in mind."

"I'll just quote the old price," Babe said. "Fifty cents a bottle."

Silence. For the first time, Babe felt the humidity of the night pouring through him. Wojak took this moment to size up Karter. The big man felt Wojak's eyes on him and, in response, took a long stride forward. He wanted Wojak and his two men to get a true appreciation of his size, his power, his menace. Babe and Karter were outnumbered two to one, but it didn't feel that way to anybody on that road.

"That price disappeared with the old guy," Wojak said. "The new price—the going rate—is three dollars a bottle."

Babe stared right through Wojak.

"Well, Mr. Wojak—To*mas*—unfortunately, it appears that you came all the way from Chicago for nothing."

Babe nodded at Karter and slowly began backing up toward the car. Right before he reached the passenger door, Wojak called, "I can do two fifty."

"Seventy-five cents," Babe said.

"You're not dealing, you're stealing. Highway robbery."

"I'm taking the whole lot. I deserve my good-customer discount."

"Two dollars. My final offer. Or we do go back to Chicago."

"I might be able to do a dollar a bottle."

"A dollar fifty. And a guarantee we lock in that price for the next shipment."

"A dollar fifty," Babe said. "And a guarantee you lock in the price for the next two years."

"You got balls," Wojak said.

"A dollar fifty," Babe repeated as he did the math in his head—a dollar fifty times twelve bottles in a case came to eighteen dollars a case, multiplied by three thousand cases—

"Fifty-four thousand dollars," Babe whispered.

"Deal," Wojak said.

Babe walked toward Wojak, his right hand extended, his left hand snaking inside his jacket, sneaking toward Pearl and Baby Girl, the twin barber's blades he kept there.

"Deal," Babe said. He shook Wojak's hand and then tipped the brim of his fedora.

"Midnight. Monday. Cuba," Wojak said. "Happy Fourth of July."

After Wojak and his men left, Babe and Karter sat in the Com-mander for a full minute without moving. Karter transferred the matchstick to the middle of his mouth and waited for Babe to speak. Babe appeared mesmerized by the dark night and said nothing.

Finally, Karter broke the ice.

"Raising fifty-four large in seventy-two hours. That shouldn't be a problem, right?"

"Nah. It's just a matter of moving some money around."

They both went quiet again, this time so long that the silence filled up the space like a third passenger in the car.

"Lot of ways to go," Babe said at last. "I'm just figuring my move."

"Yeah."

"Maybe I'll keep my investments intact. Maybe I'll squeeze my man in Cincinnati—he owes me. Or maybe I'll call in a few chips from St. Louis. Got a lot of moves, Karter."

"Always a step ahead."

"At least. You just be ready, Karter."

"Me? I was born at 'let's go,'" Karter said.

"Let's go," Babe said.

Karter parked the Commander at the corner of the alley, two or three tenements away from Babe's alley house. Karter exhaled, cursed again at his suit, and extricated himself from behind the wheel of the car. He stood outside and stretched. Babe slid over to the driver's seat. He smiled at Karter. For the briefest moment, he allowed a trace of concern to drop like a shadow over his face. He trusted Karter with his life. The trust went both ways.

"We've been in worse jams, K," Babe said.

"Not in America."

"I pressed my bet," Babe said.

Karter grunted.

"This is an opportunity," Babe said.

Convincing himself.

Karter patted the top of the Commander and watched Babe pull into a parking spot behind his house. Karter turned, rolled the matchstick off his tongue, dropped it into the gutter, and disappeared into the night.

Babe stepped inside his narrow, cramped alley house and paused in the front room. He didn't turn on the lights because he didn't want to wake anybody. He shrugged off his suit jacket, removed the holsters that housed his blades and his gun, and slipped off his shoes. He tiptoed forward and stepped on one of the kids' toys, a small metal fire engine. He swallowed a scream, gritted his teeth, and limped toward his bedroom. He stopped at the doorway. A sudden realization crept into his mind, invading his thoughts.

Forty years old. And I'm starting over?

Was that what this was about?

Or was it his time? More than half his life, lived. And now, finally, an opportunity. A chance he may never get again. Or a choice he had to make.

He peered up at the ceiling and said quietly, "Feels like I'm being squeezed."

"What?"

Rosie, his wife, rustled in the bedsheets and sat up.

"What do you mean, you feel like you're being squeezed?"

"Nothing. I think turning forty is getting to me."

"You feeling stressed?"

♠

"Nah. You know." Babe slowly rotated his head and began kneading his neck with his fingers. "Maybe a little bit."

"I know what you need. Come on."

Ten minutes later, Babe lay stretched out in their stand-alone, slipper-style porcelain bathtub that rested on stumpy, silver-plated feet resembling four silver hooves. The extravagant tub arrived one day, a gift from an appreciative state senator who was an avid Bordeaux drinker, enthusiastic womanizer, reckless craps player, and Babe's guest whenever he paid a visit to his constituents in Caruthersville. Now, nightly, or as often as he could, Babe submerged himself in near-scalding water up to his chin, his eyes pressed shut, the water stinging his skin, while Rosie sat on a footstool next to the tub and bathed him. Her hands folded inside a fluffy white washcloth, she leaned over Babe and slowly, sensually, lovingly worked her way up from his stomach, rising up his chest, arriving through a soapy wake at his right shoulder. Rosie dipped the washcloth into the water, rubbed a bar of lavender soap over it, and began massaging Babe's shoulder. She hummed softly, a blues ballad, then brushed the warm cotton cloth back and forth, back and forth, over her husband's arched and shrugging shoulder, occasionally applying the slightest pressure. Babe, lost in reverie, his mind half here, half somewhere else, moaned, his lips parting narrowly.

"That feel good?" Rosie asked.

"Um," Babe said.

Rosie leaned farther and ran the washcloth up and down Babe's neck, slowly, achingly slowly. "You want to talk about it?"

"Nothing to say. It's all good."

She wasn't buying this and he knew it. But to ease her concern, his eyes still shut, he went with small talk.

"Everybody's talking about the Fourth this year," he said. "Setting up the teams for the tug-o'-war, the relay races, the parade, wondering who's going to win Miss Caruthersville. You'd be a shoo-in based on your looks, but you'd be disqualified based on your husband and your four kids."

Rosie laughed and gently swatted Babe's head with the washcloth. She went back to massaging his shoulder. "My sister's entering the chili cook-off this year. She wants you to be her official taster."

"Her chili's like gasoline. Let her husband taste it."

"You know your brother-in-law. Montel has that queasy stomach."

"Leaky." Babe elongated the two syllables of his brother-in-law's nickname. "Always have to take care of *Leaky*."

"Oh, the kids are asking if you'll be entering the greased pole climbing contest."

Babe roared and opened his eyes. "They just want to see me make a fool of myself. Hey, maybe if I had some of your sister's chili first. Might rocket me up that pole."

"Now that would be funny."

"Pole climb is a hard no. Sonny Agnew has that locked up every year."

"Man's a legend," Rosie said.

"God gave everybody a talent."

"Climbing a greased pole. What a talent. I hope God blessed our kids with some other talent. Any other talent."

Babe raised himself up in the water and studied his wife. Light from a streetlamp splashed through the small window in the bathroom and roamed across her face. Babe peered into Rosie's green eyes and touched her almond-colored face.

"I know you pray," he said.

"I do."

"What do you pray for?"

Rosie folded her hands. "Health. For all of us."

"That it?"

"No."

"What else?"

Rosie faced Babe and stroked his cheek with the back of her long fingers. "I pray that soon we'll start building on our land. Settling in our own place. The land I bought for us. Saving my tip money, working extra hours as a midwife when called, socking away every dollar I could all those years. That land. That's what I pray for."

Babe nodded, their signal. Rosie stood and snatched a bath sheet hanging on a hook on the bathroom door. When she turned back, Babe had stepped out of the tub. She draped the big towel over him, wrapping him up, swathing him. She looped her arms around him from behind.

"That land," Rosie repeated. "That's what I want. I want what we have."

"You're right, Rosie," Babe said. "It's time."

Later, with Rosie sound asleep, Babe, fully dressed, made the rounds. He checked on his three sons—ten-year-old twins, Floyd and Lloyd, and his eight-year-old son, Melvin, who all slept in the same bed—and then he stood over his daughter, Rosetta, six, who slept on a mattress on the floor in the corner. He crouched next to her and watched her sleep. She snored softly, daintily, her mouth opened a crack, her arms clutching her favorite possession, a ragged teddy bear she called Blue. Babe had won Blue for Rosie at the Fourth of July carnival the year they'd met by shooting a toy popgun at a cardboard target of a cartoon outlaw. A varmint, the guy running the game called it. Babe hit the varmint in the center of his forehead, first shot. Now, watching Rosetta sleep, he felt riveted by his daughter's beauty, this six-year-old replica of her mother. Babe often identified aspects of her personality that also mirrored Rosie's—her whip-smart mind, her toughness, her ability to get her way with nothing more than a cute look, a pout, an eyeroll, a falling tear, all calculated. His daughter would be a force. Babe knew that already.

Back in the living room, guided by the flame from his cigarette lighter, Babe picked up the telephone and dialed a number. He waited. After hearing three rings, he hung up. He reached inside his suit jacket and pulled out his flask. He absently rubbed his thumb over the bullet hole in the center, then unscrewed the top, sighed, and took a swig. The Macallan single malt scotch, strong and rich, shocked his throat, then warmed him. He nodded, satisfied, screwed the cap back on, and returned the flask to his pocket. In the dark of his tiny front room, he shook his head and bit his bottom lip. He almost never drank, but recently he'd begun sneaking a sip a few times a day. When had he started? He couldn't remember. He had to slow down. He needed to be sharp. He strapped Pearl and Baby Girl back inside his suit, eased Honey into the other holster, and slipped his suit jacket back on. He pulled his shoes back on and checked his watch. 2:33 a.m. He left his house, quietly closing the front door behind him.

3

On the way into the countryside, Babe took another nip from the flask, and this time he held the whisky in his mouth almost as if he were about to gargle with it. Then he swallowed and shook his head.

Liquid gold.

He knew Wojak's three thousand cases wouldn't be Macallan. He'd just have to sell it as if it were, or at least something close. That's what selling was, after all—a confidence game. Making your buyers believe. Giving them confidence in your product. Ultimately, giving them confidence not in you but in themselves.

He could make this happen. All he had to do was raise fifty-four thousand dollars in four days. And then—

His own personal Independence Day.

Turning down a backroad, not far from the intersection where he and Wojak came to their arrangement, Babe considered taking another draw from the flask. As he reached inside his pocket, he heard the siren and saw the red light flashing behind him, and then the sight of a police car filled up his rearview mirror. Babe shook his head.

Cop. Out here. Middle of nowhere. Perfect.

He pulled over and waited. He heard the door of the police car open and close and the sound of heavy footsteps approaching, boots thudding on the blacktop. The footsteps stopped, and a sheriff tapped on Babe's window. Babe rolled his window down and grinned at the officer who stood a careful five feet away.

"Good evening, officer," Babe said.

"Good morning, actually," the sheriff said. "It's past three—in the fucking *morning*."

"Is that right? Time keeps on slipping away."

The sheriff frowned. "I smell alcohol. Have you been drinking?"

"Hell no. I'm a teetotaler. Might take a drink on a special occasion. Holidays and such."

"Like, say, the Fourth of July?"

"There you go. Yes, exactly, something like that. By the way, when is that this year? Is it coming up?"

"You're obviously drunk. Please exit your vehicle. Fine car, by the way."

"Thank you. I paid cash. Did you want my license and registration?"

"Do you have them?"

"I believe so."

Babe snapped open the glovebox and lifted out a sheaf of documents fastened with a rubber band. He moistened his index finger with the tip of his tongue and began sifting through the papers.

"Let's see. Birth certificate. Passport. Marriage license. Fishing license. Hunting license. Certificate to operate a forklift. Honorable discharge. Permit to carry. Notice of Purple Heart, pending. College diploma—"

"You didn't go to college."

"Barber college."

"Exit the vehicle."

"Yes, sir."

Babe grinned at the sheriff and stuffed the wad of documents back inside the glovebox. The sheriff stood, legs apart, as Babe opened the car door and eased out of the car. Babe, thin, lean, immaculately dressed despite the ridiculous hour, stood almost as tall as the sheriff, but the sheriff, whose badge read "Carl Holt, Sheriff," was built wider, broad and thick across his pale pink neck and shoulders. Even in his pressed uniform he seemed rumpled. He wore his hair in a military buzzcut. He rarely wore his required Stetson. It made him seem like a cowboy, he thought, a look that the sheriff loathed. The sheriff personified the term *local*—born and brought up in Caruthersville, quitting school in the tenth grade so he could work on the family farm, tossing bales of hay onto flatbeds from dawn until dusk for his tyrannical father. At eighteen, the sheriff got into law enforcement to both spite and escape his father. When his father died, the old man left the farm to Carl's brother who lived three hours away in St. Louis, distancing the sheriff from his family even more.

"You smell like a brewery," he said to Babe.

"That would be a distillery," Babe said. "I've had a few sips of Macallan to calm my nerves."

Hootie, the sheriff, shook his head.

"Gate," he said, slapping palms with Babe.

"Yo, gate," Babe said. "What's the word from the herd?"

"What's the word? You ring me at three o'clock in the morning? You know I got that regional director moron coming in at eight. The guest of honor. He's doing the ribbon cutting for the tug-o'-war. You know what this dumbass told me? He wants to *rehearse* the ribbon cutting."

"He's never seen a scissors?"

"This cracker couldn't find his dick with two hands and a compass."

The sheriff shook his head. He waited a beat, then shifted his weight and retucked his shirt into his pants. "What are we doing out here?"

"We got a situation, Hootie."

"We?"

"You're right. I misspoke. It's not a situation. It's an opportunity."

Babe stopped and angled his head longingly toward his breast pocket.

"Bring out the Macallan," Hootie said. "We could both use it."

"In a minute."

"All right. Tell me about this opportunity."

"The Outfit. They retired Stanley."

"Retired him?"

"Well, they didn't give him a pension. Or a gold watch. Or a warning."

Hootie whistled.

"Karter and I met with his replacement. Tommy Wojak. You know the name?"

"No."

"He's running things now. I'm sure he'll want to meet with you. Maybe right before The Outfit comes in on a hostile takeover. That's their play. That's what I see coming."

Babe paused.

"Tommy—we're on a first name basis—is bringing in a shipment by boxcar on Monday. Midnight. Three thousand cases. I told him I'd take the whole lot. He didn't really give me a choice."

Hootie raked his hand through his buzzcut.

"You make a deal?"

"Eighteen a case."

Hootie looked up and scrunched his forehead, trying to do the math.

"Don't hurt yourself," Babe said. "It comes to fifty-four thousand."

"Fifty-four—" Hootie scratched his head ferociously. "You don't have that kind of money."

"Not at the moment."

"Not at any moment."

"Hootie," Babe said, "listen to me."

The sheriff pointed at Babe's chest. Babe reached into his pocket and handed Hootie the flask. The sheriff took a swig and licked his lips.

Babe began again. "I want to ask you something." He kicked a pebble across the pavement, then took the flask from Hootie and sipped.

"We talked about this, Hootie. We've *been* talking about this. When this day came. What we would do."

Hootie swiped his mouth with the back of his hand and looked beyond Babe into a shadowy cornfield on the far side of the road. The smell of manure wafted over them.

"This is my dream, Hootie," Babe said.

"Your own Sportsman Hall. I know."

"I'm turning forty in a month."

"I know that, too. I'm right behind you."

"I want to take this shot, Hootie. It's time. I want to build that dream. Literally build it. I have to take my stand now."

"Fifty-four thousand," Hootie said. He exhaled again, feeling his knees starting to buckle. "How much do you have?"

"Half," Babe said. "Almost."

"No, you don't," Hootie said.

"Pretty near."

Hootie stared at him.

"I have twelve," Babe said. "I could sell the car, raise it to fifteen, sixteen."

"Still not half," Hootie said. "Far from it, I think."

"I'm seeing the future both ways, Hoot. It's only a matter of time before The Outfit comes in and takes over the whole thing. The Sportsman Hall, everything. They'll run the gambling. Control the liquor. Then what? Where are we?"

Babe nodded at Hootie's badge.

"I know where you'll be. You got a job."

Babe fixed his eyes on his friend.

"What I'm asking is," Babe said, "be my partner. I'm your silent partner in this Sportsman Hall. Be the silent partner in mine."

"So, cash-wise," Hootie said, squinting into the night, his face starting to contort. "Let me see."

"Twenty-seven thousand," Babe said.

"Yeah, that's what I figured, too."

For a moment, the two men stood side by side, saying nothing, soaking up the humid night.

"I know," Babe said. "It's a big ask."

"Well, it's only our lives, our futures."

Hootie again passed his hand through his buzzcut.

"I'm in," he said.

Babe exhaled from exhaustion, from relief.

"But it's actually fifty-four thousand divided by *three*." Hootie looked off again, trying to do the math. He grunted in frustration.

"Eighteen thousand," Babe said. "But why three?"

"We got a third partner on this side, Babe. You know that."

"Your daughter's husband."

"Clyde."

"Clyde." Babe frowned as if saying the name came with a foul odor. "You know how I feel. I don't trust him. I don't like him. And neither do you."

"He's my son-in-law."

"He's a gum beater. A freeloader. Among other unsavory qualities."

"Babe," Hootie said. "I have to think of my daughter. If I leave him out, she'll never talk to me again. I can't do that."

Babe bit down on his lip. He felt as if he were preparing to slug down some disgusting but necessary medicine.

"He'll be a real silent partner," Hootie said. "I promise you that. But I have to bring him in. I need to keep my family together."

Babe nodded. He knew all about Hootie's family: his difficult relationship with his daughter; his commitment to keeping Clyde employed, out of the whorehouses, and off the whiskey; his flashbacks of his abusive father and brutal upbringing; and his estranged brother who inherited the family farm and left him out.

"You know what?" Babe said suddenly. "I changed my mind. I need to do this myself."

"What?"

"I appreciate it, Hoot, but I have to go it alone. I realize that now."

"Why? We'll do it together. I'll wrangle Clyde. I'll muzzle him like a goat."

"I know, but . . ." Babe sighed. "It will complicate things."

They took another minute, standing shoulder to shoulder in silence except for the sounds of the night and their breathing.

"I have some money in the bank," Hootie said. "Not much, but some. It's yours. Pay me back later, whenever, once you start bringing cash in."

"It's okay, Hootie. You hang on to it. Let's keep it clean. It's better that way."

Hootie shifted his weight, looked off. "Have you thought any of this through?"

"Don't have time to think. Only have time to act. All I know is, I need to have my own thing."

"That decrepit mansion."

"Going to be a showplace when I fix it up. A real hummer."

Hootie nodded.

"Okay," he said, then squinted at Babe. "We good?"

"Yeah, we good."

They slapped each other's backs familiarly, acknowledging their more than half-a-lifetime friendship, a friendship that at a different time, in a different place, they might enjoy and experience publicly—at a bar, drinking together, sharing a meal, playing a sport. But now, at this time, in this place, they kept their friendship closed and secret because it had to be. They assumed that, even with that, they would always be able to keep their friendship intact. Until tonight, on that road. They knew without either of them uttering a sound, speaking even a syllable, that time had instantly, irrevocably accelerated, and that nothing, including them, would ever be the same.

After meeting Hootie, Babe called Karter from a payphone. He knew that even at this hour, Karter wouldn't be asleep. Still, he asked.

"Did I wake your big ass up?"

"I told you. I don't sleep. This town is so damn quiet, it's eerie. It's like a horror movie. I lie awake, waiting for something to jump out at me. I go to bed with my gun in my hand. I don't know how anybody sleeps here. I've been wide awake for four years. What do you need?"

"Yo, gate. Set up a game for Saturday night, afterhours, late."

"Night of the third."

"Reel in every fish you can find."

"A high-stakes craps game," Karter said.

"That's the move. You ready?"

"Got my pole, my hook, and my net right here."

"Make sure you catch me at least one big fish."

"Shoot, I'm hooking you a *whale*," Karter said.

FRONT LINE

◆

**A BET PLACED
BEFORE THE SHOOTER
ROLLS THE DICE
TO START A GAME**

4

SUNDAY, JUNE 4, 1944
FOUR YEARS EARLIER

L ying on his cot in the barracks, Babe gulped a final drag off his cigarette, crushed the butt in the plastic ashtray he balanced on his chest, placed the ashtray on the floor, and eased the letter out of his shirt pocket. He sliced open the envelope with his fingernail, reached inside, and pinched out two photographs. In the first one, Rosie wore the uniform of the diner at the Sportsman Hall where she cooked, her clothes wrinkled after work, her arms spread wide, she and their four kids occupying the living room couch. A resigned, happy grin ran across her face as the three boys climbed over her, using her as a play structure. Rosetta, the two-year-old with freckles and big red hair whom he called "Tulip," sat by herself, perched on the edge of the couch, staring straight into the camera, her eyes seemingly zeroed in on Babe. He felt he could read her thoughts, always could. Now he saw in her eyes the same question he'd asked himself: "Papa, why did they draft you at thirty-five years old? You've been gone long enough. Get your butt back here. Mama needs you more than the army."

Babe looked at the other photograph. In this one, Rosie stood alone, wearing a one-piece bathing suit, posing like a centerfold, her mouth in a pout, her index finger curled, pointing at herself, suggesting, "Come and get it."

Babe sat up, feeling himself gasp.

"'Lo, BabyLou," he said aloud, invoking her family nickname.

He studied her photo for a good thirty seconds, considering it from every possible angle—tilted, at close range, at arm's length. Then he flipped the photo over and saw the note Rosie had written in her flowery cursive: "Can't wait for you to come home."

"Damn," Babe said. He leaned over and lightly brushed Rosie's pouty mouth with his lips before fitting the photo into his shirt pocket with a pat.

"Private Boyce."

Babe searched through the darkened barracks for the man who had just spoken in a stage whisper. He made out the profile of his sergeant striding toward him. His commanding officer. His boss.

"Sergeant Ruggs." Babe sat up even straighter, debating whether he should stand and salute.

Henry Ruggs, tall, slender, taut, his shaved head glistening, his movements so fast you barely saw him move, suddenly appeared at the side of Babe's cot. Sergeant Ruggs spoke in a melodic tenor. Close your eyes and you heard Nat King Cole. But Ruggs was military all the way. Special forces. He oozed stealth, a warrior in the shadows. The man had night moves.

"How you feeling?" Ruggs asked. "You tired?"

"No, sir. Feeling strong."

"Good. Very good. Put on some pants."

"Got an assignment for me?"

Ruggs sniffed, slashed his thumb on a line right below his razor-thin mustache. "This won't take long."

Outside the barracks, another officer, another Black sergeant, sat behind the steering wheel of an idling jeep belching exhaust. Ruggs hopped in and Babe settled into the back. The cold night air bit Babe's cheeks. He shivered and rolled his shoulders. As the jeep took off, the usual midnight drizzle started.

"It's raining," Babe muttered. "Again."

"Always," Ruggs said. "England has the worst weather in the world. And I'm from Detroit."

"Food's for shit, too," Babe said, then added, "sir."

"You won't have to worry about that no more. You're shipping out tomorrow."

Babe leaned forward. "Where we going?"

Ruggs squinted into the rain. "I didn't say we."

Ten minutes later, the jeep arrived at the far end of the base and parked outside a massive oval-shaped hangar. Babe followed Ruggs and the other sergeant inside. The moment they entered they encountered a wave of noise, voices shouting, overlapping, some cheering, others hollering, cursing, and then the *clang-clang-clang* of a cowbell. The three men headed toward the sounds, as if pulled by a magnet, walking by four enormous helium-filled balloons.

"My blimp babies," Babe said, rubbing his hand along the side of one of them as he passed.

He knew this hangar well. Overseen by Sergeant Ruggs, he spent all his days and occasionally—a dozen or so times—a few minutes here at night. By day, he and a team of four worked both inside the cavernous hangar and outside on a football-field-size patch of dirt, tending to the balloons, filling them with helium, flying them on clear days at low altitude, wrangling them in gusty winds and driving rain, then hauling them inside, patching tears in their behemoth sides, repairing these temperamental helium beasts. Recently, Ruggs taught Babe to attach small explosive charges to the thick cable that anchored each balloon to the ground. The balloons would serve as cover for troops landing on and invading a beach, the purpose to draw enemy fire. If enemy aircraft attempted to fly at the balloons, the cable would snag their wings, causing the explosives to detonate, blowing up the attacking plane. At least, that was the idea. The theory. The hope.

Babe had not yet experienced any of this in action. Now, according to Sergeant Ruggs, he was about to get his chance. That thought—seeing actual combat, fighting this war—had not yet registered in his brain. Babe had slammed that idea shut. He didn't want to go there. He hated the grim, gray, cold, rainy landscape so far from Caruthersville. But he hated the idea of battle even more. A white man's war, he'd heard members of his all-Black battalion say. The army wouldn't even allow him and his battalion to mix with white soldiers. They couldn't sleep in the same barracks, eat in the same chow hall, enjoy the same entertainment at the same time as the white soldiers. But they could fight with them, bleed alongside them, die next to them, or more accurately, ahead of them. Many of his Black brothers-in-arms felt outraged. Babe felt resigned and in a hurry. He had been here long enough. He missed home. Absently, he patted Rosie's photo in his pocket.

Inside the hangar, the driver and Sergeant Ruggs flanked Babe as they came closer to the sound of the voices that rose beyond the last anchored barrage balloon. Ruggs rested his large, narrow hand on Babe's shoulder.

"This is it," he said, a little sadly. "Our last go-round. You ready?"

"Do I have a choice?"

Ruggs snickered. "Nah."

They turned the corner by the wide snout of the balloon and came to a crude, battered boxing ring, surrounded by a throng of servicemen, nearly all of them white. When the white soldiers saw Babe, they erupted in jeers, some booed, and a few started to laugh. Babe didn't look imposing. He didn't look like a fighter. He grinned, bowed slightly, and waved. The white soldiers roared and applauded.

Babe focused on the center of the ring. A brute of a man, six three at least, two hundred forty pounds, his oversize head flushed pink, prowled through the ring like a hungry, trapped animal. He raised his bulky pale arms as he walked on the fraying and stained canvas. His block of a body, white as snow, rested on two squat legs as thick as tree stumps. God had chosen not to provide him with a neck.

"Good evening," Babe said to him.

The man's eyes narrowed. He grunted, growled, and then arched a stream of spit that landed at Babe's feet.

"Seems like a nice guy," Babe said to Ruggs.

"Once you get to know him," Ruggs said. "A tip. He doesn't care for *coloreds*."

"No shit?" Babe said, shrugging out of his shirt. He folded it neatly and handed it to Ruggs. "Be careful with that." Then he added, "Sir."

"Watch yourself," Ruggs said as Babe separated the ropes and climbed into the ring. "His punch has a kick. They call him Mule."

Babe jogged along the far side of the ring where all the Black servicemen clustered. The voices around the ring rose, cascading off the walls. Babe stopped in his corner and sat on a stool as Ruggs and the driver helped him put on his gloves. In his peripheral vision, in the crowd, Babe saw arms extended, fists clutching folding money, bets shouted, money thrust at a white soldier with an eyepatch who stood between the two groups, whites and Blacks. Eyepatch was the moneyman, the bookmaker, the bank.

Babe studied Mule, sized him up. Mule glared back, snarled, and pounded himself on the chest. Then, for show, as the white servicemen screamed in approval, Mule posed, flexing both biceps, somehow making them wiggle, shake, and pop. The white soldiers shouted, applauded. Mule grinned at Babe, then he stuck his tongue out and licked his lips.

"Midnight snack," he said. "Love me some dark meat."

A white man in a T-shirt entered the ring. The referee. He pointed at Mule, who grunted again. Then the referee nodded at Babe, who stood and nodded back. The referee waved at a private in uniform standing next to the cowbell. The private pulled on the cowbell's cord.

Clang.

Mule, fists up, charged Babe, sprinting across the ring in two seconds flat. He wound up and threw a roundhouse left.

The blow connected to the side of Babe's face, snapping his head back. Babe felt the bruise forming. The crowd went insane.

Mule bellowed happily and threw a wild right.

Babe ducked.

Mule's punch whistled by Babe's left ear.

Babe bounced on the balls of his feet, ducked under Mule's third punch, a desperate left hook, then Babe pivoted and spun *around* Mule, a dance move. He could have been Harold Nicholas, whirling, twirling, "flash dancing" around his partner and brother Fayard in the film *Stormy Weather*.

Babe stepped forward and flicked a lefthand jab that caught Mule's left ear. Mule stared, stunned.

Then—blistering fast, in a blur—Babe hit Mule with a series of jabs, *flick*, stinging Mule's left eye, *flick*, his nose, *flick, flick, flick*, his right eye, his right ear, his mouth. His eyes puffed shut, Mule swung wildly, weakly, blindly, finally throwing a slow and impotent roundhouse left that wafted by Babe like a warm, pleasant breeze.

Babe spun again, danced to Mule's side, crouched, slammed a left hand into Mule's kidney, then powered a shattering right uppercut into Mule's exposed midsection. Mule moaned, his lips quivered, his breath escaping. For his finale, Babe launched a left hook from his hip that literally lifted Mule off the ground.

Mule seemed to hover in the air for a split second and then crash-dived face-first onto the canvas. He sprawled in a fetal position, barely conscious, his mouth opening and closing like a beached fish.

"Mule." Babe leaned over Mule's fallen body and whispered into his red, swollen ear, "Hee haw, motherfucker."

Behind him, the Black portion of the crowd roared while the white contingent stood in stunned silence. A moment passed and the servicemen split off, whites and Blacks, to their separate corners. Eyepatch, the banker, distributed the winnings into eager palms reaching toward him. How he kept track, nobody knew, but he always maintained accurate accounting, to the dollar. Eyepatch found Ruggs and pressed a two-inch-high wad of bills into Rugg's hands. Ruggs pocketed the cash and turned to the driver, who peered at a stopwatch.

"Thirty-seven seconds," the driver said.

"And five to one against. Not a bad night's work."

The three men didn't say much in the jeep on the way back to the barracks. The rain had let up, but Babe stayed holed up inside his shirt, keeping to himself, pressing an icepack to his purpled cheek, intermittently tapping the spot over his heart to make sure Rosie's picture remained safe in his pocket. The jeep pulled up outside the barracks door, and Babe climbed out. Ruggs swiftly, stealthily, grabbed Babe's sleeve and pulled him close.

"Here," he said.

He handed Babe five one-hundred-dollar bills.

"Your cut," Ruggs said.

Babe stuffed the money into his pocket next to Rosie's picture. "How much did you bet on me?"

"Nothing," Ruggs said. "I don't bet. I invest. Word to the wise. Find a sure thing and ride it."

"That's good advice," Babe said. "Thank you, sir."

Babe stood at attention and saluted. Ruggs returned the salute.

"At ease, soldier," Ruggs said. He reached into his shirt pocket, pulled out a pack of Marlboros, tapped the pack, and offered Babe a smoke. Babe slid out a cigarette and accepted a light from Ruggs's silver lighter.

"Much obliged, sir," Babe said.

"Call me Sarge. Everybody does. In or out of the military." He reached into his pocket again, took out a card, and handed it to Babe.

"The Rail King of the Midwest," Babe read. "First Thing Smoking."

"Hello. If something special goes by train between Toronto and Cleveland, I know about it, protect it, and take my cut."

"Nice," Babe said.

"Real nice. I can use a good man in the office, a number two, if you're interested."

"Thank you, Sarge, but I'm starting to set myself up in my hometown. Caruthersville, Missouri."

"The big time, huh?"

Babe allowed himself a laugh. "You might be surprised."

"It's a standing offer," Ruggs said. "Meantime, watch yourself over there, son, because nobody else will."

"I will, Sarge."

"At the very least, when this shit ends, if you ever make your way to Detroit, look me up. I'd like to return the favor."

5

TUESDAY, JUNE 6, 1944
Omaha Beach, France

Later, when asked to describe D-Day, Babe would call it, "A shitshow from the beginning. At least for us. The Black troops. Especially us in the Three Twenty."

Intending to draw enemy fire and provide cover for the initial wave of Allied troops, the 320 Barrage Balloon Battalion hit Omaha Beach first, their amphibious landing crafts nosing through blustery winds, roiling seas, and pelting rain. Blown and dispersed by the winds, the landing crafts—thick rubber rafts with the helium balloons trailing above them—arrived at the beach randomly. Antiaircraft and machine guns strafed the balloons, blowing most of them to bits. A hundred helium balloons departed England, crossing the English Channel. Only twenty survived.

Still, the remaining balloons served a purpose, diverting anti-aircraft fire as Allied troops hit the beach behind them. But not without consequence, casualties, chaos. Babe and his team and the other members of the balloon battalion found a beach pocked with mines, patches of jagged metal spears sticking out of the sand, and rows of half-buried barbed wire. Machine gunfire ripped through balloons and men, the white moist sand turning black with blood and strewn with bodies. Scattered body parts lay among petrified sea glass and pieces of driftwood.

It felt unreal to Babe. He felt momentarily like a bystander, almost as if he were sitting in the one movie house back in Caruthersville, watching himself on-screen, a soldier appearing in black-and-white newsreel footage. But within an instant, the blasts of artillery, the otherworldly screams, the stench of smoke, gunfire, and death wrestled him back into reality. He felt himself not acting, but reacting. He would later define this simply as surviving.

His balloon remained tethered behind him when his landing craft plowed onto the muddy shore. He was alone, his team lost, overboard, swallowed by the sea or cut down on the beach. He had to squint to see through the wall of smoke in front of him. All around him, the sound of gunfire deafened him and bullets pinged around his ears like insects buzzing, chopping the ground at his feet. By reflex and training, he rolled onto the beach, shoulder to sand. Above him, bullets tore through the balloon. Babe grabbed the rope to the balloon, trying to save it, but the balloon sailed off, drifted up, the remaining pieces of it skittering away, its body torn to shreds, pieces of it floating on the sea. Babe clasped a three-foot length of rope, holding on, all that was left of his six months in England. He wrapped the rope around his wrist. A souvenir. A memento.

Embracing his new purpose—to stay alive—Babe rolled further up the beach through an orchestra of gunfire, wails of human suffering, and artillery explosions, the sound blaring behind, in front, above, and through him, the noise itself an assault. His eardrums vibrated, closed up. His head throbbed, his field of vision swimming in an aura, burning in an otherworldly blaze of light.

I'm in hell, he thought. *This is hell.*

He crab-crawled on his elbows, heading toward—well, he didn't know. He just kept crawling, inching forward through this inferno on the sand.

Up ahead, maybe twenty yards away, he spotted a large mound. He squinted and made out what looked like a lumpen, misshapen sand dune. Curious and cautious, Babe slowed his crawling. Suddenly, the dune rose and shook, undulating, moving from side to side, then the sand groaned. Babe fumbled for his knife. He gripped the handle, pulled the blade from its sheath, and stuck the knife in his mouth like a pirate. He didn't want to stop moving. He couldn't stop moving. Stopping meant death.

He crawled closer toward the mound and made out a human form. A giant of a man. Hard to tell from this angle, but Babe measured him at six ten, maybe seven feet, and massive.

A Black man, Babe saw. *One of us. A balloon man.*

The soldier's shoes had been ripped away. Strangely, he wore civilian clothes, except for his muddy helmet. Babe returned his knife to its sheath and continued to crawl, finally arriving a yard or so away from the massive man. From here, he saw blood streaming down the giant's right leg. The man stifled a scream as he tried to pull himself up, again shaking the sand, but he couldn't put any pressure on his right side. He tried again, swore, and collapsed.

"Hey!" Babe shouted. "I'm right behind you. I got you."

The man craned his neck as Babe slid next to him.

"My leg," the man said.

"You shot?"

"No. Cut on one of them metal spits."

"Okay. I'm gonna pick you up and drag you. Then we're gonna hop off this fucking bitch."

He meant *beach*, but the huge man grunted. "I hear you, man."

Babe started to grab the man around the neck, then stopped. "Damn, you're big. How much you weigh?"

"Two of you," the man said. "And a few pounds more for luck."

"Where's your uniform?"

"Army couldn't find one to fit. It's on order. I almost hit this beach with nothing but my helmet and my birthday suit."

"Thank God the water was unseasonably warm," Babe said.

The man tried to laugh, then gritted his teeth in pain. "How we gonna do this?"

"Fireman's carry," Babe said. "Easy."

He paused, then considered the length of rope around his wrist.

"This'll work. Maybe. Can you turn onto your back?"

The man exhaled, grimaced, and using all his strength, forced himself from his left side to his back. He bit down on his lip and stifled a scream.

"Good," Babe said. "Give me your hands."

The man extended his hands. Babe looped the length of rope over and under his wrists, once, twice, tying and knotting them expertly. He pulled on the rope, felt it was tight and strong.

"That should do," Babe said. "Now we're about to get extremely familiar."

Babe rolled on top of the man, chest to chest, face to face.

"Here we go." Babe grabbed the rope around the big man's wrists, yanked, and thrust his hips forward at the same time.

He and the big man moved forward a foot. Then Babe shoved himself forward again. They managed another foot. Then another.

For the next two hours, Babe pulled the big man up Omaha Beach until somehow, miraculously, they came to an Allied soldier with a red cross on his sleeve. A medic. He'd set up a tiny medical tent at the tip of the beach behind a seawall. Babe gasped, wondering for a moment if he were hallucinating. *Is this a mirage?* But then he felt the man's actual, real human hands reaching toward him, touching him.

"I'll take it from here," the medic said, untying the big man's wrists and helping Babe roll off his body.

Babe lay on the sand, panting, his lungs burning, his head booming.

"You saved my life," the big man said.

"I lost my balloon," Babe said. "I had nothing better to do."

"I'm Karter," the big man said.

"Babe."

"Hey, Babe," Karter said. "Any chance we can go back and get my shoes?"

6

Aweek later, after doctors mended Karter's leg and treated Babe for exhaustion, they started to hear the buzz—a Medal of Honor for Babe, a Purple Heart for Karter. Nothing came of it, but Babe didn't really care. The only reward he wanted was a plane ticket home. He hoped to be back in Caruthersville for July Fourth, his favorite holiday, the annual weekend celebration and festivities that brought his hometown notoriety throughout the Midwest. But the army moved at its own pace. *Slow.* Slower than a standstill. July came and went.

Stationed now in France, Babe and Karter waited for their honorable discharge notices and their orders to go home. They remained soldiers by definition, reporting for duty at their base, but they did little else. Still waiting for a proper uniform, Karter spent his days lifting weights, hitting the heavy bag, intimidating people just for fun, and sleeping. He'd jury-rigged a bed to fit him, ingeniously lashing two cots together with some twine. Still, his feet hung over the end. But he was comfortable. Karter had a way of finding his space and not merely occupying it but overwhelming it.

Sometimes Babe worked out with him. Otherwise, he talked his way into practicing hand-to-hand knife training with some Special Forces guys. At night, Babe commandeered a jeep and with

Karter riding shotgun, occasionally won spending money boxing off base. Afterward, the two became familiar with the best local bistro, finest Bordeaux, and to let off steam, the most inviting bordel.

Mainly, though, with Karter looking on, standing guard, looming, Babe concentrated on his latest passion—craps. Babe had learned the game back home in a roadhouse gambling den tucked into the Missouri woods. But here, in France, he played the game at another level. He seemed to have a gift, a sixth sense. He became a maestro with the dice. He knew when to bet and how much, when to take his bets down, when to go with the dice, and when to go against the shooter. He always won—not usually, *always*. He shared his substantial winnings with Karter, his sidekick, his shadow, his partner, his protection. Babe didn't give him a piece. He gave him half.

"I was wondering," Karter said one night as he and Babe tasted a particularly tangy Bordeaux that, according to their officious waiter, presented a hint of blackberry, licorice, and whimsy. "What's Caruthersville like?"

"Quiet," Babe said.

"I don't like quiet. I'm used to Chicago. Hustle, bustle. Too much quiet makes me nervous. I can't sleep."

"Well, there is action. You just have to know where to find it."

"Where's that?"

"Usually where I am."

The men went silent. Babe sipped his wine, Karter swirled his glass, staring at the rippling ruby-red liquid. "If I relocated, moved to Caruthersville, I could look out for you. Be your eyes, ears. Be your—office manager."

"I could use you," Babe said.

"Good," Karter said. "That's settled."

Karter nodded into his glass. He knew he could never pay Babe back for saving his life. But becoming his man in Caruthersville? That would be a start.

One night, a couple weeks before their discharge orders came through, Babe and Karter visited a bordel they'd heard about at a dice game.

They entered the house through an alley and walked into a foyer. The place was brighter than most, well-appointed with turn-of-the-century oak furniture, bone china, crystal glasses, and antique lamps with metal bases and stained-glass shades. Their hostess, an attractive woman of fifty with snow-white skin who dressed all in black, including a veil, escorted them to the bar and offered champagne. She couldn't keep her eyes or her hands off Karter, the usual response when he entered a house like this for the first time.

"What's your pleasure?" the madam asked, waving toward a selection of women in negligees who had magically appeared, lounging near or astride the antique furniture.

"My," Karter said. "What's French for 'come and get it'?"

"You pay for it, you don't fall in love," Babe said.

"I hear that," Karter said. "Now, those two, by the armoire, the blond or the redhead? Which one?"

"I can't choose. They're both magnificent."

"You're right," Karter said, slugging down his champagne. "I'll take 'em both."

Karter winked at the madam. Babe turned away, raised his hand for a refill, and heard the two women giggling and Karter laughing. When Babe turned back, Karter and the women were gone, replaced by a thin woman in her twenties with wide blue eyes, a patch of short coiffed hair, and a surprisingly deep voice.

"Refill?"

Babe held out his champagne flute.

She poured, using both hands, filling the flute to the brim, causing some champagne to spill over.

"*Oh, je suis désolé*," she said, wiping the glass with her long finger.

"*Ne t'excuse pas*," Babe said, grabbing her hand.

"You speak French," she said.

"*Un peu.*"

"I'm Amelie."

"Floyd."

"Would you be interested in attending a private party?" Amelie said.

"I'm a married man."

"*Quel dommage.*"

"I don't know that one."

"That's a shame."

Babe nodded.

"If it makes you feel any better, I'm married, too," Amelie said.

Babe grinned.

"*Un peu*," he said.

Babe and Karter got the word. They would be discharged in twenty-one days. Their commanding officer, a sergeant they'd seen exactly twice in the past month, brought them the paperwork to fill out and sign. After that, Babe gambled even more, becoming a fixture at high-stakes, all-night craps games, most of them held in dimly lit, illegal underground casinos. He left at dawn, his pockets bulging with his winnings. When he didn't play craps, Babe spent his time with Amelie. Even though Amelie was ten years younger, she took on the role of the sophisticated, older teacher. She taught him basic French phrases and introduced him to the best French food, wine, and liquor.

To be sure, Babe felt something for Amelie. A stirring. He could lose himself with her, tumble into her world, a world so foreign and unreal that he felt safe. He felt himself falling at first, but he caught himself.

This is part of the war, he thought. *I almost died. I'm allowed a distraction, an escape.*

He half believed that. Maybe more than half. But he summoned his inner strength to take over. His love for Rosie rose up and squashed the distraction. He allowed his history with her, his future, and his devotion to his family to override whatever other feelings he had.

He'd made it through the massacre on Omaha Beach. He wouldn't capsize now. He wouldn't give up his heart, his soul, his *life*, even for someone as beautiful, as luminous, as unique as Amelie. He would keep her locked away, in his mind, in his memory, with Karter his only witness.

He said goodbye to Amelie stoically, silently, without speaking either English or French. He held her. She cried. And then he gently pulled away. When he left her, he felt light-headed, almost hungover, even though he'd had nothing to drink. *Yes, it's part of the war*, he thought again, insisted. He would not allow himself to be a causality. He would survive this, too.

He left the house and walked down the alley, leaving Amelie

standing in the doorway. As he walked, he could feel her eyes on his back, like a ray of heat. He kept walking, his head down. The moment before he turned the corner, he paused. Without looking back, he lifted his hand and waved goodbye. He never believed she had a husband.

Five days before their flight to the States, Babe walked into a small storefront that Amelie had told him about, a dusty, cluttered shop full of antiques and used books. The shopkeeper, Marcel, bought, sold, and repaired the antique lamps that the madam had purchased for the bordel.

"*Bonjour*," Marcel said.

"*Bonjour*," Babe said. "I need something special made."

"*Oui?*"

Babe slid a piece of paper across the counter. "A neon sign that lights up with these words."

Marcel squinted and read aloud in stilted English, "BabyLou's Kitchen."

"My wife's family nickname."

"*Mignonne*. What color?"

"You're the artist. I leave it to you."

"*Merci.*"

"I need it in three days."

Marcel laughed. "Impossible. I can't rush. I will send it to you."

"When?"

Marcel shrugged massively.

"*Je ne sais pas.*"

Babe stared at him for a withering thirty seconds.

"I trust you," he said finally.

Babe reached into his pocket and brought out a thick wad of bills. He began peeling them off, twenty by twenty by twenty. "Tell me when to stop."

Marcel allowed Babe to peel off one, two, or three hundred in twenties. Babe lost count.

"*Arrêt,*" Marcel said, finally, sweeping up the bills.

"*Ça peut être fait?*" Babe said.

Marcel nodded.

It can be done.

BIG RED

♦

SEVEN

7

THURSDAY, JULY 1, 1948
FOUR YEARS LATER

Rosie, holding Rosetta's hand, entered the diner in the front of the Sportsman Hall at 9:01 a.m., a minute after the diner officially opened. The Breakfast Club had already convened.

"Sorry I'm late," she said to the four men seated on stools at the counter. They chimed a greeting, a loud, respectful chorus of "Rosie" while raising their coffee cups simultaneously in her honor. A toast. A cheer. Rosie laughed, tied her apron, and helped Rosetta onto a stool. Rosetta opened the chapter book she had been carrying under her arm and tucked a leg under herself as she found her place in the book and started to read. Rosie stepped behind the counter and plugged in the neon sign that hung on the back wall above the stovetop. The sign blinked, pulsed, and settled in alternating blue and red cursive letters, "BabyLou's Kitchen."

"Four BabyLou breakfasts coming up," she shouted to the line of men at the counter, the first wave of what would be a continuing flow of customers from now until she ended her shift at two.

The men at the counter banged their coffee cups on the counter and this time shouted "Chef!" in unison. Karter, on the stool closest to the door, next to Rosetta, laughed the loudest, moved his matchstick from side to side with his tongue, and held his cup high. On the other side of Rosetta, Leaky, Babe's brother-in-law, married to Rosie's older sister, howled, his shoulders shaking, and then adjusted his glasses, fitting them more snuggly onto his nose. Anyone knowing Montel from childhood called him by his nickname, Leaky, a reference to his constantly running nose due to allergies throughout elementary school. The next two men in line, Tony, tall, strong, wearing a mechanic's coveralls with his name stitched over his pocket, and Carlyle, thick, muscled, balding, wearing a weightlifter's belt over his overalls, banged on the counter in rhythm like a conga drum. Carlyle rode shotgun on a garbage truck in the Third Precinct, on the other side of town, a Black part of town. Both men had strong opinions. Both men could *talk*.

"More coffee?"

Babe emerged from behind the counter holding the coffee pot aloft, walking down the line, topping off everyone's cups.

"I didn't hear you leave this morning," Rosie said to Babe, firing up the grill. "I was out cold."

"Late night?" Carlyle said.

"*All* night. Called to an emergency birth."

"Who?" Tony asked.

Rosie cleared her throat, hesitated. "A Galvis. Second cousin." Then, as if to justify her appearance at the Galvis farm, she added, "Baby went breech. It got complicated."

"Woman's a virtuoso with a forceps," Babe said.

"Galvis." Tony grunted, tapping a beat on the counter with his fork.

"RAF," Carlyle said, nodding in time to Tony's fork tapping and then translating for anyone who didn't know. "Racist as fuck."

"Babies aren't born hating," Rosie said. "What time you get here, Floyd?"

"Opened up at seven thirty," Babe said. "Had some early business. Thought I'd help you out. Brew the coffee."

"Well, thank you most kindly, sir. But don't expect a tip."

The Breakfast Club whooped as Babe laughed and starting filling coffee cups.

The outside door swung open and Sheriff Carl Holt, Hootie, in uniform, looking half-asleep, stepped in, removed his hat, and found a stool. "Good morning, gentlemen."

"Good morning, Officer," Babe said. "Coffee?"

"Please. Good morning, Rosie."

"Officer Holt. The usual?"

"Yes, ma'am. BabyLou, please—with Rosie Cakes."

"A man with a big appetite," Rosie said. "Coming up."

"Pancakes with a thin, crispy edge. I dream about them."

Rosie held up her coffee cup. "Here's to bigger dreams."

She pivoted toward the grill and got to work. Rosie cooked like a high-speed ballerina, bouncing on her toes, whirling, twirling, frying ham steaks, scrambling eggs, popping biscuits into the oven, then later coaxing them out and flipping them onto the grill. She kept in constant motion, never pausing, never wasting a step. Babe kept pace, taking charge of the coffee, pouring, then brewing a fresh pot, all while sipping from his own cup.

The payphone in an alcove to the side of the counter rang, stopping Babe in mid-motion.

"That's for me," Babe said, putting the coffee pot down on the warmer behind him.

Karter and Hootie watched him pick up the phone. Karter, keeping his eye on both Babe and the door, glancing from Rosie to Rosetta, was always on alert. Babe turned his back to the room and cupped the receiver to his ear.

Hootie looked over at Rosetta. "What are you reading?"

"*Doctor Dolittle*," Rosetta said, not looking up, her eyes riveted on the page of the book.

"Don't know that one," Hootie said. "What is he, a doctor?"

"No," Karter said. "He drives a beer truck. Why else they call it *DOCTOR Dolittle*?"

"He's a special doctor," Rosetta said. "He doesn't treat people. He prefers animals."

"Huh," Hootie said.

"He can talk to them."

"To the animals?"

"Yes," Rosetta said, rolling her eyes, stating the obvious.

"I had a cousin like that," Hootie said. "He talked to animals. And trees. Rocks. Pieces of furniture. Fruit."

Rosetta ignored him, or didn't care.

"He had a big head," Hootie said, sipping his coffee. "We got along good."

Babe faced them now, smiling, finishing his call.

"Thank you, Senator," he said into the phone. "And if you change your mind and you want to come to Caruthersville for the Fourth, I got you covered. A suite at the Hall, river view, couple of tickets to the show. No, not at all. My pleasure. You just let me know. Even last minute. And again, thank you."

He hung up the phone, bounced back behind the counter, and started brewing a fresh pot of coffee.

"You work it out?" Hootie asked.

Babe nodded. "Got what we wanted. No, *needed*."

"I knew you'd make it happen," Hootie said.

"Sometimes you have to bypass the locals," Babe said. "Go up the ladder. Don't accept the first *no*. Or the second. Hey, Tony, I need a favor."

"Anything," the mechanic said.

"A vehicle inspection. Top to bottom."

"Can it wait until after the holiday? Bernice has me running all over Missouri gathering ingredients for the pie baking contest. She's determined to defend her title."

"Sorry. Got to get the vehicle up and running by end of day. I know we're looking at a set of sparkplugs. Maybe new brakes."

"What kind of car?"

"Truck," Babe said, grabbing the coffee pot. "Refills, anyone?"

At that moment, a man sitting by himself at a corner table moaned and stirred. Babe had not noticed him until now. He was heavyset, sturdy, and bare chested. He absently rubbed his naked stomach and yawned. He stretched and Babe noticed that he also had no shoes.

"Tough night," Tony said to the Breakfast Club.

Leaky snickered. "Hey, Officer, what happened to 'no shirt, no shoes, no service'?"

Hootie dismissed him with a wave. "I'm off duty. I got my BabyLou breakfast coming. I have to concentrate."

Babe snatched a coffee cup and walked over to the shirtless, shoeless man who sat slumped at the table.

"Coffee?" Babe said.

"Oh, man, thank you."

"Tied one on last night, huh?" Babe said as he filled the coffee cup.

"Yeah." The man slowly lifted his head. He squinted up at Babe, shielding his eyes as if the morning light were a spotlight. "I don't remember much."

He mumbled another thank you to Babe, and then patted his pants.

"I don't have my wallet," he said. "I can't pay you."

Then Babe recognized him. His face lit up.

"It's on the house. Breakfast, too."

Babe swung back behind the counter, tapped Rosie on the shoulder, and leaned over to Hootie and Karter.

"We got us a king in the corner," he whispered.

"What?" Rosie said, distracted, her eyes fastened on the grill, never stopping her grilling, scrambling eggs, not taking a moment to look in the direction where Babe tilted his head.

"You know who that is?" Babe said.

"Yeah," Hootie said. "A half-naked vagrant who's getting a free breakfast."

"Or," Babe said, "B.B. King."

Karter spun on his stool and faced the man at the table. "I'll be damned. That is him. The immortal king of the blues." And then he crooned off-key, "Oh, oh, oh, baby, every day I have the blues."

"Don't do that, please," Babe said, returning to the man at the table. "I think we met a while ago. I'm Babe. I run things around here."

"Riley," B.B. said. "I'm sitting here, in a fog, trying to remember what happened last night. Wait a minute. That's right. There were these two women. Twins, maybe, though one was taller. We started drinking, dancing, partying."

"Did they wrestle you?" Babe said.

"Oh, yeah. They kept slapping hands and pinning me."

"Uh-huh. Like a tag team."

The Breakfast Club roared. Rosie froze and glared knives at Babe.

"What? It's my business to know the local customs."

"Shit." B.B. looked up at Babe, his eyes flickering with memory and urgency.

"I gave the tall one my guitar. Why did I do that? What if she broke it or gave it away or sold it? I have to get it back."

"You could get another guitar," Babe said.

"Not a chance. That guitar is my partner. My muse. It's part of me. I lose that, it'd be like cutting off my arm."

Riley slugged down his coffee and started to get up from the table.

"I got to go."

"You can't go like that. Let me fix you up. Whoa. You got some big feet. What size you wear?"

"Fourteen and a half."

"Karter, what size shoe you wear?"

"Twenty-one."

"Close enough. You keep an extra pair in the back, right?"

"No."

"Give me your shoes."

"My—" Karter started to object, stopped himself, and then said, "Anything for the king. But he'll be swimming in them."

"I keep an extra shirt in the closet," Babe said. "You never know. You can always get a stain. Food, wine—"

"Lipstick," Rosie muttered.

The Breakfast Club reacted as if they'd all been slapped across the face simultaneously. They recoiled, then half laughed, half coughed, all of them keeping their heads down, staring at the counter. Babe missed this. He'd disappeared into a back room, returning seconds later with a pressed white shirt on a hanger. He passed by Karter, who held his shoes out to him.

"You're going to have to stuff them with newspaper," he said.

"Try these," Babe said, handing his shirt and Karter's shoes to Riley.

"You got a way of fixing things, don't you?" Riley said.

"If I can," Babe said. "If I can."

"Here we go—five BabyLous, with extra Rosie Cakes on the side," Rose sang, slinging a few plates onto the counter. Babe handed out the rest, a plate now in front of each member of the Breakfast Club containing grilled ham steak with the round bone, scrambled eggs dripping with melted cheese, rice doused in butter, and crispy brown biscuits hot to the touch standing sentry on opposite ends of the plate.

The Breakfast Club dove in, attacking the food. The diner went instantly silent, the air filled with a kind of reverence. A holy quiet set in as the men ate. Nobody uttered a word. The only sounds were the clink and clatter of utensils scraping plates. The men didn't savor the food. They devoured it. Rosie looked on, fists slammed onto her hips, a thin satisfied grin streaking across her face.

Across the room, Riley pushed himself away from the table and stood unsteadily, barely squeezing into Babe's shirt, the buttons threatening to pop, the sleeves reaching his forearms. He looked like he was wearing a straitjacket. He could barely move his neck.

"Perfect," he said. "Like custom-made. Maybe a tad snug."

He took two steps and almost flew out of Karter's shoes. He steadied himself, slowed himself down, then kept walking, sliding really, taking one tentative step at a time. Suddenly, his legs spread apart and he nearly snowplowed into the wall. He reached back and grabbed the edge of the counter to prevent himself from toppling.

"I need my guitar," B.B. King said, standing up, inching toward the door of the diner. "Wait. How do I find her? I don't know her name."

"Lucille," Babe said. "Her name's Lucille."

8

fter two, her shift over, Rosie rode shotgun in the Commander with Babe at the wheel. She dangled her arm out the open window, a cigarette pinched between two fingers, allowing herself a pause between drags to shut her eyes.

"Tough night, busy morning," Babe said. He steered with one hand, his other hand outside his window, holding a cigarette of his own.

"I am dead on my feet," Rosie said. "Plus, this *heat*."

"This won't take long," Babe said.

"Where we going?" Rosetta whined from the backseat.

"Have to run an errand," Babe said.

"*Fine*." Rosetta sighed theatrically and opened *Doctor Dolittle* to the first page. Babe knew she sighed for effect. He caught her performance in the rearview mirror.

"I thought you finished that book."

"I did. Starting it again. It's my favorite."

"You must know it by heart."

"Yep."

Babe maneuvered the Commander through downtown, slowing his speed, cruising, taking in the stores on Main Street—The Cunningham Store Company, a block-long department store, the new Standard gas station, Henley's Drugstore, Philip Hembree's Department Store, a market, a toy store, a taxi stand, the post office, city hall. Several stores already had their Fourth of July decorations on full display—red, white, and blue banners, American flags flying, positioned on flagpoles. Some people had even placed folding chairs on the sidewalk, securing their spots for Sunday's parade.

"I heard we're having an all-time great fireworks show this year coming off the riverboat," Babe said.

"I don't like fireworks," Rosetta said. "Scares the dogs. Would scare our dog. If we had one."

"Here we go," Babe said.

Rosie laughed. "Not sure we're ready for that yet, Tulip."

"When we going to be ready?" Rosetta pouted.

"Soon."

"I may not be ready soon, or later," Babe said, sucking down the final drag off his cigarette, flipping the butt into the street.

"I thought you were working on him," Rosetta said to her mother.

"I am," she said, finishing her cigarette, too, crushing hers in the ashtray below the dashboard, giving Babe a coy glance. "It may take me a little time."

Ten minutes later, Babe drove into another part of town— more countryside, more farmland, less people, less traffic, fewer houses, many of them needing new paint, some with windows boarded up, a few with sagging front porches. As they drove, Rosie perked up.

"Let's drive by the lot," she said. "I want to see it."

"Why?" Rosetta said from the backseat. "It didn't go anywhere."

Rosetta laughed and Babe grinned at her in the rearview mirror. "How old are you?"

"Six, going on seven."

"You sure? Let me see some ID. Birth certificate? Driver's license?"

Rosetta giggled, nosed back into her book.

Babe eased onto a stretch of highway, then after a mile or so, turned down a two-lane road and pulled alongside a half acre of farmland. Rosie burst out of the car almost before Babe came to a stop.

"Come on, Tulip," Babe called to Rosetta, who sighed again, massively, for effect, before trailing after her father. Babe took his daughter's hand. They broke into a run and caught up to Rosie, who stood in the middle of the barren land, her eyes closed, her arms wrapped around her. Suddenly, she shouted into the sky.

"This is *ours!*" she hollered. Then she raised her arms and twirled in a circle. "Can you see it?" She began walking across the field, pointing at the ground, describing rooms she saw in her head. "Here's the kitchen. Stove. Icebox. Table. The living room. Couch. Daddy's armchair facing the window right here. Every dad has a chair. And here. The bathroom. Large enough for *two* porcelain tubs. Now, this big room is our bedroom, in the back, right here. Over here, the boys' room. They might have to share for now. But, look, it's a big room, double the size now."

"Where's my room?" Rosetta asked, falling into the spirit of her mother's passion and imagination.

"Well, here, at first. You've got your own little separate wing."

"I'd like a porch," Babe said.

"Back, front, or both?"

"When are we going to have this house?" Rosetta asked, causing Rosie's enthusiasm to dim, her playfulness to fade. The question silenced her parents. Babe kicked at some dirt, peeked toward the horizon, looking, possibly, for some glimpse of his future.

"Not sure yet, Tulip. Soon," he said, speaking toward a cloud.

"Took me ten years to save for this land," Rosie said to herself, but aloud. "We can wait a little longer."

"I don't like waiting," Rosetta said.

"Nobody does," Rosie said. "But sometimes you don't have a choice."

"Your mother's right," Babe said. "And yet, other times, when you least expect it, an opportunity comes along and you have to take advantage. You have to strike. It's all about timing."

"Timing," Rosie said, eying her husband. "The key to life."

Then Babe faced a different direction and pointed to a decrepit mansion in the distance. The rambling old house could have been a mirage. It seemed to shimmer in the heat. But after a moment, the mansion came into focus, a battered, barely standing reality, obscured by a dying hedge of skimpy bushes turned crispy and brown. Even at this distance, anyone could tell that the mansion was a wreck, a shambles of decaying wood, peeling paint, a sagging wraparound front porch, a ruined, hastily patched roof with shingles either missing or sliding off.

"See that old house," Babe said.

"Uh-huh," Rosetta said. "It's a dump."

"Right now, it is," Babe said. "But I'm going to buy it and turn it into a showplace. My own place. My own Sportsman Hall. You'll see."

"When? I know. *Soon.*"

"Well, you know, it's all about—"

He grinned at Rosetta, cuing her.

"Timing," all three said at once.

Rosie laughed and circled her arms around her husband's chest, the force of her hug knocking him back. He put one arm around her and then pulled Rosetta close, the three of them forming a tight huddle. They stayed that way for some time, clinging to each other without speaking, their bodies swaying, each one of them imagining their own personal futures, all of them lost in a dream, the hot afternoon sun scorching, bearing down on them.

Soon after, the mood of the afternoon changed.

Solemnly, Babe drove to another part of town, a grid of tightly packed houses where many of the area's Black residents lived. He parked at a corner, down the street from the remains of what had been a small house two days before, now a blackened, still smoking slab, a layer of ash piled on a rectangle of charred earth. Babe got out of the car slowly and approached a family huddled on the narrow sidewalk in front of what had been their home. A man his age, a bus driver named Will, stood staring into the rubble, his eyes watery and expressionless. His daughter, six or seven, Rosetta's age, held him across his midsection. His wife, Marion, looked into the empty space in front of her, her four walls forty-eight hours ago, now a smoky black void. She hesitated and then forced herself to take a few steps forward. Her legs began wobbling. Her body started convulsing. She dropped to her knees and began to wail. Will unclasped his daughter, ran to his wife, and put his arms around her. He held her, rocked her, and then gently lifted her to her feet, still holding her, not letting her go.

"I know, Marion, I know," Will said.

Babe stood to the side and watched helplessly, the sight of soot and rubble and the smell of smoke assaulting him. He drifted onto the slab, past a few ruined remains—a piece of a plate, a broken toy, a thin smoking stack of paper that he identified as the remains of a book. He walked back to Rosie and Rosetta. They, too, stared into the empty lot and then looked at the bereaved family. Rosetta and the little girl made eye contact. Rosetta wanted to say something to her, but she couldn't think of what to say. What could she say? Words—her best friends, her passion, her secret power—had escaped her, failed her.

"Lost," Marion murmured into her husband's chest.

"I'm here," Will said, holding her. "I'm right here."

"Everything," Marion said. "We lost everything."

Hootie arrived then and parked his cruiser in front of Babe's Commander. He stepped out of his car, surveyed the scene, checked his watch, and slowly walked toward the slab. He took off his hat and wiped his forehead, which had puddled up with sweat. Hootie always perspired excessively in warm weather or after the slightest physical exertion, but this perspiration pooled up from everything today—the sweltering July afternoon, the heat still rising up from the slab, the intensity of emotion he saw and felt. The anger, the frustration, the outrage shook Hootie. He patted his brow with his bunched-up handkerchief, then pressed it like a towel against his head, sopping up the sweat. His forehead pulsed bright pink. He tried to speak, but his throat burned.

"I'm . . ."

He swallowed. He couldn't find a single other word. He swabbed his forehead again. He felt himself slouching, walking in slow motion to the stricken family.

"What caused it?" he said, knowing the answer.

"A short," Will said. "Bad wiring. Or sparks from a piece of wood that rolled out of the stove when we were asleep. Or—"

He stopped. He couldn't finish. Babe finished for him.

"Or human error."

"Or human *intent*," Hootie said.

Babe checked his watch. "They're late."

"They're right behind me," Hootie said.

The *clang-clang-clang* of a fire bell rang out, jarring them, and a firetruck rumbled around the corner, a firefighter in full garb at the wheel, and Tony, the mechanic, riding next to him, leaning over, ringing the bell. In the back of the truck sat Karter, a coiled-up hose on one side, a hatchet on the other, a too-small firefighter's helmet perched on his head. He looked like an oversize child playing fireman.

"He takes up the whole back," Babe said.

The firetruck slowed, pulled in front of Hootie's police car, and parked beside the smoldering slab. Hootie sniffed, his hands idly twisting the brim of his hat. Karter stood, tossed the helmet aside, and vaulted off the truck.

"Any problems?" Babe asked him.

"Nah. A few gawkers, couple of unpleasant stares, one or two racial epithets. Nothing I couldn't handle with a look."

"Good."

"You did get a call," Karter said.

"From?"

"Chicago. They want a meet tonight. Midnight. Something about a new shipment. They want a confirmation. They're calling you at five."

"Sounds foreboding."

"I didn't like it, either."

Karter bit down on his matchstick and turned his attention to his suit. The fabric had bunched up in the ride. He muttered and slapped at the wrinkles. Babe veered off, approached Tony on the passenger side.

"You get a chance to take a look?"

"All done, Babe," Tony said. "Nothing major. I replaced the sparkplugs, and the brakes were squishier than shit. I flushed them out and put in new pads. Got this honey running like a top. Good as new."

"You write me an invoice, okay?"

Tony shook his head. "On me. Least I could do."

"I owe you," Babe said. Then he turned back to the family. They stood riveted on the sidewalk, staring at the concrete slab, the remains of their home. Babe touched Marion's arm and rested his other hand on Will's shoulder. "I can't know how you feel. I can only say I'm sorry. We'll help you rebuild. We'll raise money for you."

"We never had a fire engine on our side of town," Will said.

"You do now," Babe said.

The unspoken sentiment hung in the air.

Too late for us.

Hootie appeared next to Babe.

"Babe pulled some strings," Hootie said. "You're going to have this truck over here from now on. Going to keep it right next to the jailhouse."

"Long overdue," Babe said. He narrowed his eyes, stared at the slab. "This can never happen again."

"We're looking for some volunteer firemen," Hootie said to Will. "You know of anybody?"

Marion and Will's eyes met. She nodded. Babe could read their unspoken exchange. They had talked about this.

"I'd like to volunteer," Will said.

"You sure you don't want to take some time?" Hootie said.

"No," Will said. "I'm ready now. Let's talk to the man."

He put his arm around Marion's waist, and heads bowed, they walked slowly toward the firefighter behind the wheel. Their daughter drifted a few feet behind them. Rosetta came up alongside.

"Hi," she said.

The girl said nothing.

"I'm sorry about your house."

The girl's top lip curled down. She bit it slightly to keep from crying in front of her possible new friend.

"Everything got burned up," the girl said.

They walked a few steps in silence and then Rosetta exhaled.

"Here," she said.

She handed the girl her book.

The girl stared at Rosetta, almost not comprehending the sudden act of kindness. "No. I can't. It's yours."

"I already read it," Rosetta said.

She pressed the book into the girl's hands. The girl took it hungrily, pressing it for a moment into her chest. "Thank you."

She looked at the cover and scanned the title, *Doctor Dolittle*. She looked at Rosetta. "Is it good?"

"It's great," Rosetta said.

"I might be late," Babe told Rosie when he dropped her and Rosetta off at the alley house. "Sleep tight, Tulip."

"Kiss me and Blue when you get home," she said.

"I will."

"Don't wake us up."

"I won't."

"'Night, Daddy."

He saw then that she no longer had her book. He started to ask if she'd left it someplace but stopped himself. He somehow knew that she'd given the book to the little girl who'd lost everything in the fire.

Tulip's gonna be all right, Babe thought as he watched his daughter climb out of the backseat and wave as she ran into their house. *No matter what happens, she will be all right.*

9

Babe found a spot for the Commander in the alley on the side of the Sportsman Hall, a block up from the river, away from people and especially other cars. He intentionally took up two parking spaces. Only a few months old, the car still smelled fresh and new inside. He wanted to avoid the inevitable dings and scratches to the exterior that he knew would come in time. So far, so good, thanks in part to Karter. He cared for the car as if it were his own prized possession, washing it twice a week, dabbing on polish when he saw a blemish, buffing out dings until they disappeared, spit-shining the exterior until it glowed.

"You don't have to do all that," Babe told him.

"It relaxes me," Karter said. "Not that I need to relax around here. All I do is relax. You're doing me a favor. Polishing your car is the main excitement I get."

They took the side entrance into the building. They walked through the diner where Rosie worked nine until two, Monday through Friday, then headed through the second restaurant, The Café, a casual lunch spot with tables and a few booths, then proceeded into the third restaurant, Le Restaurant, a larger, fancier, white-tableclothed eatery for special occasions and moneyed guests who wanted to make an impression. They passed the main entrance to the Sportsman Hall, walked through the lobby, breezing by the front desk where hotel guests checked in and out. Babe and Karter walked briskly, with purpose, greeting everyone they encountered. The staff smiled when they saw Babe, exchanged a handshake, a laugh, some small talk, remarking about the stifling heat, the upcoming Fourth, the parade, the Miss Caruthersville pageant, the floats, the pie-eating contest, the greased-pole-climbing competition, the other festivities, the fireworks. People reflexively retreated a few steps when Karter came upon them, allowing him as much room as he needed. Babe and Karter engaged waiters, cashiers, busboys, hotel clerks, bellhops, delivery men, security guards, all dressed in uniform, some in suits.

Eventually they came to the back of the building. They shouldered through two large French doors leading to a wide banquet hall. Babe slowed his pace and eyeballed the vast, empty room— the plush carpeting, chairs lined up and stacked against the far wall, a large oak table pushed to the side, a grand piano in the corner. *My world*, he thought.

Babe looked at his watch. "We're good."

Karter consulted his watch. "Fifteen minutes."

Babe strode to the back of the banquet hall and went into a well-lit hallway with several more doors. One opened to a kitchen, another led to a pantry, another to a storage closet, and beyond that, at the end of the hall, two massive metal doors rolled up and opened outside to a loading dock. The delivery entrance. Items too oversize or too numerous came through here, whatever the particular event in the banquet hall required that evening—extra tables and chairs, trays of catered food, elaborate floral arrangements, musical instruments, and in particular, cases of beverages for wedding receptions, birthday celebrations, election night victory and concession parties, and holiday galas.

Babe controlled these doors. Babe commanded the loading dock. At his signal, the doors opened afterhours several nights a week. These nights Babe repurposed the banquet hall into a full-service casino. Babe rolled up the metal doors, and he and Karter oversaw a parade of men hauling craps tables, blackjack tables, poker tables, roulette, slot machines, and one Big Six Wheel. Some nights, Babe and Karter turned the banquet hall into a boxing arena, helping to carry up the four corner pieces, rope, and a cushy square of canvas making up the boxing ring they set up in the center of the banquet hall for unsanctioned cage fights.

And one night a week, never the same night but always after ten and often past midnight, Babe and Karter cut the lights and led the way with flashlights, guiding men up the ramp to the loading dock, burly men in suits from Chicago wheeling wooden cases of whiskey on hand trucks, the primo stuff, not the lesser grade poured in Le Restaurant. Babe bootlegged only the best, offloading cases to his buyers—distributors throughout the Midwest, liquor store owners, restaurant owners, and a handful of very wealthy clients and collectors in the private sector who demanded only the finest for their individual use, especially when it came to scotch and bourbon. Strictly speaking, this activity stretched beyond the law. But while Babe was breaking the law, he also ran his bootlegging operation with the full cooperation of the law. Hootie stationed himself on one side of the men unloading the whiskey while Karter loomed on the other. Hootie never looked away. He focused full attention on the delivery, counting each shipment case by case, verifying Babe's order. He had to. He was Babe's partner. Occasionally, Babe or Hootie ripped open a case with a crowbar, uncorked a random bottle, and Babe sampled the contents. The men from Chicago would glare at him.

"Don't be offended. Just doing my due diligence," Babe would say, sniffing the whiskey, then closing his eyes and taking a pull from the bottle. "Ah. There it is. A hint of vanilla and right behind that a touch of butterscotch. Um, *um*. Tastes like Kentucky. Sorry for the interruption, gentlemen. Please continue."

Babe came back into the banquet hall and checked his watch again. He liked wearing a watch. Since the army, he had become obsessive about time, the concept of time, the meaning of time, everything to do with time. Timing. Good timing and bad. Keeping time. Knowing the right time. *Feeling* the right time. He made it a point to arrive at appointments ten minutes early. He couldn't abide being late and rankled at people who were late to meet him. He felt disrespected. He considered tardiness a flaw in a person's character.

"Five minutes," Karter said. He poked his head into the hallway to make sure that nobody came near the payphone on the wall across from him.

Babe waggled his hands at his side and shrugged his shoulders. He moved over to the piano and sat down. He bent over the keys, closed his eyes, and began to play. He launched into Memphis Slim's upbeat boogie-woogie dance number "Trouble in Mind." But Babe went the other way. He turned the tune into an achingly slow blues ballad. Reflexively, Karter moved to the music, slightly, briefly, always keeping an eye on the back hallway and the payphone. Babe played for a couple of minutes, his fingers curled, lightly caressing the keys, his eyes squeezed shut, his head bobbing to the rhythm.

The payphone rang.

Babe's fingers froze in midair over the keys.

He waited.

The phone rang again.

"You take it," Babe said.

Karter crossed the room into the hallway, arriving at the phone on the wall in two strides. He picked up the receiver and murmured, "Yeah."

He rounded his shoulders, dug in, and listened.

Inside the banquet hall, Babe's fingers landed softly on the piano keys. He closed his eyes again and began playing a Chopin nocturne. For the briefest moment, he felt transported back to Paris, to that house in the alley. He pictured himself at another piano, a shaky upright pushed against a wall, illuminated by the muted blue and red of a stained-glass pattern from an antique lamp on an end table next to his elbow. Amelie loved Chopin. Babe learned the introduction to a couple of nocturnes. A few bars, that's all he knew. Enough to get by. Enough to impress.

That's all you have to do. Enough to get by.

To keep yourself going. To get in.

To keep yourself alive.

Karter murmured goodbye into the phone and walked deliberately back into the banquet hall, taking his time. Babe didn't look up from the piano, but he felt Karter's massiveness surrounding him, blanketing him like a shadow.

"They're on their way from Chicago," Karter said. "The meeting's on."

"Where?"

"The four corners. I designated the location."

"Something's up," Babe said.

"I don't like it."

"You said you wanted some action."

"Careful what you wish for, right?" Karter said.

The big man rolled his bottom lip over his matchstick. He seemed to swallow it whole, and then the matchstick reappeared in a different position, hanging at the corner of his mouth. A magic trick. Karter liked to make things disappear.

"Something is definitely *up*," Karter said, and whistled low.

But he didn't seem unhappy.

After the midnight meeting with Tommy Wojak, his more-than-implied threat, and making the deal to acquire the entire allotment of three thousand cases of whiskey—a boxcar full—Babe and Karter drove back to town and sat in the Commander a few tenements away from Babe's alley house. Karter sighed, squirmed in his suit, and then settled in uncomfortably. He peeked into the night.

"Fifty-four thousand dollars," Babe said, his voice hushed. "Three thousand cases of bourbon."

"Lot of hootch, lot of cash," Karter said.

"An opportunity," Babe said.

"Early birthday present," Karter said. "Dropped into your lap."

Babe nodded. "You turn forty, you should change some things, right?"

"I expect so," Karter said.

"You'll see when you get there."

"I will." He paused. "So we're clear, I am planning to move

back to Chicago. This place is too slow. Look up *boring* in the dictionary. You'll see a picture of Caruthersville."

"When you going?"

"After this deal," Karter said.

He grunted and hauled himself out of the Commander.

STROKER

◆

**A PLAYER WHO MAKES
OVERLY COMPLICATED BETS
AND CAUSES DEALERS
TO WORK HARDER,
UNNECESSARILY,
USUALLY PISSING THEM OFF**

10

FRIDAY, JULY 2, 1948
10:07 A.M.

Friday morning of Fourth of July weekend.

The last chance to score a BabyLou Breakfast and a stack of Rosie Cakes for two days.

The diner swelled with customers, standing room only, an eager line clogging the doorway and snaking out to Main Street. Rosie, with her apron flapping, working solo, sprinted from the grill to the counter and back, swooping up the coffeepot, balancing plates of breakfast on her forearm, her silhouette splashed with the glow of "BabyLou's Kitchen" in neon red and blue mood lighting pulsing over her. As she slid plates piled high with her signature ham, bacon, eggs, biscuits, and cornbread onto the counter, a medley of contradictory thoughts smashed through her mind—

I love this.

I LOVE that these people line up for my food.

Where the hell is Floyd?

I'm getting too old for this.

My feet are killing me.

Feels like there's a knife being twisted into my lower back.

I'm getting WAY too old for this.

I'm ready to "retire" (ha ha) and start building on my land.

I'd like a do-over. A new beginning. It's time.

WHERE THE HELL IS FLOYD?

The bell above the door dinged, and as if reading her thoughts, Babe, preceded by Hootie, threaded his way into the diner, ducking and weaving past customers in line. Hootie, a blocking back, ran interference. Tony, Leaky, and Carlyle saw Babe arrive and saluted with their coffee cups from their stools at the counter.

"Good morning," Babe sang softly and immediately stifled a yawn.

"Good morning, *Floyd*," Rosie said, emphasizing his given name, never a good sign. "You left rather abruptly last night. Excuse me. This morning. *Early.*"

"No rest for the weary," Babe said. "Where's Tulip?"

"My sister's," Rosie said, nodding at Leaky.

"She's helping Carla prepare her world-famous chili," Leaky said, and then mumbled, "Better her than me."

"Morning, Rosie," Hootie said.

"Morning, Officer. Breakfast?"

"Thanks, no. Got a meeting. Official Fourth of July business. In other words, I'm being held hostage. I'll take a coffee to go."

"I got you," Babe said, squeezing behind the counter. As he moved toward the coffeepot, he brushed hips and locked eyes with Rosie. She paused and then lifted her face, allowing Babe to brush her cheek with his lips. She caught some tentativeness in his kiss. She pulled back and studied him. She saw exhaustion, distraction, and something else. Something she hadn't seen before. A new emotion. She read—concern. She and Babe spoke in a rushed whisper.

"You okay?"

"Fine," Babe said.

"You don't seem fine."

"It's always something."

"Said the King of Vague."

"I got a situation. It could be either a lucrative business proposition or a life-changing opportunity. Jury's out."

"Oh, okay, as long as it's nothing *serious*."

"Probably won't be. Then again, maybe it will. Fifty-fifty."

"Should I be worried?"

"It won't help."

Somebody shouted for more coffee. Rosie shouted, "Coming up!" to the room and touched Babe's arm. "You'll have to elaborate after the breakfast rush."

"I have to leave in a minute. I'll say this. We might be having a big celebration bash for my fortieth."

As they spoke, Hootie's attention drifted toward a large white presence taking up an entire corner table. A nervous butterball of a young man with a crewcut and pale skin bordering on pink *tap-tap-tapped* the table with his chubby, fidgety fingers.

"Clyde?" Hootie said.

The young man ducked his head, snorted, and waved. "Hi, Carl."

"I've never seen you in here before."

"Yeah, well, I know you come in for breakfast sometimes."

Hootie tilted his head toward Rosie. "Best breakfast in town. Give it a try."

Clyde sniffed. He peered at his tabletop, then looked up at Hootie. "I need to talk to you."

"Can't it wait until we get home?"

"It's private."

Hootie laughed, nodded at the crowd in the diner. "Not my idea of private in here."

Clyde snorted again. His cheeks flushed so red they looked scalded.

"Why don't we step outside?" Hootie said.

Clyde pushed himself up from the table, scraping his chair across the floor, creating a noise loud enough to silence most of the room.

"Sorry," he said to the floor.

"Here you go," Babe said, handing Hootie a to-go coffee.

"Thank you. Thanks, Rosie," Hootie said, reaching for his wallet.

Rosie waved a spatula. "On the house."

"That might be considered a bribe," Hootie said, dropping a dollar onto the counter.

"'Lo, Clyde," Babe said.

"Mm."

"I'll walk you out," Babe said to Hootie. Near the door, Babe pivoted toward his guys at the counter.

"Word to the wise," he said gravely. "You can't make pork-chops out of bacon."

He tipped his hat and cut through the line at the door, ducking, darting, Hootie and Clyde at his heels, trying to keep up.

Tony, Carlyle, and Leaky watched Babe go, his words falling on them with heft, with purpose, with insight. Carlyle kept his knife poised over his ham and biscuits as he contemplated Babe's wisdom.

"Think about that," he said, diagramming the sentence in the air with the blade of his butterknife. "You. Cannot. Make. Porkchops. Out. Of. *Bacon*."

Tony nodded at his plate and poked the two strips of bacon he had left. "True."

"Deep," Leaky said, his mouth full. He waved at Tony with his knife. "Babe has a way of cutting through shit and slicing it into bite-size, easy-to-digest *morsels*. You know what I'm saying? He gets down to *it*."

"You can't make porkchops out of bacon," Carlyle said again, with emphasis, with reverence.

"No way," Leaky said. "You can't do it."

"Cannot happen," Carlyle said.

"So deep," Leaky said.

"Pithy," Tony said.

"What does it mean?" Carlyle said.

"Well," Tony said, twirling his knife in a circle. "If you have bacon—I'm saying, *if* you have it—but you may not, you understand? You may not have any bacon."

"Uh-huh," Leaky said, nodding, listening, considering.

"But if you do have bacon, you are *limited* to bacon, you follow?" Tony said. "You don't have porkchops. You cannot *have* porkchops. And that is a life lesson."

Carlyle waved his knife in sync with Tony's knife and said, "Babe has smarts *and* wisdom. Two separate things."

"Totally different," Leaky said. "That's why he's so deep."

"He's been places," Carlyle said. "England. France. You know, in the war."

"Serving his country," Leaky said.

Carlyle shifted his position at the long counter. "I, too, would have served my country if I hadn't been turned down because of my medical condition."

"Medical condition?" Leaky said. "You have flat feet."

Carlyle ignored him, looked dreamily into the neon sign. "That's my biggest regret. Not serving my country. My only regret, really. I've had a good life. A steady job with health benefits, vacation time, a pension. I have everything a man could want. I'm blessed."

Tony stared at him. "You're a garbage collector."

Carlyle arched his back and sat straight up on his stool. "*Sanitation consultant*. I am a city employee. I serve the people of my community. I keep our streets clean and free of pestilence and infestation. This year, so far, I have only been bitten by a rat once."

"Congratulations," Leaky said. "What the fuck does that have to do with anything?"

"*Montel*." Carlyle lowered his voice. "I might *like* to turn these two puny strips of bacon into a couple of thick, juicy porkchops, but that will never happen. It's impossible. It's a pipe dream."

"In other words," Tony said, "accept your lot in life."

"Hel*lo*." Leaky slapped the counter. "Be thankful for what you have."

The three men went silent for a long count of ten. Finally, Tony said, "I don't think that's what it means."

"I don't, either," Carlyle said.

"Definitely not," Tony said.

"So deep," Leaky said.

11

After Hootie and Babe left the diner, they turned sharply up the alley, Clyde huffing behind them, trying to keep up. They pulled up along the side entrance of the Sportsman Hall and found a spot in the shade of an awning. Clyde held his hand up, a stop sign, then wiped his forehead with the back of his hand. He exhaled heavily and rested his palms on his knees.

"Ten in the morning and it's already a sweatbox," Clyde said.

"What's going on, Clyde?" Hootie said. "Everything all right with Helen?"

"Fine, she's fine, everything's fine."

"I missed you at Sunday dinner."

"Yeah, I know. Sorry about that. I had a previous commitment. Couldn't get out of it."

"Uh-huh. I like having the whole family together for Sunday dinner. The one thing I ask."

"I'll definitely be there Sunday."

"This Sunday's the Fourth."

"Oh, yeah, right."

Hootie sniffed, made eye contact with Babe, who kept his eyes on Clyde.

"So, Clyde, what did you need to talk to me about?"

Clyde looked at Babe, hesitated. "It's, you know, business. Well, it's personal, really. Family."

"I'll leave," Babe said.

"No," Hootie said. He took a step toward his son-in-law. "Babe's my partner. Anything you have to say, you can say in front of him. Especially if it has to do with business."

Clyde clumsily patted his sizeable belly. "Fine, fine." He started to address Babe directly and then backed away and turned toward his father-in-law. "The fact is, in terms of business, we've had the same definition of terms for something like five years now."

"By definition of terms, you mean what?" Hootie said.

"Partnership." He looked at Babe now. "A third, a third, a third."

"Yeah?" Hootie said.

"I'd like to redefine my terms."

Clyde tried to keep his eyes on Babe, but Babe's icy stare froze him. Clyde lowered his eyes to the pavement and kicked at a shadow.

"And how would you like to redefine the terms?" Babe asked.

Clyde kept his head down. "I wasn't talking to you."

Babe shifted his weight. He felt his fingers ease toward the twin leather holsters holding his barber's blades. A reflex. He would never harm Hootie's son-in-law. He would never draw on him. But he could feel his rage rising. It felt like a heat ray beating directly down on him. His neck started to sweat.

"Let's hear it," Hootie said, his voice laced with anger and pain. "Your new terms."

"Forty, forty, twenty," Clyde said, his voice small, shaking.

"You want to reduce me to twenty percent," Babe said. He tried not to laugh. He tried not to scream.

"It's only fair," Clyde said. "It's only right."

"Fair?" Babe said, cocking his head at Clyde. "I'm curious. What exactly do you do right now to justify getting even a third? Besides not fucking up your marriage to Carl's daughter."

Clyde licked his lips, raised his head. Then he turned toward Hootie, stepping in front of Babe, making a point to keep his back to him.

"Why do you carry him?" Clyde said. "You don't need him. He's not one of us. He doesn't belong—"

"Watch yourself," Babe said.

"Where is this coming from, Clyde?" Hootie said. "Who've you been talking to?"

"Nobody. I've just been thinking."

"That would be a first," Babe said.

Clyde took a step toward Babe. Then he caught a different look in Babe's eye—a murderous look—and he retreated.

"I hear you're running with some new boys," Hootie said.

"I don't know what you mean. Like who?"

"You know who. I have eyes. I have sources. I see. I hear. People talk to me."

Clyde snorted. He swiped at the sweat that had begun to pool up on his forehead.

"I'm hearing Johnny G. The Farm Boys. That group."

"I mean," Clyde said, clearing his throat. "We had some beers. Played some cards. A couple of times."

"Johnny G," Hootie said. "I knew his old man. Both RAF."

Clyde squinted. "RAF?"

"Racist as fuck," Babe said. "Farm Boy Mafia. They make the Klan seem like a singing group."

"He put you up to this?" Hootie said.

"No. Like I said, I've been *thinking*—"

"I'm going to let you two work this out," Babe said. "But for the record, Clyde, not only am I keeping my thirty-three and a third, but you're lucky I don't unleash Pearl and Baby Girl and eviscerate you right here on the street."

"Babe," Hootie said. "About what we talked about earlier. That investment opportunity. I'd like to revisit that conversation. I seriously want to invest. Without any limitations. No withdrawal penalties."

"Are you sure?"

"Yeah," Hootie said, eyeing Clyde. "I've been *thinking*."

"Let's schedule an investor's meeting," Babe said. He took a couple of steps down the alley, spun suddenly, and glared at Clyde. He lifted Pearl from her holster, allowing the blade to sparkle in the sun. Then he pulled an apple from his suit pocket, tossed the apple straight up, flicked the barber's blade, and with the precision of a surgeon and the moxie of a magician, sliced the apple perfectly in half, catching both pieces in his palm. With a flourish, he returned Pearl to her holster and popped half the apple into his mouth.

Babe tipped his hat toward Hootie and continued walking. "Later, officer."

"Who the hell are Pearl and Baby Girl?" Clyde asked Hootie.

"You just met Pearl. She and Baby Girl are twin barber blades with inlaid gold handles, sharp as cold steel. You know what *eviscerate* means?"

Clyde shook his head.

"Gut you like a fish."

Babe came out of the alley and headed right for the Com-mander. He opened the door, got behind the wheel, and drummed his fingers on the dashboard. He stared ahead, thinking of Clyde, Johnny G, and Hootie. He felt as if time had accelerated and begun to career out of control. In his mind, the events of the past twelve hours came barreling at him like an avalanche—the meeting with Wojak, the deal he made to buy the whole lot of whiskey for fifty-four thousand dollars, and now Clyde wanting a bigger cut of his partnership in the Sportsman Hall. He felt knocked back, thrown off-balance. Babe, the consummate, careful fighter, a boxer not a brawler, always kept his footing. He planned his punches, plotted his moves, always staying two, three, four steps ahead—of everyone, always. Until now.

Babe glanced at the glove compartment. He licked his lips and snapped open the compartment. He reached in past his mound of bound-up papers and pulled out the flask. The Macallan. His courage. He needed a sip to calm his nerves. A swallow. A taste. He looked at the flask, rubbed his finger over the worn but still jagged edge of the bullet hole. This flask had saved his father's life. His father fought as a member of the 369th Infantry Regiment in France. A squad of German soldiers set upon him and his battalion while the African American soldiers repaired a bridge. His father's unit had been trained to fight, but once overseas, they mainly patched roads, dug latrines, and rebuilt bridges. He used his rifle butt more often as a hammer than a weapon. During the ambush, Babe's father took a bullet in the leg and one in his chest. Remarkably, neither bullet killed him. The first bullet ripped up his leg and eventually left him with a limp. The other bullet tore through his uniform, his T-shirt, knocked him back into some reeds, and got embedded in the flask, inches from his heart, saving his life. Babe touched the bullet hole again and thought, *This flask symbolizes a miracle.* He drew the flask to his mouth, but his fingers started to tremble.

"Ten o'clock in the morning," he said aloud. "What are you doing, Babe?"

He tucked the flask back behind the documents and slammed the glove compartment shut.

He leaned back against the seat and closed his eyes.

He pictured an event from his past. A memory. A moment.

A stifling Saturday night twenty-three years ago.

He saw a craps game in the middle of the woods.

He saw the beginning.

TAKE DOWN

◆

REMOVING YOUR BETS

12

FRIDAY, JUNE 12, 1925

uane, a white farm boy who worked at the farming supply store outside town, told him about the game. Babe, self-appointed caretaker of the family farm, had gone to the store to pick up supplies—seeds, beans, fertilizer, a bundle of wooden stakes, a hoe. Duane, in his early twenties, a few years older than Babe, liked to pontificate and brag, especially about his unmatched gambling prowess. Every week, when Babe drove the truck to the store, Duane regaled him with stories about his winning streak at an illegal dice game outside town—how he held the dice for forty-five minutes, making point after point, how he doubled up on the hard eight and how the two fours had come in five straight times, how he placed all the numbers in the box, and how those hit again and again. The way he described his winnings, Duane should have been a high-stepping, tuxedo-wearing riverboat gambler lighting fat Cuban cigars with five-dollar bills instead of being a gangly twenty-three-year-old with torn overalls and dirty fingernails selling fertilizer at a farming supply store.

"Where's the game at?" Babe asked him one afternoon.

Duane frowned at Babe. "How old are you?"

"Sixteen. Seventeen in August."

"You're not legal."

"The game's not legal."

Duane wiped his hands on his overalls. "Do you know how to play?"

"I can pick it up."

Duane sniffed. He looked Babe over, deciding whether or not Babe would be worth a trial. "Meet me here tonight at ten. It's hard to find. You can follow me there. We could always use another chump."

"I appreciate the invitation," Babe said.

That night, driving the pickup, Babe followed Duane off the highway to a two-lane road, then down a narrow, twisting, barely paved single lane into the woods, arriving at a well-lit cabin in a clearing. Babe saw twenty Model Ts and a cluster of pickups parked tightly in a grassy area to the right of the cabin. Beyond them, three brand-new Cadillacs were parked on the lawn at the back of the cabin. A driver sat inside one, smoking, watching, waiting.

Babe parked up the road, away from all the other vehicles. At this distance, it looked like he'd arrived at a used car lot. He wanted to be able to leave at any time should this night go bad. Duane parked among the other cars as if a spot close to the cabin identified him as a member of an exclusive club, a regular, a player. He hustled out of his pickup and rushed inside, leaving Babe to find his own way. Babe hesitated and then climbed out of the cab of his pickup. He knocked on the front door. A large white man wearing a suit, a scar, and a scowl opened the door. He sized Babe up, nodded, and stepped aside, barely allowing Babe to ease in. He slammed the door behind him.

In front of him, Babe saw a craps game in progress, players and spectators packed two and three rows deep around the table. Babe walked closer to the table as a roar from the crowd erupted, followed by a burst of cheering like you'd hear at a baseball game after a walk-off homerun. Babe stood on his toes and saw that the dice shooter had made his point. The shooter grinned and accepted slaps on the back and a kiss from a busty and heavily made-up woman at his side.

Babe scanned the room. This was a restaurant, he realized, during normal business hours. Tables and chairs had been stacked up and pushed to the side. Tonight—and maybe most nights—the place hosted a craps game and offered a full bar. A thick cloud of cigar and cigarette smoke formed a second ceiling, and Babe winced from the smell of whiskey and sweat. Despite Prohibition laws, the liquor here *flowed*, streaming nonstop as if from an open spigot. Young women, pouring beer and shots into tall frosted glasses, sashayed among the gamblers. Still fighting to get his bearings, Babe stood his ground. A woman wearing a tight-fitting and skimpy outfit appeared, handed Babe a glass, and poured him a beer that spilled over. She blew him a kiss and slinked away into the crowd. Babe watched her go and then turned his attention to the craps table. He felt mesmerized, immobilized, immersed by everything around him. All of it. Choking on cigar smoke. Drinking whiskey without hesitation or fear. And the game itself. Laughing, shouting, roaring—each roll of the dice filled with hope, leading to instantaneous triumph, riches, or heartbreak. It made him dizzy. The setting felt surreal. He felt as if he had stumbled into a casino at the end of the world.

Babe took a long drink from the glass, set it aside on the bar, and maneuvered his way through the packed rows of people until he managed to wedge his way into an opening at the craps table. Duane stood on the opposite side, already half-drunk, hungrily exchanging a fistful of cash for a stack of chips.

Later, when thinking about that night, Babe wouldn't trace his affinity for craps to the first time he rolled the dice down the green felt, watching them tumble over each other and ricochet off the back wall and with the sound of a kiss land on six shiny black dots next to five shiny black dots, the crowd roaring as the stickman announced, "Winner. *Eleven.*" No, Babe fell in love with the game even before that first roll. And he fell hard. It was love at first sight. He fell in love with every aspect and nuance of the experience— the energy in the packed room, the shoulder-to-shoulder contact of the players around the table as if they were participants in an athletic event, the cool touch of the small cubes in the palm of his hand, the subtle windup that he made with his wrist before he launched the dice in an arc as if he were lobbing a softball or throwing horseshoes. Yes. He loved all of it.

But mostly he fell in love with the idea of making instantaneous decisions, on the spot, those choices being part of the game, the most crucial part, knowing when to press up his bets and when to take his bets down and which numbers to play. Duane boasted, but Babe knew. He just knew. Tonight, his first time, he began with his favorite number—eight—his birthday, August 8, the eighth day, the eighth month.

Midnight came, went, and Babe felt flush, both because of the actual warmth in the cabin as more and more players arrived and packed the room and because he continued to win. Again and again, roll after roll. At one point, the house ran out of chips, and Babe played with cash, laying folding money on the table—fives, tens, and then twenties. After one ridiculously long roll that ended with him making his point, an eight, of course, and the crowd screaming insanely, Babe caught Duane across from him bashing his fists onto the side of the table, swearing, and then shouting, "Beginner's luck!"

"No doubt," Babe said. "How long did I hold the dice? About an hour? Did I beat your record?"

Duane smacked the side of the table again, then bulldozed through the crowd and headed toward the door. He stopped, whipped around, shoved back through the crowd, and bumped his thick shoulder into Babe's side, jarring him.

"You knew how to play," Duane said.

"I didn't," Babe said. "I guess I just have a feel for the game. You leaving? I'll head out with you."

"Find your own way," Duane said.

♠

13

At a clearing in the woods, a mile or so from the cabin, a young man, seventeen years old, Babe's age, lay on a blanket and watched his girlfriend snap her bra back on and then shimmy her lightweight summer dress over her body.

"Wow," Carl said. "The moonlight hits you just right."

Tammi laughed, dropped down, and snuggled into Carl's side. He wore jeans and a T-shirt. He'd left his shirt on the seat of his pickup that he'd parked at the tip of the clearing. For a while, he and Tammi held on to each other, listening to the night sounds, a breeze rippling through leaves, critters skittering, snapping twigs. Mainly, they listened to the low hum of their breathing and the beating of their hearts.

"I wish we didn't have to do this," Tammi said.

Carl half sat up. "If you don't want to—"

Tammi swatted Carl's chest. "No, fool, I love *this*. I mean sneaking around, driving ten miles out of town so we can be together."

Carl put on a scary voice he'd heard on a radio show. "Their love. It is forbidden."

Tammi giggled, but then she went quiet.

"I'm serious," she said.

"I know," Carl said. "But what can we do?"

"We could stop," Tammi said.

Carl leaned forward onto his elbows. "Do you, I mean, do you want to?"

"No."

"Good," Carl said. "Me neither."

Carl pulled Tammi closer to him. He rubbed her back and brushed her tightly curled hair. For some time now, months at least, he had wanted to tell her something, but he hadn't been able to formulate the words. Or he hadn't been able to summon the courage. But tonight, he thought he might try.

"Um," he said.

Then—nothing.

"There's more," Carl said.

"I hope so."

Tammi waited. Carl started to speak, then stopped.

Tammi bit her lip, forcing herself not to burst out laughing. "Does he speak?"

"I'm trying to tell you something serious."

"I'm serious. I'm very serious. Look at me."

He leaned forward. Tammi had put on a fake, cartoony expression. She ran her finger over her bottom lip. "See? Serious."

She laughed.

"Okay, really, I'm ready," he said.

And waited.

Finally, Carl exhaled. "Here goes. I want to tell you that I, ah, um, I—love. I, ah, *love*, um—"

Tammi lost it.

She roared, laughing out of control. Then she waved her hands rapidly in front of her, fanning herself.

"I'm sorry, I'm sorry, no, no, please, go on—"

She breathed in, out, composed herself, exhaled again, and then burst out laughing.

"Well, if you're gonna laugh—"

Carl began tickling her.

"Stop it, you *Jeff*, you know I'm ticklish. *Stop*."

He didn't stop. He tickled her harder, frantically, all over—her sides, under her arms—then amped up the tickle attack even more until Tammi thrashed helplessly, panting from laughing, Carl joining her, laughing as hysterically as Tammi. They laughed this way, in sync, breathless, their tears of sheer joy streaming down their faces, their laughter, separate and together, pounding in their ears.

Which is why they didn't hear the men coming out of the woods.

Five of them.

In their early twenties.

Farm Boys.

Thick, heavyset, deliberate.

White.

They carried bats and knives.

One held a noose.

They came through the trees, fanned out, circled the edge of the clearing, and started to close in. Carl sensed them before he saw them. He could feel their presence. Their menace. Their violence.

Carl gently pushed Tammi behind him and scrambled to his feet. At this point, he identified them only as five pale rounded body shapes outlined in the night. But in a matter of seconds, his eyes adjusted, and he could make out their features. He didn't know them. He may have recognized one. He wasn't sure.

"Y'all having a party?" one of them said.

Carl drew himself to his full height. He was tall, broad-shouldered, and strong from baling hay and working the farm. He stepped off the blanket for better traction and balled up his fists at his side. He could hear Tammi trembling behind him. One of the Farm Boys stepped closer to her. Carl kept his focus on him, but behind him he heard Tammi whimper.

"What have we here?" the guy Carl recognized said. He stepped past the first man. In the moonlight, Carl now made out his face clearly. He knew of him. Johnny Galvis. The Farm Boys called him Johnny G. He was a few years older than Carl. Twenty, twenty-one. He had a reputation. Thief. Brawler. Drunk. Son of a major domo in the Klan. Total loser. All-around piece of shit.

"Who you hiding behind there? Is that a *girl*?"

Johnny G stepped closer, the other four at his back, tightening the circle around Carl and Tammi.

"Oh, no, my mistake," Johnny G said. "It ain't a girl. It's a female nigger."

He cackled. Carl smelled liquor on his breath.

"What are you two doing out here, all alone?" Johnny G's speech came out slurred and loud. "Wait, no, you ain't. You can't be. Are you—*fucking*?"

Carl glanced at Tammi. She had somehow curled herself up, almost into a standing fetal position. She started shaking violently. Carl could hear her lips chattering.

"You want a piece of me," Carl said. "Let's go. Leave her be."

Johnny G made a gurgling sound in his throat, swirled saliva in his mouth, and launched a missile of spit at Tammi. She tried to duck, but a wad of yellow spit spattered the side of her face. Johnny G hollered and slapped his leg. "Bullseye!"

The other four laughed with him. Johnny G turned to them.

"We don't want a piece of him, do we?"

They shouted, started coming closer, bearing down on Carl.

"Nah," Johnny G said. "We want *all* of y'all. Y'all breaking the law. We can't have that. You know who we are? Law *enforcers*."

Carl shifted his weight and looked at each of the five men, trying to decide who to go at first. Maybe the leader. Johnny G. That might be his best move. His only move.

"Just so you know," Johnny G said, "we have a plan. We're gonna string you up so you can watch the five of us fuck her, and then we're gonna slice her up before we burn her. Then we'll lynch you both. Side by side."

He pulled a knife out of his pocket. A switchblade. He sprung the blade open and tossed it from hand to hand. Carl kept an eye on the knife as he watched Johnny G's face. He raised his fists in a boxer's stance. He didn't back up. To Johnny's surprise, he stepped forward, *toward* Johnny G. Thrown off, Johnny G backed up a step and then thrust the knife at Carl's face. Carl leaned out of the way, the knife blade zipping past him. He came back, flicked a jab at Johnny, catching the side of his jaw. Shocked, Johnny howled. Then he went crazy. He charged Carl, and the other four swept in behind him, onto the blanket. One guy grabbed Tammi. Carl spun away from Johnny and smashed a right cross into this guy's throat, then he cracked him with a left to his jaw. The guy fell. Tammi wailed, but then another guy grabbed her and lifted her off her feet. She screamed at the top of her lungs as Johnny G and the other two men pulled their own knives and descended on Carl.

14

riving with his windows down, Babe squinted through the pickup's windshield at the twisting road ahead. He could swear he'd been down this road before—ten minutes ago. He felt as if he'd been driving in a circle.

"Where the hell am I?" he said.

Then he heard the screams.

Spilling out of the night.

Jolting him.

Someone shouting, followed by a howl. Then, unmistakably, a woman screaming. A panic scream. High-pitched. Filled with terror.

The screams stopped, but then he heard another scream, a follow-up scream. It sounded muffled, swallowed, defeated. The screams came out of the woods, to the right of him. Babe pulled over, reached into the glovebox, and found Honey, his father's gun. He flew out of the pickup. Illuminated by moonlight, Babe ran into the woods.

The darkness blanketed him, blinded him. He ran aimlessly for ten seconds or so, then stopped at a tree stump. He waited for his eyes to adjust to the night, only a few more seconds, and then, using his cigarette lighter, he felt his way through the woods, sliding from tree to tree. He veered in the direction of new sounds—the rise and fall of voices. Garbled words. A shrill shout. Another scream. Grunting, groaning, shouting. Crying. The moonlight spread before him, and Babe found a path leading through the trees until he came to a pickup truck parked at the edge of a clearing. He pocketed the lighter and ducked behind the pickup's tailgate. Before him he saw two white guys his age pounding on another white guy, who fought back hard but took a blow and fell forward onto the ground. He instantly sprang to his feet, blood spurting from his nose and mouth. He swung his fists desperately, trying to fight off his attackers. One of the attackers reached around him, grabbed one of his arms, and pinned it behind his back. A third white guy stepped into Babe's line of vision. The leader. Babe could tell by the way he held himself. He took an arrogant stance. He rolled his shoulders and started to laugh. Then Babe heard a sickening sound to his right. He peered over there and saw another white man punching a young Black woman in the face.

Babe felt bile rise into his throat. He wanted to vomit up his rage. He wanted more than anything to make this fight even, but he knew he had to calm himself. Measure his moves. Be smart. Be precise. He couldn't let his emotions rule. *Ice*, he told himself. *You need to become ice.*

He nodded, exhaled, counted to three, and stepped into the clearing. He shot his pistol into the air.

Everyone froze.

Babe darted toward the two guys pummeling the man on the ground, then he suddenly swerved and sprinted at the white man who was pummeling the Black woman. He got to them in what seemed like a blink. He pointed his gun at the guy's temple.

"Back away from her," Babe said.

The guy stood stone still, breathing deeply.

Babe cocked the trigger. "You have one second."

The guy didn't move.

Babe lowered his gun and shot the guy in the kneecap. The guy screamed and crumpled to the ground, blood gushing from his leg.

"Next one goes in your eye," Babe said.

"We all got knives," Johnny G said, ten feet away, standing behind Carl, pressing his switchblade to Carl's throat.

"Me, too," Babe said.

Babe reached into his coat and with a flourish brought out a barber's blade, longer than any switchblade. The barber's blade gleamed in the moonlight.

"I'd rather not use it," Babe said. "I'd rather kill you with my bare hands."

One guy bellowed and came at him.

Stupid move.

The guy lunged, his fingers clawing the air. Babe sidestepped, whirled, tripped him, and rode him facedown into the ground. He felt a second guy coming, about to pounce on him. Babe rose, ducked a punch, then launched himself. He slammed a left hook into the second guy's kidney. The second guy gasped for air, his knees buckled, and he collapsed into the grass. Babe went to the first guy. He lifted the first guy's head by his hair and placed his blade at his throat. He shouted at Johnny G who still stood with his switchblade at Carl's neck.

"You cut him? I'll kill these two. Then I'll kill you."

Johnny G hesitated for half a second.

That's all Babe needed.

He threw himself on the ground, rolled, aimed his gun, and shot Johnny G in the shoulder. Johnny G fell backward, the knife sailing out of his hand.

But behind him, Babe didn't see the first guy stand. He crouched and came at Babe with his knife.

Carl saw him. He took three long strides, leaped, and tackled the guy. Carl wrestled him to the ground, got astride his chest, and slugged him in the face. Then again. And again. Carl hit him one more time, knocking him unconscious. He got off him, stood up, staggered, retrieved his balance, and went over to Tammi. She knelt on the blanket. Her eyes looked glazed and far away. Blood streamed from her nose. She seemed in shock. Carl put his arms around her, rocked her gently, whispered, "It's all right."

Babe walked over to Johnny G and stood over him. He poked him with his shoe. Johnny moaned and tried to slither away. Babe stayed with him.

"Klan?" he said.

Johnny G grunted, cursed, tried to spit at Babe.

"He said he was going to lynch us," Carl said. "He said—"

"Don't," Tammi said.

Babe squatted, grabbed Johnny G by the collar, and pulled him to a sitting position. "I'm going to do humanity a favor. I'm going to reduce the world's population by one less racist piece of shit."

Babe raised his gun.

"Don't kill him," Carl said, arriving at Babe's side.

Babe stopped.

"Let me," Carl said.

He took Babe's gun and shot Johnny G.

Babe waved his blade in the direction of the other four. Two were out cold, two were semiconscious, watching in terror.

"I want to take out these four pieces of garbage, too," Babe said.

"Leave them."

"All right. I don't agree. But let's go."

Carl ran to Tammi. He lifted her and carried her to the truck. Babe gathered up the blanket, checked the five Farm Boys on the ground. They wouldn't be able to move for a while. He saw that Johnny G, while bleeding heavily from the stomach, was still breathing. Carl hadn't killed him. *He'll bleed out*, Babe thought. He would learn later that Johnny G would survive, miraculously. His racist animus would only grow.

Carl helped Tammi into the front seat of the pickup.

"I'll ride in the back," Babe said.

"No, you won't," Carl said. "Sit in front with us."

They squeezed in, Tammi in the middle, Babe riding shotgun.

"Plenty of room," Tammi said. Her voice sounded weak, tiny.

"How did you find us?" Carl said, starting up the pickup.

"I was on the road and I got lost. I heard screams. I pulled over and ran into the woods. Pure luck."

"We were the lucky ones," Tammi said.

"I have to know." Carl swallowed. "Why? I mean, why did you help us?"

"I'm a gambling man," Babe said. "I didn't like your odds."

Carl put the truck into reverse. Before leaving the clearing, he took a final look at the five guys on the ground. Carl turned to Babe and extended his hand. "Carl Holt. My friends call me Hootie."

"Floyd Boyce. My friends call me Babe."

They shook hands, keeping their grip on each other for a long time before they let go.

Carl gunned the pickup. They fishtailed out of the woods.

♠

HI-LO

◆

A BET ON TWO
OR TWELVE

15

FRIDAY, JULY 2, 1948

T *ap-tap-tap.*

Fingers drumming on the driver's side window.

Babe jumped, jerking out of his daydream. The sound of fingers tapping jolted him. Seeing Karter's face filling up his entire field of vision jolted him even more. Babe rolled down the window and narrowed his eyes at Karter. The noon heat made him squint. Karter stood and wiped his forehead with a handkerchief the size of a chamois cloth.

"It is *hot*," Karter said. "Feel like I'm a piece of charcoal inside a grill."

"That's what Caruthersville is famous for in July. Humidity. Read the brochure."

"Game's set," Karter said. "Ten o'clock, tomorrow night."

"You work fast."

"Nah. You spread the word that Babe Boyce wants a serious game, the fish come to the top of the tank like it's feeding time."

"You hooked my whale?"

Karter patted his sopping face. He hadn't made much progress drying the lake of sweat that had pooled on his forehead. He'd mainly managed to soak his handkerchief. "Guy named Hanford. From St. Louis."

"He easy to spot?"

"Should be. He's loud and they call him the Fat Man."

"Nice work."

"Doing my job." Karter grunted and wriggled uncomfortably in his suit.

"You know, in this heat, you could lose the suit."

"And wear what, shorts and flipflops? Please."

"Your call."

"Also, some news." Karter paused, then nodded in the direction of the alley next to the Sportsman Hall. "Hootie's son-in-law? He's tight with Johnny G Junior. Inner-circle tight."

"That's concerning."

Karter began wringing out his handkerchief. He popped a fresh matchstick into his mouth. He rolled it over with his tongue before tucking it into the corner of his mouth. "Hootie and Tammi. That was what, twenty years ago?"

"Give or take."

"That's over, right?"

"She's married. Three kids."

Karter folded his dried and stiff handkerchief into four precise triangles. "You didn't answer my question."

"Long over," Babe lied.

Babe always thought that if he were making a movie and needed someone to play the part of a banker, he would cast Oswald Middlebrooks III, the vice president of First State Bank and Trust

Company of Caruthersville. Ozzie, as Babe and everyone who knew him well called him, dressed, acted, and looked the part. He was tall, gangly, grim-faced, stoop-shouldered, and carried a permanent scowl, due, no doubt, to his recurring ulcer. He wore three-piece suits, flashy red suspenders, a colorful pocket square, and shoes buffed, shined, and squeaky. When Babe walked into the bank's lobby gripping his leather briefcase, Ozzie burst out of his office and rushed toward him, his loudly squeaking shoes piercing the quiet of the bank.

"Mr. Boyce," Ozzie shouted, slapping Babe on the back.

"Mr. Middlebrooks," Babe said.

The two men shook hands, Ozzie keeping the handshake going, pumping Babe's hand as if it were the handle of a well or slot machine. "Visiting your money?"

"Yes and no."

"Opening a new account? You're in luck. Fourth of July special. Open a new account, take home a free toaster."

"Excellent incentive, but I need to get to my safe deposit box."

"By all means," Ozzie said, resting his bony hand on Babe's shoulder. Ozzie was physical, a toucher. Babe didn't mind because Ozzie was also a frequent attendee at Babe's afterhours casino, a heavy drinker, a free spender, a skirt chaser, and best of all, a terrible craps player. Ozzie was far more than a business associate. He was one of Babe's favorites. A cash cow.

Ozzie steered Babe toward the side of the lobby, away from the row of tellers and the desks where bored loan officers and account managers sat, pretending to go through paperwork. Ozzie released a massive key ring from his pocket, jangling dozens of keys. He began sifting through them, one at a time, in search of the key leading to the backroom vault and safe deposit boxes. Babe shook his head. "I never met anyone with so many keys. Except the school janitor."

"Guess you never been to prison," Ozzie said.

Babe looked at Ozzie, wondering if he had, thinking, *Nah, he wouldn't last five minutes.*

Ozzie clicked his tongue triumphantly, finding the key he needed. He rubbed Babe's back. "Looking forward to tomorrow night," he murmured.

"Sorry it was so last minute," Babe said.

"Not at all." Ozzie lowered his voice. "Will there be women?"

"If you're referring to Monique, that can be arranged."

Ozzie's craggy face flushed. "Unlike most men, I admit to my vices."

"The bare minimum in your case," Babe said. "Three, tops."

"A manageable number," Ozzie said. He yanked open the door to the vault and allowed Babe to step inside first. They walked through a tight maze of safe deposit boxes, floor to ceiling. Ozzie went straight to the far corner, stopping at a metal box in the bottom row. Babe reached into his wallet and dug out a single, solitary key. He handed it to Ozzie. Ozzie squatted and opened the box with the two keys—the bank's and Babe's. He eased out the rectangular metal box and handed it to Babe.

"I assume you'll want some privacy," Ozzie said.

"I know the way," Babe said.

He tucked the safe deposit box against his side like a football and waited for Ozzie to leave the vault. Ozzie bowed regally and turned away. Babe walked to a small table separated by a curtain. Babe stepped in, closed the curtain, placed his briefcase on the table, and set the box down next to it. He pulled up a chair and opened the lid of the box.

The safe deposit box was filled with cash.

Our nest egg, Babe called it.

Savings for a rainy day.

Thursday, midnight, at the meet with Wojak, the rain had come.

Fourth of July weekend, temperatures in the midnineties, sweatbox humidity, no precipitation predicted for a week, but in his mind, all Babe saw was a torrential downpour.

He rested both hands on the stacks of cash before him fastened with rubber bands in thin piles of hundreds. He closed his eyes. He wanted to pray, but he couldn't find the words, couldn't summon the ask.

He opened his eyes, folded his hands on the money, and looked at the piles of cash again. He knew how much sat in front of him. He counted it and recounted it every time he added another stack earned from bootlegging or gambling. Rosie deposited her money—her weekly paycheck from the diner and earnings from midwifery—with one of the tellers in the other part of the bank. She may even have walked home with a toaster once. Babe kept this money separate, here, in this metal box, away from anyone, away from the government—away from him.

But now, tonight, he needed it.

He needed the twelve thousand for his stake.

He whistled out an arrow of air and reached for the stacks of cash.

He hesitated.

He felt his mouth go dry.

I won't take all of it, he thought. *I'll leave five grand for—*

For?

He couldn't think of a reason.

Slowly, methodically, he stuffed the twelve thousand dollars, stack by stack, into the bottom of his briefcase. He slid the last few remaining stacks into his jacket and pants pockets. As he lifted the last stack of twenties, he stared at something else—a legal document folded on the bottom of the safe deposit box.

The deed to Rosie's land.

Untouchable.

Unthinkable.

Babe lowered the top of the safe deposit box and started to pull back the curtain.

But—

He stopped.

With his fingertips, he placed the safe deposit box back onto the table.

He lifted the metal lid delicately as if any sudden or rough movement might damage the deed or dent the box.

Then for the briefest moment, Babe gasped.

He caged his breath, settled himself, and then he picked up the deed. He put it inside his coat, in his breast pocket, behind a stack of bills.

He yanked back the curtain, walked to the corner, and replaced the empty safe deposit box back in its slot on the vault's floor.

He left the backroom, clutching his briefcase. He waved at Ozzie and started toward the front door.

"Wait," Ozzie said, jogging after him.

"I put the box back," Babe said, nearly choking on the words.

"I need to check—"

"I put it *back*," Babe hissed.

He absently massaged his breast pocket, feeling for the deed, touching it, imagining its crease, and then he left the bank.

Coming outside, his head down, his arms hanging rigidly against his side, Babe nearly collided with Leaky. They danced around each other, their shoulders banging slightly. Babe grunted, motored past, muttered, "Excuse me," and kept going. Leaky looked offended.

"*Babe.*"

Babe halted and turned around. He sized up his brother-in-law, then squinted at him.

"I didn't see you, Leaky."

Leaky poked his glasses back onto his nose. "That's okay."

"I'm in a hurry. Preoccupied. Had some bank business."

"I hear you. I don't have much cash lying around, either—" He dropped his voice to a whisper, even though there was nobody around. "For tomorrow night."

Babe cocked his head, took a step toward his brother-in-law.

"What about tomorrow night?"

"The game," Leaky said. "Word's spreading like a grease fire. High rollers only."

"That's right, Leaky," Babe said. "So, you're out. You can't play. Game's serious."

"I'm a grown-ass man. I can play if I want to. I have free will."

"Since when? You're married to Carla."

"Touché. But cold."

"Leaky, listen to me. You have to be invited. It's one of those games. You hear me? Invitation only."

Leaky sniffed, looked past Babe at something imaginary in

the distance, then came back to him. "You should invite me, Babe. We're family."

Babe exhaled. "It's not like that," he said, again lightly tapping his breast pocket.

"You keep patting your pocket," Leaky said. "What you got in there, your life savings?"

Babe's mouth went dry. He grabbed Leaky's arm. "I won't lie to you. This is more than a big game, Leaky. It's *the* game. All in. You cannot play."

Leaky started to speak. Babe pressed a finger over Leaky's mouth.

"But I need you there. I want you to be my second."

"What does that mean?"

"Stick by my side. Watch me. Watch everything around me. Be my eyes and ears."

"You got Karter."

"I need you, too."

Leaky tilted his head. He studied Babe for a second, trying to sniff out the bullshit. Once again, Babe absently tapped his pocket.

"What do you mean, an all-in game?" Leaky said.

"I'm putting everything on the line. Risking it all."

"I still don't understand—"

"I'm turning forty in a month," Babe said, louder, and with a fire Leaky had never heard before. "I got to take a stand before it's too late. I got to go my own way. Now or never. I'm choosing now. I'm willing to risk it all tomorrow night. Everything, Leaky. Everything."

"You're scaring me."

"Can I count on you?"

"Sure. I mean, I guess so—"

"Leaky!" Babe shouted.

Montel jumped. Babe spoke again, slowly, as if to a five-year-old.

"Can I count on you?" Babe said.

Leaky nodded once, twice, and then said, "Yes."

Babe clapped Leaky on the back and darted past him. He kept his hand pressed over his pocket.

16

At six thirty on the dot, as usual, Rosie and Babe sat down for dinner with the kids.

In most households, four kids, ages ten and under, seated around a table spelled chaos.

Not with Rosie, the leader, sitting at the head, with Babe at the far end, the closer, the enforcer, the consigliere. Tonight, though, he seemed barely present. He picked at his plate with his fork, stacking and restacking his string beans, his thoughts on the backroom at the Sportsman Hall and on the twelve thousand dollars that he'd moved inside the pockets of his suit jacket, folded on the bed in the next room.

Fifteen minutes into the meal, noting that their father seemed away on some mental vacation, the ten-year-old twins, Floyd and Lloyd, started taking liberties, toying with their food, poking each other, and hassling eight-year-old Melvin simply because they could. Rosetta, six, going on seven, the only girl, often appearing to be a third adult in the room, glared at them. Also, she ate slowly and carefully because she didn't want the book that she was reading to topple off her lap and hit the floor. Rosie noticed this. "You reading at the table?"

"Me?"

"Who else?" Rosie said.

"Fine, yes, I'm reading." She stabbed her knife toward the twins. "What about them? They're misbehaving right and left. It's annoying and cacophonous."

"Ca-ca what?" Floyd said.

"I don't even know what she's talking about," Lloyd said.

"Yeah," Melvin said, shoveling food into his mouth, eating enough for all four of them.

Rosie fixed her eyes on Babe. She cleared her throat, loudly. "Oh, Floyd, Senior."

Babe didn't respond. He kept staring at his plate.

"*Helllooo.* Mr. Boyce. Yoo-hoo. Where are you?"

Rosetta swatted her father's arm. He looked up.

"Huh?" Babe said.

"Are you even here?" Rosie said.

Babe pushed his plate away and absently tapped his shirt pocket. "I'm sorry. I got a lot on my plate."

Rosetta pointed at his nearly empty plate. "You have exactly seven string beans."

The other kids roared as Rosetta grinned.

"That was good, Tulip. Very clever," Babe said. "Quite droll."

Rosie, at the other end of the table, couldn't stop laughing, either.

"I misspoke. I have a lot on my *mind*," Babe said. "In fact—"

He flipped his wrist and looked at his watch.

"I have to check in with some people."

He started to push himself away from the table but caught Rosie's look, which stopped him cold.

"I'm sorry," Babe said. "May I please be excused?"

The four children looked at Rosie. She nodded.

"Yes, you may," the four kids and Rosie chorused.

He folded his napkin, cleared his plate, and walked over to Rosie before he left the room.

"These individuals you're checking in with?" Rosie said. "Would this be about that life-changing opportunity we were going to discuss?"

"Could be."

"Are we now playing twenty questions? About our life?"

"I don't think so."

"Kind of feels like it."

"I'll see you later."

Babe held off lowering his mouth to Rosie's cheek for half a second, taking the pause to gauge her anger. But she grabbed him by the neck and pulled him toward her. They kissed deeply.

"Ewww," the kids sang, Floyd pretending to gag.

Rosie and Babe kept going—ten, twenty seconds of a lip-locked, eyes-slammed-shut, time-stopping kiss. Finally, Rosie pushed Babe's chest gently and he broke away. He clutched Rosie's hand, squeezed, unkneaded their fingers, then waved at his family before heading into the bedroom to get dressed for the evening.

Babe inched into the small closet in the bedroom, swatted away Rosie's work clothes, then knelt, his knee creaking, his head brushing the hem of Rosie's best Sunday dress. With his fingertips, he pried up a floorboard and lifted it away. He leaned the floorboard against the back wall, past his suits, and looked into a rectangular space beneath the floor. He placed his briefcase, now bulging with stacks of cash—his life savings—into the space below the floor, a hole he'd dug out, squared up and flattened precisely with the back of a trowel, and then lined with a double layer of newspaper. His mouth dry, Babe snapped open the briefcase. He slid the deed to Rosie's land inside the back flap of the briefcase, safe in its own private compartment, sequestered from the stacks of bills. He closed the briefcase and carefully laid it into the hidden compartment. Then he fit the floorboard over it. He rose to a squat and backed out of the closet. He straightened up all the clothes, attempting to flatten any obvious wrinkles, shut the closet door, dusted himself off, and sat on the bed. He suddenly felt inundated by exhaustion. He yawned massively and allowed himself to topple over, crashlanding onto his pillow.

"I'll just close my eyes for a minute," he said. "Collar a nod."

Two hours later, he walked into the living room, his head throbbing, his suit jacket slung over his shoulder. He found Rosie stretched out on the couch, fighting to keep her eyes open.

"I conked out," Babe said.

Rosie nodded.

"Long day for you, too," Babe said.

"Every day," she said. "Way it is with four kids."

"They in bed?"

"Where else they'd be?"

Babe laughed and shook his head. "I have to go out. Need to check on a few things at the Hall. Mainly for tomorrow night."

He started to leave. Rosie reached out and snatched his wrist.

"You'd tell me, right?" she said.

"What?"

"If things went bad."

Babe said nothing. He couldn't agree to that, not honestly.

"I'd protect you," he said eventually. "Or die trying."

She took this in.

"You'd tell me what you had to," Rosie said.

"I'd tell you the truth."

Rosie squeezed his hand, urgently.

"Don't be late tonight."

"I won't," Babe said. "I promise."

Babe met Karter at the Sportsman Hall. He sat down at a desk in the corner of the ballroom and went through all the arrangements for the craps game that would be held in the backroom of the Hall the next night. He ran his pen down a checklist he'd made, making sure he hadn't missed anything. He'd ordered the whiskey, the beer, the mixers, extra olives for Ozzie. He'd handpicked the croupier, Leon, the guy he called Stick Man. He'd made sure his special people received invitations—a couple of local congressmen who drank and gambled to excess, the state senator who gifted him the used firetruck, and a trio of high rollers he counted on to build every pot, keeping the table flush with bets.

And he'd arranged for the women. He had Karter contact Monique, who ran the town's most exclusive and popular brothel, making sure she provided a dozen of the sexiest and most beautiful women in the county both to relax the players and to offer a distraction and a reason to stay at the table and keep betting even when the dice turned cold. Babe bankrolled Monique. He prepaid for her services and her women, but Monique made it clear that she and her employees greatly appreciated tips.

Babe went over the checklist, then went over it again, this time from bottom to top, and then, to be extra certain, pored over it a third time. Satisfied, he checked his watch. He whistled at the time.

Nearly eleven. Not late yet, but on the verge. He flicked at the checklist with his finger and closed his notebook. He was eager to get home to Rosie, as promised.

"We cover everything?" he asked Karter.

"To *death*," Karter said, squirming in his suit. Karter felt Babe's eyes sliding over him like a searchlight. "What?"

"After the holiday, we're going shopping."

"We'll see."

"I wasn't asking."

"They don't make clothes in my size."

"Not off the rack," Babe said. "You need custom-made. I got a guy."

Karter grimaced, loosened his belt, shook his head, then tightened his belt.

"Maybe," he said.

Babe looked around the room, peeked at his watch again.

"Where's Hootie?"

"Haven't seen him."

"I expected him to drop by."

"Probably detained by an urgent law enforcement matter," Karter said.

"No doubt," Babe said. "Our hard-earned taxpayer dollars at work, working overtime."

But he and Karter exchanged a look that suggested something else, something they both knew and neither wanted to say. Babe stood up. "I'm heading home."

"Right behind you," Karter said, sliding his ever-present matchstick to the other side of his mouth, narrowing his eyes.

17

2:11 A.M.

In an upstairs bedroom tucked in the middle of the hotel wing at the Sportsman Hall, a couple held on to each other, entangled beneath the creamy, satiny linens of the king-size bed. They lay motionless, their eyes locked on each other. After the second time they made love, they had gone silent and still, basking in the quiet and fullness of each other. At this point in their lives, after years—decades—they didn't dare waste their precious time together on small talk. Their bodies, entwined, *almost attached*, they both thought, said everything that needed to be said, anything that mattered, all without words.

"Carl?" Tammi whispered.

"Yeah?"

"Nothing. It's just—"

"What?"

"I don't suppose we could spend the night."

"Probably not a good idea," Hootie said after giving the idea some consideration.

"I know."

Tammi rustled in the sheets and squeezed even closer to Hootie.

"Can you believe it?" she asked.

"What?"

"This. Us. After all these years."

"We're still going," Hootie said, gently kissing Tammi's now closed eyelids. "We never stopped."

"A few interruptions along the way," Tammi said. "One or two complications."

"You mean, your husband, my wife, our kids, and pretty much every resident of this town?" Hootie said. "Other than that—"

Tammi laughed, again adjusted herself in the sheets. "How long we been together?" she asked. "Ever do the math?"

Hootie frowned. "The math? Well, no. But, okay, let's see. The math. I'd say—I don't know, Tammi. I'm terrible with numbers."

"How about this number?" she whispered. "One."

"One?"

"Yeah. As in one more jelly roll before we go?"

"I can definitely count to one," Hootie said.

He brought her lips to his and then he pulled the sheet over them, enclosing them under the tiny elegant satin tent he made. Once again, they clung to each other beneath the sheets in a bed not their own, as they had so many times over the years, more times than Hootie could count, if he could count.

Lost in themselves—disappeared from the space they occupied—they never heard the click of the lock on the door being released and the door swinging open. They never saw the man with the gun enter the room.

"Sheriff Holt!" the man shouted.

Hootie jumped out from under the sheet and sprang to a sitting position. In the moonlight streaming through the upstairs window, he instantly identified the man with the gun. He was the replica of a young man he'd encountered decades before—a lifetime ago—in a clearing in the woods. The mirror image of Johnny Galvis, who had attacked him and Tammi when they were teenagers.

"Johnny G *Junior*," Hootie said.

"This is what you call a compromising position, ain't it?" Johnny G said. "Don't worry. No one will ever know."

He pointed the gun at Tammi.

"No," Hootie said.

Johnny G fired at the same moment Hootie pushed Tammi aside and shoved himself forward.

Hootie took the bullet in his arm.

Blood gushed from his biceps and showered the bed. Tammi screamed.

"Why'd you do that?" Johnny G said, coming closer. "What's one less colored in this town?"

"Put the gun down, Johnny," Hootie said.

"Or what?"

Johnny waved the gun around menacingly, pointing it at Tammi, then swinging it back to Hootie, then back and forth from one to the other, cackling as he did.

"Or *what*?" he screamed.

Johnny G stepped farther into the room until he stood three feet away from the bed.

"You would rather die instead of her?" he said. "Fine by me."

He thrust the gun ten inches from Hootie's head and thumbed the hammer back.

A deafening boom echoed off the walls.

The back of Johnny G's head exploded and caved in. Blood sprayed the walls, the bed, the floor.

Johnny G's legs gave out. He crumpled onto the floor as if he were made of paper.

Behind him, Karter stood in the doorway, the barrel of his .38 still smoking and directed toward what was left of Johnny G's head.

"Karter," Hootie said.

"That's a lot of blood," Karter said.

Karter's voice rose an octave and sounded thin and far away. His tone went flat when he spoke a few seconds later.

"You think he's dead?" Karter said.

Hootie hopped off the bed. He took one step, grimaced, and grabbed his arm.

"Carl," Tammi said, wrapping the sheets around her and coming to him.

"He just nicked me. I'm all right."

"You're bleeding bad. You have to take care of that."

She tore off a piece of the sheet with her teeth and circled it around Hootie's arm, creating a makeshift tourniquet.

"The room's a mess," Hootie said, stepping over Johnny G's corpse.

"I'm pretty sure he's dead," Karter said, his voice flatlined.

"Karter," Hootie said, wincing, resting his hand on the big man's shoulder. "Get Babe."

Karter blinked rapidly as if he were trying to make out Hootie through a dense fog. He didn't move. He stood cemented to the bedroom floor.

"Now," Hootie said.

"Yeah," Karter said.

He lowered the gun to his side and looked down at Johnny G's body as if he'd just noticed the dead man at his feet. He raised the gun.

"No more," Hootie said, intercepting Karter, blocking his arm. Biting his lip to relieve the pain shooting up his arm, he eased the gun out of Karter's hand.

"We got to clean up this mess," Hootie said.

"Babe," Karter said.

"Hurry," Hootie said.

WRONG WAY

WAY

BETTING AGAINST
THE DICE

18

abe ran. His heart pounding, his cheeks puffed, he lowered his head and bolted through the darkness, running on a road leading deep into the night. The darkness enveloped him. He shoved his hands in front of his face, but he couldn't even see his fingers. He ran faster. He sprinted, hitting a gear beyond any speed he'd ever run before. He ran so fast he thought he would lose his footing, trip, and fall. He began to pant, his breath piercing his lungs. He thought his chest would explode. Then the road ended. He ran toward a wall. The wall rose in front of him. He couldn't see the top. He saw only the wall, rising, rising. He reached both hands toward the wall to prevent himself from crashing into it. He touched the wall. It felt cold. Frozen. A wall of ice. He rubbed the wall. Rough. Jagged. *Cold*. He looked up, craning his neck to see the top of the wall. He saw only a black cloud slithering above him. He decided to climb the wall. He searched for somewhere to grip, but his hands slid off the craggy and frozen surface. He tried again, digging in his nails. He found no place to hoist himself. He jumped and fell backward. He slapped the wall in frustration. He realized then that he had come to the end. He was trapped. Stuck. He had nowhere to go. No outlet. No escape. He felt suffocated. He heard a noise behind him. A murmur. A hum. Then a low growl. He turned away from the wall and faced the sound. Something came at him. A shape. A shadow. He heard the growl again, louder, and then he heard an otherworldly howl. The hairs on his neck stood up. He felt hot foul breath brushing his face. Then he saw a feral white dog, its coat dirty, matted. The dog bared its fangs, drooling saliva. The dog roared, lunged, and—

Babe shot up in bed.

He sucked in a breath and tried to shake off the dream. He twisted the sheet around his waist, found it soaking wet, sopping with his sweat. He unrolled the sheet from his body and looked at Rosie curled into a question mark next to him, asleep, her breathing slow and soft. In the stifling heat, she'd kicked her blankets off.

Then he heard the noise.

Ping.

Low. Insistent.

Ping.

Something hitting glass.

Then, again, louder.

PING.

"Tell him to go away."

Rosie. Muttering.

Babe turned to her, astonished.

Was she talking in her sleep?

"Who?" Babe said.

"Karter," Rosie said. "He's going to break the window."

Babe reached for his watch, saw the time—2:37 a.m. He cursed softly and vaulted out of bed. He crouched at the window and saw Karter outside, his massive form filling up what looked like the whole street. Karter cradled a mound of pebbles against his chest like a baby. He chose a tiny stone and lobbed it at the window. Babe ducked.

Ping.

"I hear you," Babe said, flagging Karter. "I'm up."

Karter saw him and shot up his index finger.

Babe held up five fingers.

Give me five minutes.

Karter stared at the window, motionless. He seemed dazed.

Babe started to back away from the window but moved in closer to get another look at Karter outside. Karter dumped the pebbles into the gutter and began talking out loud, engaging in what appeared to be a heated conversation with himself. He tilted his head back, opened his mouth in a roar, shook his head, and walked in a circle. He spun around and faced the window. He wore rumpled sweat clothes and looked disheveled, as if he'd arrived at Babe's window after a long, breathless run.

Something's wrong, Babe thought. *The man wears a suit to take out the trash.*

Babe found his pants bunched up on the floor. He wrestled them on and put on a clean undershirt. He strapped his holster over his undershirt, patted Honey, his gun, and then eased into a short-sleeve button-down shirt. He stuffed his wallet into his back pocket. As he buttoned his shirt, he glanced at Rosie. She had fallen back asleep. She murmured and turned onto her side. Babe leaned over and kissed her cheek.

"That was more than five minutes," Karter said as Babe approached him.

"Damn," Babe said. "I forgot my watch. I'll just run back inside—"

"No."

Karter grabbed Babe's arm, hard. Babe winced as pain shot up like an electric shock from his wrist to his elbow. He looked into Karter's eyes and saw something he had never seen before.

Fear.

"We got to go," Karter said, releasing Babe's arm.

"Where?"

"The Hall."

Babe rubbed his forearm and tapped his wrist. He felt naked without his watch. Even more, he felt unsettled, adrift. He wanted to go back inside for his watch, but another look at Karter told him that he'd better do what the big man said. He sensed urgency now, desperation. Without a word, they headed toward the Commander, which Babe had parked one block away. As they walked, Babe felt a heaviness to Karter's step, as if he were dragging a block of iron behind him.

"You ever wear a watch?" Babe asked.

"No," Karter said, and then the man not known for loquaciousness began to ramble. "Don't need a watch. Never saw the purpose. If you need to know the time, someone will tell you. Or if you open yourself to the universe, time itself will let you know."

"Deep," Babe said.

"For real," Karter said. "Ever hear the expression *time will tell*?"

"Wish I had my watch," Babe said, his eyes fixed on Karter as they arrived at the Commander. He seemed—peculiar. In some kind of state. Babe opened the passenger door, assuming as usual that Karter would drive.

"You drive," Karter said, tossing Babe the keys, coming around to the passenger side.

"Why?"

"I can't."

"What happened tonight?"

Karter tried to answer, but the words caught in his throat. He swallowed, licked his dry lips, and tried again.

"I—"

He stopped. Shook his head.

Babe spoke gently. "Tell me."

"Johnny G."

Karter lowered his head.

"I shot him," Karter whispered.

Babe waited.

"How bad?"

"Bad."

"*How* bad?"

Karter shook his head again, slowly, painfully, back and forth, back and forth. Babe saw Karter's eyes go wide and wild and then fill with tears—tears of horror, tears of fear.

"I killed him."

"He's *dead*?"

"Dead as shit," Karter said.

"Get in," Babe said.

Karter stood as rigid and still as the frozen wall in Babe's dream.

"Karter!"

"I had to, Babe. He was about to shoot Hootie."

"Get in the car."

"I never killed anyone before. I've messed people up. I enjoyed that, but I never killed anybody. Never had to."

"Ease up on yourself," Babe said, quietly.

"Trying to."

"Johnny G's racist as fuck. Klan scum. You did the world a favor."

Karter held his right hand straight in front of him. His fingers began trembling.

"I'm shaking," Karter said.

"First time's the hardest," Babe said.

19

In the guestroom at the Sportsman Hall, lit only by moonlight flowing through the windows, Babe walked in, the man in charge. He eyeballed the scene in the bedroom, surveyed the damage, then walked over to Hootie and took a long time assessing the sheriff's wound. Then he began triage. He started with Karter, who had gone stone-cold again, his eyes filmy and distant.

"Karter," he said, staring into his eyes.

Babe got no response. Karter looked past him.

"Karter!"

Babe slapped the big man across the face, an openhand flick, and then hit him again, a stinging backhand across his face in the other direction. Karter's head snapped back. He balled up his fists reflexively. He stared at Babe, astonished. Karter's mouth opened, closed, opened again.

"Snap out of it," Babe said.

Karter still didn't respond.

Babe flicked Karter's earlobe. Karter grunted, closed his mouth, held his lips in a line, and looked at Babe with an expression that finally resembled recognition.

"You hit me," Karter said.

"Had to," Babe said. "You're no good to anyone as a seven-foot, three-hundred-fifty-pound statue. I need you. Now. You back to earth?"

"Not yet," Karter said, alternately rubbing his cheek and patting his earlobe. "Fighting through it."

"You saved two lives," Babe said.

"True," Karter said.

"You feel any better?"

"Coming back. Hootie and Tammi would be dead, huh?"

"Yes."

"I think I'm back."

"You have to be," Babe said. "We're wasting time."

Karter blinked and sighed loud enough to suck all the air out of the room. "What you need, Babe?"

Babe held up a finger as if testing for wind and began walking the circumference of the room. He studied the walls, the bed, the floor, and then squatted next to the corpse on the floor. After ten seconds, he stood up, eyed Tammi, nodded at her, and took another long look at Hootie. Hootie scratched his head with his good hand, avoiding Babe's stare.

"Déjà vu all over again," Babe said. "Have you two been sneaking around since you were teenagers? Or was tonight the twenty-year reunion?"

"We never stopped," Tammi said. She retreated to a corner, wrapped her arms around her midsection, and hugged herself tightly.

"Y'all starring in the adult version of *Romeo and Juliet*," Babe said. "You know how that ended, right?"

"Unless it was the cover story of *Farm Journal*, I haven't read it," Hootie said.

♠

"I'll summarize," Babe said. "They both die."

"Babe, we got to move," Karter said.

"Yeah, you're back," Babe said. "All right. Now."

He took another quick turn around the room. He stopped again at Johnny G's dead body and kicked his lifeless foot. "How did he know?"

"He must've followed me," Hootie said, and then turned to Karter. "How did you know?"

"I figured something was up when you didn't make it to the Hall tonight," Karter said. "I waited outside. Set myself up across the street in the shadows of a tree. After a couple hours, Johnny G showed up, hellbent on destruction. I followed him inside."

"Glad you did," Hootie said. "That's an understatement."

Babe kicked Johnny G's foot again.

"How did *he* know?"

The room went quiet. Babe waited for Hootie to admit what he and Karter had figured out and feared.

"Clyde," Hootie said. "Had to be. Son of a bitch. He told Johnny to follow me."

"I'm afraid so," Babe said. "We will deal with the Farm Boys shortly. Right now, we got to get to work in here. How much time we got?" He looked at his naked wrist. "I wish I had my damn *watch*."

Hootie plucked his watch off the night table. "Nearly three. The morning shift comes in at six."

"If we push, we can clean this up before then. Gonna be tight. Now, here's what we need." Babe moved to the side of the bed and rattled off a list, ticking off each item on his fingers. "A bucket, a scrub brush, as many towels as we can find, and two bottles of disinfectant soap."

"Bleach?" Karter said.

"No. Bleach will rub the blood in."

Babe bent down again and palmed the floor. "Hardwood. That's good. This rug is soaked through. It's as gone as Johnny G. Burn it. We'll need a new rug, sheets, pillowcases, blankets, a whole new setup. Karter, raid the linen closet and attack the bed. Hootie, let me see your arm again."

"He has to go to the hospital," Tammi said.

"No," Babe, Hootie, and Karter said together.

"I'll call Lionel Durbin," Babe said. "He owes me a favor."

"Doc Durbin?" Hootie said. "He's a veterinarian."

"He takes care of large animals. Cows, horses, pigs, mules. He can fix you right up. Meantime, you stay out of sight until I deal with the Farm Boys. And your son-in-law."

"Not him, Babe," Hootie said. "You can't."

"I can," Karter said. "I'd like to."

"We have to get serious with them, Hootie," Babe said. "They'll keep coming otherwise."

"Spare Clyde. I'm asking you."

Babe felt his fingers tinkling the tip of the leather holster inside his shirt. He allowed his hand to settle over the grip of his gun. He caressed Honey. He looked into Hootie's eyes, at his wounded arm, then back into the pleading expression on his friend's face. He reluctantly released his hold on his gun. He took a long, deep breath to calm himself.

"All right," Babe said.

"Thank you," Hootie said.

"I should exterminate that fat ugly pale piece of excrement once and for all, but for your sake, I won't," Babe said. "Against my better judgment. And your future health and safety."

"I have to take that chance," Hootie said.

Babe turned to Tammi. "And Tammi? What about her? They could come after her next. Her alone."

"Make sure they don't." Hootie scratched his head furiously and nearly spat the words. "Rough him up. Scare him. Leave a mark. But don't kill him."

Babe looked at Karter. Karter grunted and tried to tamp down his disappointment.

"Fine. I'll rough him up and leave it at that," he said. "I'll just have to kill somebody else."

Babe looked at him.

"I need to get that second one out of the way," Karter said.

Babe circled his naked wrist absently as he rattled off instructions. "Karter, call Carlyle. Tell him to wake up Tony and get over here fast. They have to dispose of the body. Then use my car and bring Tammi home and drive Hootie to Monique's. Call ahead. Make sure she sets him up in a private room upstairs in the back. Hootie, wait there for Doc Durbin, and don't move until you hear from me. I mean it. Stay there."

"Babe, Sunday's the Fourth. I have to show up on Main Street for the parade. If I'm not there, everybody will talk."

"You'll be there." Babe stared at the telephone on the nightstand. "I got to call Rosie."

"Why do you want to involve her?" Hootie said.

"I can fix most things, even with a clock ticking, but nobody can clean up a mess like her."

"When do we visit the Farm Boys?" Karter asked. Outside, the moonlight had begun to fade, but Babe could see the big man in the shadow of the bedroom, cracking his knuckles and rolling his matchstick in his mouth eagerly.

"Soon as you get back from Monique's," Babe said. "I'll stay here and help Rosie with the cleanup."

Karter crossed the room in two strides. He swooped the telephone off the nightstand and cradled the receiver between his shoulder.

"Give me an outside line," he said, the calm, authority, and menace returning to his voice.

"Clyde a heavy sleeper?" Babe asked Hootie.

"He once slept through a tornado that blew through every room in the house, including his bedroom."

Babe caressed his holster again. "That tornado wasn't as loud as the rumble Honey's going to make when I fire her right past his ear."

"I trust you," Hootie said. He grimaced as he noticed that the piece of satin sheet that Tammi had ripped away to fashion the tourniquet had pooled up with blood.

"I know you do," Babe said, applying light pressure to Hootie's arm. He quickly began redressing the wound with another piece of satin that he tore from a pillowcase.

Karter rested the telephone receiver on the nightstand against his chest. "Carlyle and Tony will be here in thirty minutes. Rosie's on her way."

"You tell her to bring my watch?"

Karter grunted, returned to the phone, and redialed Babe's number.

Framed in the doorway, wearing a worn, faded housedress, Rosie rested her hands on her hips and surveyed the crime scene.

"This is a world-class *mess*," she said, mostly to herself, her eyes bouncing from Babe to Hootie to Tammi. "I don't even want to know."

Rosie stepped into the room and handed Babe his watch. "You'll be needing this."

He accepted the watch with a smile and an eyeroll of relief and strapped the leather band over his wrist. Rosie pulled an apron out of her housedress pocket and tied it around her waist.

"Got to clean this up before the kids wake up," she said as Karter walked into the room holding a bucket packed with towels, a scrub brush, and two bottles of disinfectant.

"Fill the bucket halfway with warm water," Rosie said.

Karter placed the towels on the floor away from the puddle of blood and disappeared into the bathroom, returning shortly with the half-full bucket. In seconds, Babe and Rosie, husband and wife, now partners in crime cleanup, dropped to their hands and knees and silently began scrubbing the blood off the floor, their movements crisp and in tandem like a well-rehearsed dance team. Every so often, Babe's eyes drifted toward Hootie and Tammi, now sharing an armchair. He addressed Tammi.

"Soon as Tony and Carlyle show up, we'll bring you home and get Hootie fixed up," he said.

"Only a flesh wound," Hootie said, for Tammi's benefit. She clung to his good arm. Babe could see that the pink had left Hootie's face, replaced by a pallor only a few notches above Johnny G's whiter shade of death.

Tony and Carlyle, wearing gloves and coveralls, arrived fifteen minutes later. Tony whistled when he saw Johnny G's body, and Carlyle emitted a sound that fell between a curse and a chuckle. The car mechanic and sanitation consultant wasted no time. Tony unrolled a black drop cloth that he used to slip beneath customers' cars when he changed the oil. Carlyle, accustomed to hoisting heavy loads of garbage, strapped on his weightlifter's belt, nudged Tony aside, lifted Johnny G's body, and rolled him onto the drop cloth. Their eyes cold, devoid of emotion, Tony and Carlyle wrapped Johnny G up like a mummy, making sure to cover his bloodied face and the remains of his blown-away head.

"Over my dead body, right?" Carlyle said.

He and Tony slapped hands.

"Where's his final resting place?" Babe asked.

"The car cemetery," Tony said.

"Junkyard by the dump?"

"Yeah. We got a new machine," Tony said. "A car crusher."

Carlyle grinned. "It's sweet. It can smash a Lincoln Continental into the size of a suitcase. We're going to pulverize Johnny G and then bring him to the dump and incinerate him."

Babe looked at Rosie who stayed focused on the blood-sopped floor, her jaw jutted, her fingers gripping the brush to death as she scrubbed. "Rosie, you all right?"

"No."

"She's fine," Babe said to the room. "I'll walk you guys out."

Carlyle performed a weightlifter's squat and hoisted Johnny G's swaddled body over his shoulder. Tony swung the door open and allowed Carlyle and the body to pass. Babe caught up to them in the hallway.

"Put him down," he said.

Carlyle lowered the body to the hallway floor, and before he or Tony could determine what Babe had in mind, they caught a flash of metal cutting through the dark above the drop cloth. Glistening cold steel. A glimmer of light coming off Pearl, one of Babe's barber blades.

"I need evidence," Babe said.

He dug under the drop cloth and pulled out Johnny G's lifeless hand. Babe pressed it flat on the floor. He brought the blade up.

"Damn," Carlyle said, turning his head.

"Shit," Tony said, squinching his eyes shut.

Neither saw Babe chop off Johnny G's ring finger.

"Is he bleeding?" Carlyle asked, his eyes still closed.

"He's dead, fool," Tony said.

"Scientific fact," Carlyle said. "A body can bleed up to six hours after death."

"Thank you, Professor Garbage," Tony said.

"Done," Babe said.

He tucked the finger into a piece of satin sheet he'd torn from the bedding in the Sportsman Hall bedroom.

"That's all I need," Babe said. "Now go pulverize his racist ass."

Only then did Tony and Carlyle open their eyes.

Karter took the wheel of Babe's Commander, Tammi rode shotgun, and Hootie sprawled across the backseat, keeping his arm raised. Except for Tammi murmuring directions in a monotone and Hootie muttering "I can't miss the Fourth" like a mantra, nobody spoke. Karter bit through one matchstick, started another. Shortly, Karter pulled up to a rowhouse not far from the site of the fire he and Babe had visited two days before.

"That's my house," Tammi said, and Karter put the car in park. Tammi twisted toward Hootie in the backseat. Pain roaring through his arm, biting back a howl, he inched himself forward. He leaned over to Tammi. They brushed lips and then Tammi grabbed the back of Hootie's neck, pulled him close, and kissed him long and hard. Tammi pulled away, opened the door, hesitated, turned back to Karter.

"Thank you," she said. "I know that's not enough—"

"Line of duty," Karter said.

"Still, we owe you," Hootie said.

"None of my business," Karter said, "but maybe you two should cool it for a while."

"You're right," Tammi said, smiling as she exited the car. "It's none of your business."

20

Farther into the countryside, Karter drove down a dirt road and parked in front of what everyone called a roadhouse—a speakeasy in the woods, similar to the cabin-restaurant where Babe first played craps so many years ago. This place, a rustic, wooded dive bar that supposedly served beer and burgers, fooled you. You saw nothing special from the outside. But inside, you entered an immaculate front room, ornate and elegant, especially if you were a fan of the color red. Karter led Hootie in by his good elbow. Hootie moved heavily, his steps slow, deliberate, more from exhaustion than pain. The moment they entered the roadhouse, five sexy, scantily clad women converged. They all knew Karter, intimately.

"Not tonight, ladies," Karter said, holding up his hand.

"We know," the tallest woman said, the spokesperson. She wore heavy makeup, recently applied, a massive blond wig, and teetered on treacherously high stiletto heels. Behind the phalanx of the five ladies, the welcoming committee, a busty woman in her midthirties watched, hovered, calculated. She took a moment and then stepped toward Karter and Hootie as the other five women parted, allowing her to approach. She wore a mink coat over a sheer negligee, revealing her curvaceous body in snippets as she walked, each sashay a preview and a promise, a look that made Karter nearly swallow his matchstick.

"Monique," Karter said.

"Heard you had quite a night," she said. "May I offer a beverage, a smoke, some company?"

"Raincheck. Babe and I have business."

"I imagine," Monique said, eyeing Hootie from head to boot, her gaze landing on his arm. "Doc Durbin's waiting."

"The man's a veterinarian," Hootie said in meek protest. "He deals with livestock. Plus, he's on the north side of eighty."

"You should see his needle," Monique whispered. "I have, many times. He may be eighty, but he's uncommonly virile. He'll mend your arm, shoot you up, and you will sleep well. Let me show you to your room."

Hootie moaned and slowly followed Monique up the plush, red-carpeted staircase.

"Can you make the stairs?" Monique cooed. "Or do you need a hand job?"

The five other ladies roared. Hootie laughed—he couldn't help himself—but then he grimaced, grabbed the railing, and began rambling as he deliberately climbed the stairs. "Make sure I'm up by eight. I have to be on duty tomorrow. Have to make sure everything's set up for the parade. Every Fourth is the same. Drunk and disorderly all day. Law enforcement's third busiest day, after New Year's Eve and Halloween. I hate Halloween. Stupid holiday. Everybody in costume, hiding behind their masks, causing havoc. The perfect day for a holdup. Nightmare. I feel light-headed."

He started to topple over.

Monique caught him.

"Come on, big man," she said softly and guided him up the rest of the stairs.

Clyde wanted to join the rest of the Farm Boys and celebrate with Johnny G after his triumphant murder of the Negro whore, his father-in-law's harlot, but Johnny and his first lieutenant, Huell, a redneck with a literal red neck and a belly the size of a haystack, insisted that he stay home.

"Otherwise, you're a suspect," Huell said. "This way you got an alibi. Unlike some people, you were home, in bed with your *wife*."

Clyde had to admit that the argument made sense. He joined his wife, Helen, Hootie's daughter, in bed around midnight and tried to stay awake, but as soon as his head hit the pillow, he fell into his usual sleep coma. Which is why he never heard Babe and Karter pick the lock of his front door, enter the living room, stuff a sock into his wife's mouth, tie a burlap bag over her face, and lock her in the hall closet. Babe interrupted Clyde's snoring by placing his gun in Clyde's mouth. Clyde started choking on the barrel, waking himself up.

"Where the Farm Boys at?" Babe said.

Clyde coughed, gagged. Babe removed the saliva-soaked gun from Clyde's mouth and aimed it an inch from his right eye.

"You got five seconds," Babe said.

"You don't have to tell us," Karter says. "Unless you want to live."

Clyde's voice cracked, "I don't know what you're talking about."

"See, Clyde, I would shoot you," Babe said. "It'd be quick. I'd blow your brains out. In your case, I'd only need a small caliber pistol. But I'm not doing it. Karter is. And he's going to take a different approach. No gun. No knife. No weapon. He's going to tear your heart out of your chest with his fingernails."

"I'm gonna hurt you," Karter said.

"Where are the Farm Boys?" Babe said. "You got one second."

Clyde started to cry.

"BOW," he whimpered.

"The Bucket of Whiskey?" Babe said. "Makes sense. Worst piece-of-shit bar in the state."

"They're waiting on Johnny G," Clyde said.

"I'm betting he doesn't show," Babe said.

"How many?" Karter said.

"I don't know. They didn't tell me," Clyde said.

Karter formed a claw with his fingers and dug his hand into Clyde's chest.

Clyde screamed. "Five, maybe six."

"Let's go," Karter said to Clyde, slightly lessening his grip on Clyde's chest.

"I'm in my pajamas."

"Oh, you want to brush your teeth, floss, maybe put on your slippers?" Babe asked.

Karter shoved a sock into Clyde's mouth, hard, and then stuffed his head inside a burlap bag and tied it tight. Karter lifted him out of bed and tossed him over his shoulder like a sack of grain. Clyde convulsed and wailed.

"Cry now if you want," Karter said, "but it's gonna get worse."

The Bucket of Whiskey, a dilapidated dive bar in the woods, made the outside of Monique's roadhouse look like the Ritz. The BOW was a rickety, paint-peeling shack with a tin roof at the end of yet another dirt road deep in the countryside. The building looked like an oversize, dented tin can. One man wearing overalls and a stained ballcap stood outside the front door, cradling a rifle. The lookout. Drunk and exhausted, he tilted and yawned, constantly peering at his watch, bringing his head within an inch of his wrist. Even though the July night was stifling, the lookout shivered.

Karter stood a hundred feet away, obscured in a clump of trees, Clyde hogtied with clothesline at his feet. Clyde tried to say something, but with the sock stuffed into his mouth, he could only make a tiny, barely audible *um* sound.

"Clyde," Karter whispered, "I really feel like killing you."

"Umm," Clyde moaned desperately.

"Babe wouldn't care. Hootie might, I guess, even though he hates the sight of you. Man, after tonight, I'd love to be a fly on the wall at your next Sunday dinner."

A snap of a twig. A rustle of leaves on branches. Footsteps thumping a dirt path. Babe appeared. "The dumb fucks have all the lights on, so it's easy to see inside. I counted five, six with the lookout. Moron, the son-in-law, was telling the truth."

"He's too dumb to lie," Karter said.

"There's a back door. Nobody's covering it. But it's locked."

Karter shrugged. "Not a problem."

Babe pulled out his gun, checked the chamber to make sure Honey was fully loaded. "Let's go."

The lookout yawned again. He tried to shake off his fatigue by slapping himself in the face. He grunted, shivered from head to toe, took a couple steps to his right, and froze. He heard a noise.

Unmistakable. Something moving. An animal? No. He heard foot-steps. Someone running. He gripped his rifle.

"Who's there?"

Silence.

He raised his rifle, squinted into the night, searching, looking to his right.

Babe appeared on his left.

He knocked out the lookout with one punch to his jaw.

Babe caught the rifle before the lookout hit the ground.

He dragged the lookout away from the front door, then, con-sulting his watch, waited twenty seconds. He lowered his shoulder and burst through the front door of the seedy bar, the lookout's rifle in one arm, his gun in the other.

Four men sat around a table, playing cards, drinking beer, waiting.

They started to stand.

"Don't move," Babe said. "Where's your other man?"

"Right here."

The fifth man slithered out of the shadows and stepped into the smoky light of the bar. The place stunk of beer, cigar smoke, flatu-lence, and piss.

The man pointed a shotgun at Babe.

"Put your guns on the floor," the man said.

He looks like all the rest of them, Babe thought. *What a cliché.*

Pasty, heavy-set, thick around the middle, shaped like a pear, sur-prisingly strong from a lifetime of baling hay and working farmland.

"I said, put your guns down."

Babe looked at the man.

He should be stepping toward me. But he's standing back. He's un-sure. He's scared.

"No," Babe said.

"What did you say?"

The man shouted, to give himself courage, but Babe could hear the catch in his throat.

Instead of backing up or standing firm, Babe came toward the man. He swept the lookout's rifle at the four men sitting at the table and kept his pistol—Honey—aimed right at the man with the shotgun.

"I'm warning you," the man said, but now his voice trembled.

"Johnny G didn't kill the sheriff or his friend," Babe said, still coming. "He missed. We didn't."

The back door splintered and exploded. The building shook.

Karter roared into the room with Clyde slung over his shoulder. Karter heaved Clyde onto the card players' table. The players yelled and stood, just as Babe went low, flinging himself into the standing man's legs, wiping him out with a crisp, flying tackle. The man howled and went down in a heap. Karter covered the four card players with his gun, keeping them at the table, their hands raised. To the side of them, Babe subdued the man with the shotgun in five seconds. He kicked the shotgun toward Karter, locked his arms behind the man's back, and forced him to his feet. Babe stuck his gun into the base of the man's neck and kicked him in his substantial ass for the hell of it. He pointed him toward a chair and pushed him down.

"Have a seat," Babe said.

"Put your hands on the table," Karter said to the others, moving his gun slowly from face to face, making sure everyone took a seat.

"Y'all know Clyde?" Babe asked, ripping the burlap bag off Clyde's face. The men leaned back to make room for Clyde's slumped, fleshy body. He squinted and squirmed and started to hyperventilate.

"Stop woofing, Clyde, or I'll pull your tongue out for fun." Babe dragged over another chair. "Sit down."

Clyde, petrified, rolled off the table and scrambled onto the chair.

Babe scanned each white face, studying them, measuring them. He gave no clue as to what he was thinking. He just stared. Nobody held his gaze. Finally, he spoke.

"Johnny G won't be joining us," he said. "But he left something for you."

He tossed Johnny G's severed finger onto the table. The finger knocked over a pile of poker chips.

One man screamed. Another stood up and retched. Another flew backward, kicked away his chair, and tried to run. Karter clotheslined him with his forearm, sending him sprawling to the floor.

"Nobody *move*," Babe said.

One of the Farm Boys, the youngest and fattest among them, wearing overalls and a pathetic blond stubble he called a beard, shifted his substantial weight over the too-small seat of his chair.

"Where's, ah, the rest of him?" he said.

"My best guess?" Babe said. "Hell."

The bar went quiet.

"Here's the score," Babe said. "Five of you. Two of us. You got the numbers, but we got the big man and all the guns. I'm betting on us."

"You're winning right now," the Farm Boy said. "But the second you walk out that door, the numbers shift in our favor, and you're gonna lose. Especially if you kill us."

The silence blew in harder. The air in the roadhouse felt stifling and sticky. Babe searched the faces of the white men in front of him, looking for a softening, a modicum of compromise, a sliver of cooperation, anything resembling even a narrow path that both sides might possibly travel. But with the silence came a piercing stench, and Babe saw only what he had always known and feared, and he felt sickened. He saw—and smelled—hatred, followed by a sad and profound hopelessness.

"You despise us," Babe said. "Can't stand the sight of us."

"Ain't our fault," the Farm Boy said. "We're born one way, you're born the other. You got a raw deal. We're white. You're colored. Luck of the draw."

"I prefer *Black*," Babe said. "The French used the term during the war. A sign of respect. My preference. I am a Black man."

Babe brushed the barrel of his gun across the young Farm Boy's neck.

"You hear me?" Babe said.

The Farm Boy stiffened, narrowed his eyes. "If you're gonna shoot me, go ahead—*Negro*."

Babe tickled the trigger, held his breath, and lowered the gun. "Too easy."

He slowly took in the faces around the table.

"It appears that we've come to an impasse," he said.

The men looked at him with confusion. Nobody knew the word.

"It's from the French, meaning no way out, a *cul de sac*. A dead end."

"You kill Johnny G, what do you expect us to do? Nothing? We're coming for you," the Farm Boy said.

"We'll kill the five of you first," Babe said.

"You'll never kill Hootie's son-in-law."

"I will," Karter said, putting his gun to Clyde's temple. "Happy to."

"Please," Clyde said. Then he lost it. He gasped and stared at his pants. "I think I wet myself."

"You can't win a war," the Farm Boy said.

"I don't want a war," Babe said. "Too costly, too exhausting, too many casualties. Extremely unproductive and time-consuming. And, to be honest, there's no money in it."

"So, you're in this for the money?"

"Absolutely," Babe said. "Isn't everybody?" He paused. "Look. I have a proposal. I can offer a temporary way out."

He took two quick steps toward Karter, then turned back to the men around the table. "A truce. Fourth of July. We celebrate the holiday, then we go our own way. Retreat to our respective corners. We start fresh. We let this go. All of us."

"What about the sheriff?"

"He took a bullet in the arm. I think I can convince him to say that while cleaning his weapon, he accidentally shot himself. Unfortunate. Clumsy. Accidents happen. I'll make sure he doesn't come after any of you. *If.*"

"If?" the Farm Boy said.

"You accept the fact that Johnny G suddenly decided to move away. In the middle of the night. Without telling you why or saying goodbye. People do unexpected things."

"A truce," the Farm Boy said, trying it on.

"We take it slow. Day at a time," Babe said.

"Plus, a bonus," Karter said. "Y'all get to live."

"Nobody here wants to die," the Farm Boy said. "But if we did die here tonight, I promise you that our boys and the Klan will start a war within the hour. Hell, even if you let us go, we'll be coming at you hard. Even harder than usual."

He paused.

"So, even though you got the guns and the muscle, in a strange, crazy way, we got the advantage."

"Guess so," Babe said. "If you're willing to die for your so-called cause. Whatever the fuck that is."

The Farm Boy cleared his throat. Babe heard a guttural honk from his twenty plus years of chewing, spitting, and swallowing tobacco.

"You're right," the Farm Boy said finally. "We got us an impasse. Don't see a way out."

"Here's my proposal." Babe nodded at the stack of cards on the table. "You've heard the expression *it's in the cards*? How about we let the cards decide?"

The Farm Boy scratched his head. "What do you mean?"

"We'll cut for it. Me against the five of you. High card wins."

"I don't follow."

"Everybody here picks a card from the deck. If I pull the highest card, we call a truce. If any of you beats my card, then you can come at us."

"But we kill them, right?" Karter said.

"Might as well," Babe said. "As he said, won't matter either way."

The lead Farm Boy scratched the side of his face, his nose, and then patted his substantial belly like a drum.

"Well?" Babe said.

"I'm thinking it over."

"Let me understand this," Babe said. "I'm offering you a way out—five against one, overwhelming odds in your favor—and you're deciding whether you would rather die than agree to a truce with us . . . *because we're Black*?"

"Yeah," the Farm Boy said. "Tough call."

"Fuck it and fuck them." Karter yanked back the hammer on his gun and pointed it at the leader of the Farm Boys.

Suddenly, one of the men at the table, the oldest among them, a red-faced bear of a man with steely blue eyes, stood up slowly. He rested his palms on the table and leaned toward Babe. His knees buckled, creaked.

"Huell," he said to the big Farm Boy.

Huell faced the man.

"Uncle?"

"This here runs deep," the man said. "Deeper than you know."

Babe fixed his eyes on the man, studied him for a solid ten seconds as if seeing him for the first time. "What's your name, gate?"

"I'm not your friend, boy," the man said. "My name is Huell, too. I'm his uncle."

"Huell Galvis, right?" Babe said.

Uncle Huell licked his dry bottom lip and nodded.

"What do you mean, deep?" Huell said.

"We got a tie to this man," Uncle Huell said.

"I think I know," Babe said, "but you tell him."

"What *tie*?" Huell said, spitting the words.

"My wife," Babe said.

"The midwife," Uncle Huell said to his nephew. "She delivered you. It was—touch and go."

"What do you mean?"

"The umbilical cord got wrapped around your neck," Uncle Huell said. "Strangled you. The midwife—"

"Rosie," Babe said. "My wife."

"She untangled the cord, pulled you out," Uncle Huell said, and then added, softly, "saved your life."

Huell blinked furiously, then slapped his bulging stomach repeatedly. "Wait a minute, wait a minute. Are you saying—that a colored woman—*a Negress*—birthed me?"

"More than that," Uncle Huell said. "If it weren't for his wife, you wouldn't be here."

Huell kept blinking.

"This Negress put her hands on me when I was born."

He nearly choked on the words.

"You wouldn't have *been* born," Uncle Huell said.

"Let me say it slow so you understand," Babe said. "You would have died. You wouldn't exist."

Huell stammered. "That Ne—your—wife—"

"Rosie," Babe said.

"Saved your ass," Uncle Huell said.

"Saved my *life*," Huell said a beat later, five times softer, his voice quivering.

"Changes things, don't it?" Karter said.

Babe nearly blurted, *Wish she'd pulled that cord tight and strangled your white supremacist neck,* but instead he said, "About that truce."

"You got no choice," Uncle Huell said, and lowered himself back onto his seat.

Huell turned away from Babe. He looked at the floor, then at the ceiling, then at his hands. His lips moved as he mumbled to himself, trying on this new information, repeating the sentence, "This man's wife—a Negress—saved my life." Finally, he stared into Babe's eyes.

"Let's cut the cards," he said through a scowl, the words leaving a residue of filth sloshing inside his mouth.

Babe nodded, reached for the cards, and started to shuffle. Huell extended his hand, palm up. "I'll shuffle."

"Suit yourself," Babe said.

Huell began shuffling the cards, sliding the deck over itself, slowly. He finished his shuffle and then shuffled again, and again—nine, ten, a dozen times.

"I know your reputation," Huell said. "I don't want no funny business."

"By all means. Shuffle your heart out."

Huell, shuffling now with fierce concentration, finally stopped.

"You sure that's enough?" Babe said.

"No," Huell said, pushing the deck to the guy sitting next to him. "I want my cousin Huell to shuffle now."

"Your cousin is named Huell, too?"

"Four of us here are related. All named Huell."

"What about him?" Babe said, pointing at the guy at the far end of the table. "You're not Huell?"

"No. Too confusing. I'm Howell."

One of the Huells took the deck and shuffled more expertly, with a flourish, making the cards rise and fall. He cut the deck, then offered the deck to the third Huell, who shuffled twice and cut the cards as well.

"All right, let's do this," the first Huell said, spreading the cards all over the table. "Pick a card. Huell, go first."

He nodded at Huell, his cousin, who fished a card from the deck and spread it on the table. Then each of the Farm Boys in turn picked a card, leaving the first Huell and Babe as the only ones left to select a card. Huell looked at the sea of cards in front of him and, keeping his eyes fixed on Babe, chose his card. He slid it across the table and placed it in front of him.

"Now me," Babe said. He reached across the table for a card, stopped, hesitated, then selected a different card. He dragged the card across the table with his index finger and put it in front of where he stood.

Huell ran his thumb across his lips.

"It's not that I don't trust you," he said. "But I don't trust you. I'm keeping your card right in front of me, where I can see it. Next to mine."

"Up to you," Babe said. "The cards don't lie."

"Flip 'em over," Huell said to the room. "One at a time."

Huell, his cousin, turned his card over.

Ten of diamonds.

The other three followed.

Jack of hearts.

Six of clubs.

Nine of spades.

"Now you," Babe said to Huell.

Huell started to turn over his card. He stopped, hovering his palm over his card, then he dropped his hand onto Babe's card.

"I'm gonna look at your card first."

Karter moved toward him just as Huell picked up the corner of Babe's card and took a peek. He slapped the card down.

His face turned red as blood. After a count of three, a crooked smile spread across his pulsing, maroon face as he turned over his card.

The king of hearts.

The other four Farm Boys whooped. Huell started to laugh, a hacking guffaw, his shoulders rumbling.

"I can't help myself," he said. "Your game, your idea. The cards don't lie. It ain't in the cards. Go ahead, Boyce. Turn your card over."

The Farm Boys amped up their laughter to match his.

"Well, Huell, since you already know my card, you turn it over," Babe said.

Huell allowed his laugh to subside to a chuckle. He shrugged massively, shouted "Read it and weep," and flipped over Babe's card.

The ace of spades.

The room went quiet as a coffin.

Huell stared at the ace of spades for ten seconds—an eternity—without speaking. He didn't seem to be able to breathe.

"No," he said.

He pounded the table with his fist.

"That wasn't your card. It was a red five. The five of diamonds."

"I'm seeing the ace of spades," Babe said.

"That's what I see," Karter said.

"You turned it over yourself," Babe said.

"I saw a red *five*. A red FIVE."

"Like you said, Huell. The cards don't lie. I guess we have a truce."

Babe extended his hand.

"How did you do it?" Huell said. "How the fuck did you do it?"

"Do what? You turned over my card. You lost. Now, do we have a truce? We all have places to go."

"I ain't gonna shake your hand," Huell mumbled. "Unless—"

"Unless what?" Babe said.

"You tell me how you did it."

"I got lucky, Huell. But not as lucky as you. Because we're going to take your guns, and we're going to back out of here. We're all going to leave here in one piece. Even the sheriff's useless piece-of-shit son-in-law."

"When did you switch the card? I had my eye on you the whole time. Where the hell is that red five? It was the five of diamonds."

Huell frantically began flipping over the remaining cards in front of him, tossing several over his shoulder, finally sweeping the remaining cards onto the floor.

"Enjoy the Fourth," Babe said.

He gathered the three shotguns and started backing out of the Bucket of Whiskey. Karter hoisted Clyde onto his shoulder and headed out of the BOW with Babe providing cover with his handgun and the lookout's rifle. Huell kept staring openmouthed at the cards on the table as Babe and Karter arrived at the front door.

"I saw the card!" Huell shouted as Babe and Karter broke for the Commander. "It was the *five of diamonds.*"

Outside, Karter rolled Clyde, moaning and still hogtied, into the trunk. He slammed the trunk down, eased behind the wheel, and started the car while Babe kept the guns trained on the front door of the Bucket of Whiskey.

"Let's go," Babe said.

Karter gunned the Commander. The big car kicked up gravel and swerved away from the trashcan of a roadhouse.

In the car, Karter drove steadily, not speeding, concentrating on the narrow, twisting backroad illuminated only by moonlight, biting down intently on his matchstick. Babe kept an eye on the sideview mirror, looking for the first glint of headlights from a car coming up behind them.

"That was the move, letting them go," Karter said, his voice cracking slightly with uncertainty. "Right?"

"Buys us time," Babe said. "Maybe they leave Hootie and Tammi alone for a while. Still got to watch our backs."

"Always do."

"We got to survive this weekend," Babe said. "Got to focus on the game tonight. Let's see where we land. Lot on our plate."

"Bigger fish to fry."

"A big, big whale."

"Damn," Karter said. "The matchstick broke off. The nub's stuck in my teeth. You got a toothpick?"

"Try this," Babe said.

He reached into his suit jacket pocket and flipped something at Karter.

A playing card.

Landing on Karter's lap.

The five of diamonds.

Karter grunted, sniffed, then rubbed the rim of the card with his fingernail to make sure.

Yes. The five of diamonds.

Karter sniffed again, paused, and casually spoke out the side of his mouth. "How'd you do it?"

"Can't tell you," Babe said. "Cardsharp's credo. Can't reveal how it's done."

"Come on, man. It's me. Tell me."

"Sorry. I swore an oath."

"I respect that."

"I know you do."

"Was it sleight of hand?" Karter said, on a mission, his words flamethrowing out of his mouth. "You had a second deck tucked under your sleeve, right?" Karter nodded, grunted again. "Yeah. That's it. Sleight of hand. Am I right?"

"Could be," Babe said.

"Okay. Yeah. No. It was sleight of *mind*. I get it. Mental judo.

You had them thinking one way, manipulated their minds, had them leaning left, but you swerved *right*, mentally, twisted them into knots, went the other way. Uh-huh."

Karter took a last glance at the five of diamonds, then flipped the card back at Babe.

"Fine. Don't tell me."

"Wish I could."

"*Fine*," Karter said. "Doesn't matter, anyway. I don't really care."

"You do."

"Do not."

Karter drove in silence for a long thirty seconds.

"Just tell me this much," he said. "Was it sleight of hand or sleight of mind?"

"Karter," Babe said, glancing again at the sideview mirror, checking for the all clear, then, satisfied, facing forward, settling in for the ride. "When you're under pressure—when you're being squeezed, waiting for the chips to fall, dealing with life and death—you need to utilize every tool in your toolbox."

"I knew it," Karter said. "It was both. A combination. Sleight of hand *plus* sleight of mind. What I thought."

"Exactly," Babe said. "Both."

After a moment, Karter whispered, "Fuck the credo. Tell me."

"Not even on my deathbed," Babe said.

EASY WAY

◆

ROLLING FOUR, SIX, EIGHT, OR TEN WITH ANY COMBINATION, EXCEPT FOR DOUBLES

21

SATURDAY, JULY 3, 1948

Babe and Karter spent the next two hours—approximately 4:00 to 6:00 a.m.—rushing from place to place, operating on fumes, a methodical and determined cleanup crew of two, barely speaking. They drove from the Bucket of Whiskey to Monique's roadhouse. They bull-rushed Monique's five-member scantily clad and extremely distracting security detail, bolted up the stairs, rousted Hootie—his wound cleaned and dressed, his arm in a sling, groggy from pain medication and mental and physical exhaustion—who followed them dreamily down the stairs and outside toward the Commander, where he nosedived into the backseat, instantly passing out.

They drove to Clyde's house next. They removed him from the trunk, where he lay curled up, hugging the spare tire. They stood him up, pulled the burlap bag off his head, stuffed a sock into his mouth, carried him inside, and launched him onto his bed. They unlocked the closet, brought out Helen, removed her gag and ties, and deposited her next to her lump of a husband.

"You two have a lot to talk about," Babe said, leaving them

stretched out and tangled up on the bed, both momentarily traumatized into silence. "Happy Fourth."

Then they made a return visit to the Sportsman Hall, leaving Hootie still unconscious and snoring in the backseat of the car. Karter and Babe wound their way down the alley at the side of the building, to the service entrance, taking the back stairs and entering the guestroom, the scene of the shootings. Using a flashlight with a wide beam, Babe pored over every inch of the room like a health inspector. He walked the perimeter, then got down on his knees and combed through every speck of the carpet, clicking his tongue in admiration.

"You'd never know two men had been shot in here," Babe said. "Blood all over. The floor, the walls, the bed. All clean."

"Spotless," Karter said.

Satisfied that not a speck of blood remained in the room, Karter and Babe left the Sportsman Hall and drove Hootie home. They pulled up to the sheriff's front door as the first light of day broke. The moment the car stopped, Hootie sat up, bleary-eyed and blinking, his lips caked, his mouth dry.

"You need help?" Babe asked over his shoulder.

"I'm fine," Hootie said, groaning, his voice crusty. He rolled out of the Commander. "Just another day at the office."

"Sleep it off," Babe said. "Big night tonight. Big day tomorrow."

Hootie held his hand up, a backward wave, and trudged toward his front door.

"He's got to reassess his *life*," Babe said, and then added in a low voice, "We all do."

"I hear that."

"Meantime, I'm going to collar a nod, try to get a couple hours' sleep," Babe said as he and Karter drove away.

"Same."

"I thought you couldn't sleep in this town. It's too quiet."

"No more," Karter said. "Everything changed last night. This place makes Chicago seem like a sleepy little village."

Babe barely remembered collapsing onto the bed next to Rosie. He checked his watch, whistled at the time—5:45 a.m.—and tucked himself next to his wife. He didn't hear her get up or feel her kiss on his forehead, but at 9:00 a.m. sharp, after he'd dissolved into three hours of stone-cold sleep that resembled death, all four of the kids, led by Floyd and Lloyd, twin ten-year-old torpedoes, dive-bombed onto the bed, attacking his unconscious and vulnerable body. A second later, Melvin followed, plowing into him like a tiny tank, and finally Tulip came onto the bed with the ultimate blow, climbing onto his back, walking over him, tiptoeing and preening like a ballerina.

"Y'all kidding me?" Babe said, knocking Rosetta onto the mattress, throwing a pillow over his face.

"Get up!" Tulip shouted. She vaulted onto his back again and began tickling him.

"No," Babe said, now under siege by all four of his offspring. He tried to protect himself with the covers, halfheartedly fighting back, swatting, tickling, grabbing, corralling each child, cradling them, hugging them, all of them howling with laughter. At one point, Melvin fell off the bed, landing on the floor with a thud. He looked stunned, slightly hurt, but the other three kids and Babe roared so loudly that Melvin shook off any injury and jumped back onto the bed to resume the battle.

"Got to get up," Rosetta finally said, the voice of reason, the adult in the room.

"Who says?" Babe said, reaching for her.

His daughter giggled and darted away.

"Mama."

"Oh, she the boss?" Babe said.

"Um, *yeah*," Rosetta said, and the boys howled even louder.

"She told us to wake you up and bring you to the café," Floyd said, the messenger.

Babe yawned and shook his head, trying to burst through his fog of fatigue. He needed coffee and food. He craved a cigarette and a shot of Macallan. He kicked off the covers. "I always listen to the boss. I don't want to get fired."

By late morning, the family had taken over the café. They were the lone diners, the red and blue neon colors of the BabyLou's Kitchen sign flowing over them. The kids had shared and devoured three BabyLou Breakfasts, and Babe had guzzled nearly a pot of coffee himself. Rosie, quieter than usual, slow danced from counter to grill and back again, parceling breakfasts to her family. She didn't work weekends at the café, but this Saturday before the Fourth, she made an exception. She needed to fortify her family before they headed out.

Thirty minutes later, Babe sat at the far end of the counter, nursing yet another cup of coffee, keeping an eye on the boys, making sure they didn't drift away or get bored and start jumping on each other. So far, so good. Tulip sat on a stool to his left, in her usual position, her head in a book, one leg curled beneath her. Even though Rosie only worked Monday through Friday, Babe half expected most of the Breakfast Club to show up, except for Leaky. Babe figured he would be running errands for Carla all day, but

Carlyle and Tony, after their busy and unscheduled late night, might actually make an appearance. Strenuous work often resulted in an empty stomach, at least for those two. As confirmation, the bell over the door jangled. Carlyle and Tony slouched in and took up residence at their stools at the counter, the ones they'd claimed years ago.

"Rosie," they said in tandem.

"Gentlemen," Rosie said, sliding coffee cups in front of them and pouring a steady stream of black coffee, fresh and steaming, into their cups.

"Thanks," Carlyle muttered.

"Um," Tony said.

"And how are you two this morning?" Babe asked.

Carlyle stared into his coffee cup. "Living the dream."

"Your constant, unwavering optimism is admirable," Tony said.

"We've been blessed with one life," Carlyle said. "Might as well make the best of it."

"That's what I'm talking about," Tony said.

"It's all about attitude," Carlyle said.

"Uh-huh. And how was your morning?" Babe asked.

"Doing what I do, taking out the trash," Carlyle said.

Tony raised his coffee cup. "Ain't nobody better."

Carlyle spun on his stool and faced Babe. He spoke quietly, gravely. "I've been thinking about something you said."

"Oh?"

"Yeah." Carlyle parsed out the words, leaning on each one. "You. Can't. Make. Porkchops. Out. Of. Bacon."

"No," Babe said. "You can't."

"It's deep," Tony said.

"A life lesson," Carlyle said.

"Pithy," Tony said.

"Are you all serious right now?" Rosie said.

"Well," Babe said. "I meant—"

"He didn't mean anything," Rosie said. "He meant you add bacon to dress up a meal. On the *side*. An accompaniment. Not a meal itself. Porkchops are a meal. Bacon is not. That's it. The end."

"Oh," Tony said. "I get it."

"Well, when you put it like that," Carlyle said.

"Still deep," Tony said.

He, Carlyle, and Babe raised their coffee cups and toasted Rosie.

"To the voice of reason," Carlyle said.

"To the one who knows," Tony said.

"Amen," Babe said.

A short time later, Babe took over the grill. Carlyle and Tony had waddled out together, each having Hoovered their BabyLou Breakfasts, on the house, coffee, pancakes, and biscuits included. Now, Babe, with the family as his support team, began grilling and constructing what would result in dozens of fried bologna and cheese sandwiches. The kids packed the sandwiches, Rosetta, the youngest, taking on the role of mini mom, sandwich supervisor, and quality control. While they worked, Rosie holed up in the corner booth, shouldering the far wall, sipping coffee and picking at a plate of scrambled eggs and toast. She occasionally looked up and watched her family putting together the sandwiches, her eyes fluttering, her thoughts somewhere else. Usually, she took charge, but today, after Tony and Carlyle left, knowing what she did about their late night and early morning activities, she felt unmoored. Out of balance. Finally, the sandwiches completed and neatly packed next to wedges of dry ice in a couple of large coolers, Babe walked over to her.

"How you doing?"

Rosie held her cup with both hands, finding the coffee's warmth soothing, even in the middle of this early July afternoon.

"Trying to get last night out of my head," she said.

"I didn't want to involve you. But given the time factor, I didn't see a choice."

"Floyd." Rosie spoke dreamily, looking outside at nothing. "I'm never doing anything like that again."

"Understood. You won't have to."

After a long while, she said, "You talk to Hootie?"

"Leaving him alone," Babe said. "He'll be around later, same as always. Count on that."

"He's living on the edge," Rosie said.

"The life some people choose," Babe said. "The life he chose."

Rosie's stare burned into her husband's eyes.

"Not the life I chose," she said. "Not a life I could live."

22

*T*he Commander hummed along, taking up most of the narrow country road as Babe drove deep into the farmland, heading toward the cotton fields. On a typical July day, the brutal Midwestern humidity torched you, but today's heat felt both blistering and suffocating. Babe fiddled with the air conditioning knob on the dashboard, trying to work the fancy option he'd purchased with this year's model, the "air-flow" system. But instead of filling the car with crisp, cool air as promised by the slick car salesman at the Studebaker dealership in St. Louis, the air-flow system blasted a torrent of hot air through the evilly grinning vent next to the car radio. A while ago, after several futile tries, Babe gave up, and the family rolled down all the windows, hanging their arms outside. Still, as a matter of principle and factoring in his stubbornness, Babe tried to get the air-flow system to work. *I have to ask Tony to take a look*, he thought and then amended himself. *Maybe give him a day or two after disposing of Johnny G's remains.*

Rosie fanned herself with her wide-brim hat and rode shotgun. The kids spread out in the backseat, the coolers filled with the fried bologna and cheese sandwiches at their feet, a slight yet pungent smell of the lunchmeat rising from the floor. Stifled by the heat in the car, Babe yawned. He didn't feel simply exhausted. He'd gone way past that. He worked his jaw muscles and bugged his eyes out, an exercise he'd learned in the army to keep himself alert while on night patrol. The exaggerated movements encouraged the adrenalin to kick in. Still working his jaw, he focused on the road and kept his mind on his mission: the delivery of the sandwiches, a monthly ritual. He even thought that after delivering the sandwiches and returning home, he might try to nap. He nearly laughed out loud. After last night, he doubted he'd ever nap again. And then, of course, the game. Tonight.

Tonight.

Only the most important night of his life.

"What's funny?" Rosie said.

"Was I laughing?"

"Not out loud. I can read your mind."

"I swear, Rosie, sometimes I think you're a witch."

She looked at him, shook her head, and smiled. Then she reached across the leather bench seat, sticky from the heat of the day, and grabbed Babe's hand. She brought it to her lips and kissed his knuckles gently. She held his hand to her face, gently pressing his fingers against her cheek. He steered the Studebaker with one hand.

Her hands, he thought. How often he'd kissed her hands. How often he'd watched her using those hands, holding their children, caring for them, working the grill, plating breakfasts, dancing along the counter at the café, on her feet, weaving, finding a second wind, dialing up her energy. She kissed his hands again and released him.

"Concentrate," she said. "Both hands on the wheel."

Not an order. Not even a suggestion. Simply a reminder. Be careful while operating heavy machinery. Be safe. You've got your lifeblood in the backseat.

They arrived at a cotton field, a square patch lined with dozens of rows of green plants bounded by dirt paths on all four sides. The plants were waist-high, containing prickly branches of white puff balls, each topped with a pink flower. Babe drove the Commander as close to the edge of the field as he could, the big car rising and falling into a couple of divots in the dirt while kicking up clouds of dust before he parked. Babe exhaled, the heat now more than a factor, a presence, heavy and insistent, living inside the car like an uninvited relative nobody cared for and who wouldn't leave.

The family exited the car. The kids lugged the coolers of sandwiches, dropping them onto the dirt, slamming the car doors behind them. The first signal. Then Babe pressed the horn. The second signal. Within seconds, a parade of workers emerged from the field. Cotton cutters. Men and women, their kids trailing, all dressed alike in overalls. Some wore white T-shirts underneath to soak up their sweat. Some wore only the overalls. Despite the heat, nobody rolled up their pants. They needed to keep their legs covered to protect against cotton burrs and swarms of insects. They all wore gloves. The cotton boll edges were nasty and hidden, sharp as razor blades. All the workers wore floppy hats. All were Black.

Pulling off their gloves as they walked, the cotton cutters approached the Commander. Babe greeted the cutters. He knew most by name, and they knew him. They called him "Mr. Babe," and many shook his hand. Beyond that, everyone kept conversation to a minimum. The heat made talking an effort, a drain of energy.

Rosie took the tops off the two coolers, and she, Babe, and the kids began handing out the sandwiches. A few words floated in the air. *Thanks. Much obliged. Happy Fourth. Hot enough for you?* Some of the cutters brought their sandwiches to a spot in their row of cotton plants. Others ate the sandwiches immediately. Most of the cutters brought canteens or thermoses filled with water. It took only a few minutes to empty the coolers. After they'd distributed the last of the sandwiches, Rosie shielded her eyes with her hands and watched the cotton cutters disperse. Rosetta came up to her mother and linked her arms around her mother's waist. Rosie rocked her daughter gently, the two of them watching the cotton cutters in the field. Babe moved beside them, draping his arm over both his wife and his daughter.

"They're hungry," Rosetta said.

"Least we can do," Babe said.

"Will we come back next month?" Rosetta said.

"Every month," Babe said.

The family went quiet on the way back to Caruthersville, and eventually the kids fell asleep in the backseat. Rosie leaned her head against the passenger-side window and she, too, nodded off. Babe fought to keep his eyes open. The cooling air-flow system seemed to have kicked in slightly. As he drove, images appeared in his mind like pictures in a photo album—Wojak meeting him on the road; Hootie in the hotel room, his arm bleeding; Tammi curled up fearfully in the corner; Johnny G lying dead on the floor; someone shuffling a deck of cards; a close-up of the five of diamonds; someone slapping the ace of spades onto a table; and, the last photograph—a pair of dice, rolling and tumbling down a narrow carpet of green felt, people roaring, the sound as deafening as a bomb. Babe blinked as he felt the Commander weave across two lanes. He opened his eyes wide and worked his jaw muscles up, down, and sideways to keep focused and awake.

"I have to sleep before the game tonight," he said.

I have to be ready.

But when Babe got home, he couldn't sleep. Instead, he lingered over dinner and then obsessed over what suit to wear, what shirt, what tie, and once he decided, he stressed over how to transport the money. He considered bringing his briefcase, nixed that, then thought of dividing the money into two wallets, rejected that, and chose to distribute the cash into the various pockets of his suit jacket and pants. Finally, with the clock ticking, dressed in his lightweight linen suit, the cash packed away, he studied his reflection in the bedroom mirror. He fixated on several recent lines he discovered that had appeared across his forehead. Recent evidence of aging.

Forty. How the hell did I get here?

He kissed the kids and Rosie before he left. She started to say something to him, stopped, and merely murmured, "Good luck."

"Thanks, but I won't need it," he said on his way out the door, which is what he always said before he left to play craps. He said that, he realized, for luck.

Outside, illuminated by the streetlamp, taking his time, he walked toward his car, which was parked around the corner.

I'm doing what I do, he thought. *Nothing different, nothing special, nothing momentous.*

Saturday night, July 3, 1948.

Just another dice game.

He wanted to believe that.

23

A few minutes before nine, Babe sat behind the wheel of the Commander waiting for Leaky to come out of his house. He lit a cigarette, lowered his window, edged out his elbow. With his other hand, he flicked his lighter on and off, on and off, *clack, clack, clack.* He slipped the lighter into his jacket pocket and piano-ed his fingers on the steering wheel, hearing a Fats Waller tune in his mind.

"Come on, Leaky," he muttered, bobbing his head anxiously. "Let's go."

Carla and Montel lived two streets over from him and Rosie. The two women spent most of their nonworking hours traveling back and forth to each other's houses, carting food, baked goods, laundry, or one or more of Rosie's kids.

"I'm remodeling the front entrance, putting in a revolving door," Babe said to the sisters several times a year. "Like they have at Philip Hembree's Department Store downtown. Save you two the inconvenience of knocking and waiting five seconds."

"I don't go to your house that much," Carla said.

"Oh, *no,*" Leaky roared.

Carla, taller, broader, louder, and more intimidating than Rosie, looked offended for a second and then burst out laughing, to Leaky's relief.

"The thing about your sister," Babe said to Rosie privately. "You never know where you stand with her."

"I know where I stand with her."

"Maybe you do. I feel like I walk on eggshells."

"I can see that. Make sure you stay on her good side. Follow a simple rule. Don't cross her. Trust me."

"I would never cross her. And I do. Trust you."

Leaky, though, especially after too much to drink, occasionally fell into a shaky pattern of playing it fast and loose with his marriage. More than one time, after Leaky had lost his mind, Babe had bailed him out.

A few years ago, at 2:00 a.m., as Babe and Rosie slept pretzeled in each other's arms, the phone rang.

Babe jerked awake, vaulted out of bed, and answered the phone on the table in the hall. "Hello?"

"Are you two alone?" Carla said.

"Of course."

"Well, as I suspected, he's not at your place."

"Who?"

"Who. Bing Crosby. *Montel.* Where is that son of a bitch? You better tell me or I swear—"

Babe bolted upright. Rosie untangled the bedclothes and leaned back against the headboard.

"Carla, calm down. I'll find him."

"Oh, I'm calm. I am very calm. You just bring him home alive. When you do, I'm gonna very calmly kill him. Very calmly and very slowly."

"I'm sure there's a simple explanation—"

She hung up.

"Hello?"

Babe ran back to the bedroom.

"Leaky's gone missing," he said.

"I'm surprised. It's not like him to go catting around."

Babe searched the floor for his clothes. "Where's my pants?"

"Is it?"

"What?"

"*Is* it?" Rosie considered Babe as he rushed around, frantically pulling on his clothes. "Leaky doesn't step out on her, does he? He's not a *player*, is he?"

"Leaky?" Babe laughed as convincingly as he could. He could see that Rosie wasn't buying it. "I'm sure he had one too many and he's passed out at the Hall."

The phone rang again.

Carla.

"Don't bother looking for him."

Her voice dripped with rage.

"It's all right. I'm dressed. On my way."

"No, I mean, *don't* look for him. I'm going out to find him. And when I do—"

The phone clicked off.

"Shit." Babe yanked on his pants and frantically pulled on his coat. "Carla's on fire. She's going out to look for him."

"Well, she'll sober him up and take him home."

"Yeah, that's all it is—too much to drink."

Rosie tilted her head so she could see Babe from a different angle. She studied him fiercely. "He wouldn't be at Monique's, would he?"

"*Leaky?* No way."

Babe raced out of the bedroom. He came back two seconds later.

"Forgot my shoes," he said, stepping into them.

He left the room without tying them.

Leaning forward in the Commander, Babe chain-smoked two cigarettes back-to-back as he sped past the Sportsman Hall and headed out of town and into the countryside. He knew exactly where Leaky would be.

"Damn it, Leaky," Babe said aloud. "You got to quit this. You're gonna destroy both our marriages."

He turned down a dirt road and parked in front of Monique's roadhouse in the woods. Babe shouldered his way out of the Commander and charged inside the roadhouse. The five sexy, half-naked women who congregated by the door converged, knocking Babe back. Babe took a boxer's stance to settle himself, then he stood tall, took off his hat, smiled, and bowed slightly.

"Good morning, ladies."

The five women answered in unison. "Good morning, Babe."

"Where is he?"

One of the women stepped forward. "Of whom do you speak?"

"Please. Is Montel upstairs?"

"Monique has given us a hard do not disturb. *Hard.*"

The ladies behind her laughed.

Babe fished a twenty out of his pocket and stuffed it into the woman's bra, which appeared an inch away from Babe's eyeline. "We have to move fast. Carla's on her way. She's extremely un-happy. As in, she may be packing."

That got the women's attention.

"I'll inform Monique," the first woman said.

Babe brushed past her, taking the stairs behind the bar two at a time. "I know the way."

At the landing at the top of the staircase, Babe sprinted to the end of the hall and flung open the last door on the left. Leaky and Monique, her hair piled high on her head, lay entangled in a swirl of maroon sheets on her king-size bed. Seeing the door fly open and Babe rush in, Monique rolled off the bed, taking the sheets with her. Leaky fumbled for his glasses on the ornate nightstand, dropped them, reached down, picked them up, and opened his mouth to speak just as Babe balled up his pants and rifled them at him. The pants hit Leaky in the face.

"Move it, Leaky. Carla's right behind me. Good thing she's got a slower car."

Leaky pulled his pants off his face and scrambled into them. Monique fashioned the sheets around her like a serape and started to leave.

"Monique, wait."

Babe grabbed her hand and enclosed her fingers around a one-hundred-dollar bill.

"You haven't seen him," Babe said. "You haven't seen him in *months*. Okay?"

She nodded.

"None of the girls has seen him," Babe said. "When Carla asks, you heard through the grapevine that he passed out at the Hall."

Monique nodded again.

"Forget your shoes, Leaky," Babe said. "Let's *go*."

"Monique, I'll call you," Leaky said.

"No, you won't," Babe said.

He handed Monique another hundred.

"This stops here. This stops now."

Leaky looked at her. Monique caught his eye, then turned her head away. "Where's my cigarettes?"

"Monique," Leaky said.

From downstairs, they heard a commotion, a crash that sounded like a chair being overturned, then shouting, and then Carla's voice, wailing at a register usually associated with hog-calling contests.

"Take the backstairs," Monique said.

"Let's book," Babe said, pushing Leaky out of the room.

Babe spun back into the bedroom and took Monique's arm. He squeezed her forearm until she winced and then groaned.

"I'm not asking you," Babe said. "I'm telling you. It's over. Deal?"

She bit her lip and nodded. He released her forearm, peeled off another hundred, and pressed it into Monique's hand.

Outside, behind the roadhouse, Babe and Leaky sprinted to Babe's car. Babe shoved Leaky into the backseat. "Get down."

Babe got behind the wheel and drove away, slowly. He didn't turn on his lights until they reached the highway.

"Can I sit up?" Leaky said from the backseat.

"No."

"Where we going?"

"Sportsman Hall. You're going to a room upstairs. You've been there all night, you got it? All *night*. You hear me?"

"I hear you."

"I'll have flowers sent to Carla with a lovely note."

"You think that'll work?"

"No. But it can't hurt you worse. Better she throws a bouquet of flowers at you than shoot you." Babe paused. "Leaky, you have to quit Monique."

"I can't, Babe."

"Listen to me. She's not going to see you again."

"Yes, she will. We're in love."

Babe whirled on him. "Leaky, I paid her to quit you. I bought her off. She won't see you anymore."

Folded into a fetal position in the backseat, Leaky looked stricken. "Why would she agree to that?"

"She's a businesswoman." Babe turned his attention back to the road. He shook his head and then spoke quietly. "It's business."

Neither spoke again until Babe parked in the alley next to the Sportsman Hall. As Babe helped Leaky out of the backseat, Leaky swayed drunkenly. Babe caught him, prevented his brother-in-law from falling. He put his arm around him and guided him toward the side entrance.

"How much did you pay her?" Leaky asked.

"Three hundred."

Leaky sniffed. "I never paid her that much."

MIDNIGHT

◆

TWELVE

24

At last, Leaky walked out his front door and got into the Commander. He adjusted his glasses, pushed them back on his nose, and grinned at Babe. "I'm feeling lucky. You feeling lucky?"

"Don't know how I feel," Babe said as he pulled the car away from Leaky's alley house. He thought he caught a glimpse of Carla's shadow in the window, tracking them, watching them go.

"I feel—different," Babe said.

"I hear you," Leaky said, pointing two fingers at Babe, then back at himself. "I'll keep my eye on you."

"Tonight, tonight, I'll never forget tonight," Babe said.

"That's a song, right?"

"Yes, it is, Montel," Babe said. "It's a song."

Babe shut down after that, his mind a whirl of thoughts, strategies, images, and sounds—dice being thrown, clacking, people shouting, waving fistfuls of money—and faces. His children. Hootie. Karter. And Rosie, smiling that afternoon two days ago, bending over her land. Their land. Their future. He saw her face, the smile stitched on, slowly expanding and coming closer, and then, behind her smile, Babe could see tears, big, lumpen, full, rolling down her cheeks in slow motion. Her face became wider—and wider—until her face filled up his entire sightline and he could only see her tears.

11:58 P.M.

Babe couldn't lose.

Bet after bet went his way. Pass line bets, backup bets, come bets, the field, all the hard ways—the ten, four, six, and especially the hard eight—they all came in. *Reeling in these fish*, Babe thought, trapping the high-stake gamblers who came to this game from all over the Midwest, specifically to go up against him, to take on the man some called the Missouri Mechanic. They arrived hopeful and flush, their faces crimson from their pulses racing, their hopes dashed, their losses mounting, betting against Babe, believing the odds were dramatically in their favor, while every time Babe broke their hearts and thinned their wallets. Babe keep stacking his growing piles of chips in front of him, so many chips that the croupier, whom Babe called Stick Man, handed him his own tray. And when Babe filled that up with his winnings, the chips spilling onto the felt like a small black river, Stick Man handed him a second tray, and Babe started slamming chips into that one, too. The dice came back around to Babe.

"Let's do the hard eight again. Eight's my lucky number. August eight. My birthday. And the day I got engaged. Eight, eight. Come on, *eight!*"

He tossed the dice and—

"Eight again! And he made it the hard way," Stick Man shouted.

The crowd around the table roared. Babe shyly ducked his head, gave the room a *What-can-you-do?* shrug, and allowed a grin to snake across his face as Stick Man slid thirty more black chips—worth a hundred dollars apiece—across the felt toward Babe. Babe snatched them away as fast as a magic trick and slid them into his tray with a *clack*.

"Guess tonight's my night," Babe said.

A cheer went up.

At midnight, the bell from the church at the end of Main Street clanged twelve mournful times, like a dirge, and Babe felt the energy in the casino shift. He actually saw it coming first, a shadow creeping across the craps table like a dark mist, hanging there for a moment as the entire room went dark.

Then the new day started—July Fourth—and Babe couldn't win.

25

SUNDAY, JULY 4, 1948
1:12 A.M.

even out."

Pandemonium.

The crowd, three deep around the craps table, erupted. The room itself tilted, and the walls shook.

With the crowd roaring at his back, Stick Man dropped his curved wooden stick onto the table, and with a flick and a flourish, raked the dozens of small hills of chips across the green felt and deposited them with a *clang* into a hidden depositary somewhere below the table. Thousands of dollars of promise gone, disappeared, evaporated. In a blink.

In the hazy, steamy light of the banquet hall turned casino behind Le Restaurant, Babe hunched over the top of the craps table and studied the corridor of green felt before him as if searching for answers. Or a way out. He seemed to be staring into an abyss.

Then he reached down and rubbed his palms over the empty felt below, caressing the now barren pass line. His mammoth stacks of chips, his personal mountains—his life savings—had been among those scooped away. Obliterated.

"I lost," he said.

He could barely formulate the words.

He sneaked a glance at his watch. The hands blurred, then slowly came into focus, and he read the time.

1:12.

"An hour and twelve minutes," he murmured. "I had it all set up. The way I do. When I lose."

Then he corrected himself.

"When I *seem* to lose."

He looked around the room, up and down the craps table, at the those faces again, those flush faces, cigars popping from cherry-red lips, thick fingers tapping on the wooden rail of the table, building the pots exactly how he planned. Heavyweight gamblers unwittingly detaching themselves from their money. Stepping into his trap. Snared. Helpless. Hooked. Just like he *planned*.

Except—

This time, Babe, who controlled the dice like they were extensions of his fingers—

Lost.

He felt blind.

Blindsided.

"I lost," he said again, chewing on the words.

Then he mumbled in French, the real truth.

"Je suis perdu."

I am lost.

This sensation—this sense of total loss—felt raw and rare. Those moments you experience only once in your life.

The first time you make love. The first time you go to jail because of the way you look. The first time you get shot.

"I don't," Babe said, "*lose.*"

"Babe."

He heard somebody calling his name as if from a far distance. He couldn't hear where it was coming from, couldn't place who was speaking.

"*Babe.*"

Babe leaned toward the sound.

Leaky.

Montel—his brother-in-law—came into focus. Babe took him in. Tall, bespectacled, his body thin and taut as a leather strap, standing next to him. His second. His backstop. His voice of reason. His conscience.

"Leaky," Babe said, as if recognizing him only now. Babe eyed his brother-in-law, freezing him with a look of sheer ice.

"I lost," Babe said.

"I know." Leaky swallowed. "We have to leave."

"That was all my money. Every dime. It's impossible. It cannot happen. I don't lose."

"It's a first. Nobody has ever seen that before. It was a freak thing. But now we got to go."

Babe straightened up and eyeballed Stick Man, and then he stared at the obese man at the far end of the table. The big winner since midnight. Hanford. From St. Louis. Karter's designated whale.

"Dice had to be loaded," Babe said.

Babe slowly brushed the front of his three-piece linen suit, and then he took a deep breath, seemingly guzzling all the air in the room.

"Dice are coming out," Stick Man announced.

People around Babe leaned down, stacking chips on and behind the pass line. Babe felt jostled, arms leaning past him, over him, bumping his shoulders, his head, random elbows knifing him in the ribs.

Leaky swabbed his dampened forehead with his palm and spoke in a deep, stern voice, a schoolteacher admonishing a wayward student. "I'm serious, Babe. We have to go. You lost everything."

"No," Babe said. "I lost all my money. I didn't lose everything."

He uttered the words so low that Leaky cupped his ear to hear. Then Babe lifted his head and allowed himself a long peek at the crowd crammed shoulder to shoulder around the table. The cramped room reeked of cigarette and cigar smoke, whiskey, sharp cologne, and strong perfume. He squinted through the smoke and glanced at the people in the room. They shouted almost as one, a thundering chorus of encouragement and excitement, even in their collective drunkenness. They were looking at him. He was their center. Their focus. Their main attraction. The bull in their bullfight. And for Hanford from St. Louis, The Fat Man, his target.

Babe blinked and the ocean of faces swam together. Karter, positioned in a corner near him, surveyed the room like a searchlight, taking in every detail, every movement. Karter quickly rolled his neck and shoulders. *That damn suit*, Babe thought. Karter looked uncomfortable because it didn't fit right. Or maybe because he was packing two pistols.

Babe blinked again and the faces blurred. Mouths, noses, eyes, ears, chins, cheeks, foreheads, hairlines melded into a foggy backdrop. The faces shimmered, dissolving into a kind of powder. Men, mostly, except for a few women squeezed into sequined evening gowns, their bodies tucked in tight to their male companions. Dancers. Singers. Hookers. Babe knew these women well—

some too well. He watched them gripping a biceps, massaging a shoulder, caressing or licking an ear, their long, thin bejeweled fingers creeping up a thigh on a beeline to a bulging wallet.

Babe knew the men, too, most of them forever, some since childhood. But a few—the most important ones like the Fat Man—he'd met tonight. They'd been invited here for the occasion, for the contest, the show, this game, *the* craps game, their travel arrangements, hotel rooms, dinners, and bar tabs comped. Babe considered these men more than marks. They were the point. Expensive pigeons, a friend called them. Meat, said another. Prey. Babe first called them fish, whales, investors, but then he corrected himself.

"My way out," he said. "My lifeline. Tonight, I make my final move. Tonight, I put it all on the line."

"Place your bets," Stick Man said, looking straight at Babe.

"After midnight," Babe said. "My time."

Leaky squinted, not understanding.

"When the dice aren't going your way, you go theirs," Babe said.

"Babe," Leaky said, his voice cracking. "Walk away."

Babe's tongue slid over his suddenly dry, caked lips. "Walk away?"

"You ain't bet yet. Say goodnight and let's book."

"I can't," Babe said. "This is it."

Leaky frowned. "This is what?"

"It," Babe snapped. "Everything. The end. The beginning," and then he caught Stick Man's eye and said loudly enough for the room to hear, speaking directly to the Fat Man, "I'm going all in."

In the haze and smoke-filled air of the casino, Babe kept his eyes on the felt below him on the craps table. Without looking up, he spoke solemnly to his brother-in-law.

"I didn't want to do this," he said. "But I have to."

♠

He slowly reached into his breast pocket and lifted out the crisply folded document. For a moment, he stared at the paper in his hand.

The deed. The deed to Rosie's land. The document of his future. His and Rosie's.

Fishlike, Leaky's mouth opened, closed, opened again. He faced Babe, feeling a lump rising in his throat.

"You can't do that," Leaky said. "It's all you have left. The only thing you and Rosie have to your name."

Babe snarled. "I am doing it."

"Think about me for one second, Babe. My wife is your wife's sister. Carla. My wife. I told her I would look out for you. You put me in charge. If you do this, it'll destroy my marriage. She'll leave me."

"She'll never leave you. She'll kill you, but she won't leave you."

"Babe, please. For her sake, for my sake, for your sake, for Rosie's sake, for everyone's sake, walk away."

"Not going anywhere."

Leaky slid in front of Babe, blocking him from the craps table.

"I can't let you."

"Move aside, Leaky."

"Staying right here, Babe."

Babe gripped Leaky's biceps with such force that Leaky's eyes started to water.

"You owe me, Leaky. If I didn't step in when I did, you'd have no marriage, you'd have no life. Now, this is *my life*. Step aside."

Leaky felt his entire body slump. Then, a moan escaping from his lips, he allowed Babe to move back to his place at the table. Leaky shook his head, and then he shouldered his way through the crowd and weaved his way to the side door that led to the street. He paused at the door, but he didn't turn back. He lowered his head and his entire body quivered. He opened the door, and a blast of hot air rushed into the room. Leaky tried to force himself to turn around, but he couldn't move. He shook his head one last time and exited to the street. Then, amid the shouting and the brown haze of cigarette and cigar smoke that floated and hovered over the table like a dirty brown cloud, Babe wiggled his fingers over the edge of the table and dropped the folded document onto the pass line.

"Place the twelve," he said.

"What is that?" The Fat Man said.

"The deed to my land," Babe said. "It's worth twenty thousand dollars."

The din in the casino descended into a cavernous silence. A pit of quiet.

The Fat Man broke the silence.

"It's your lucky night. I'm a real estate developer. Let me see it."

Stick Man flicked his wooden stick toward Babe, scooped the deed across the green felt, and dragged it in front of the Fat Man. The Fat Man reached for the deed, and with both of his stubby pinkies extended, held the document an inch from his flushed, oval face. He studied the paper for an endless thirty seconds. Finally, he looked at Stick Man and nodded.

"It's good," he said.

He dropped the deed back onto the felt. Stick Man swept the document neatly onto the square with two dice each showing six black dots.

The twelve.

Boxcars.

Midnight, some gamblers called it.

"Boxcars pays thirty to one," Stick Man said.

The Fat Man fixed his eyes on Babe. "If you're betting for, I'm betting against. Here's twenty thousand on seven come eleven."

He leaned down and pushed four stacks of chips toward the croupier. Stick Man set them neatly onto the come line.

"Babe going for twelve, craps, on the come-out roll," Stick Man announced and then chanted like a pitchman, "Place your bets. Two sixes. Boxcars."

Boxcars, Babe thought. *My whole life has come down to that. Boxcars. I hit that twelve, I pocket six hundred thousand. Game over.*

Then, like a starting pistol going off, the shouting resumed and the action came, a torrential shower of chips raining onto the felt, Stick Man swirling his stick and scooping them all up and placing them in squares and circles on the table, a few bets backing Babe, most going against him. In a second, towers of chips covered the table and an uneasy, ragged silence settled over the space. Babe felt a sort of reverence as if the casino had transformed into a chapel.

"I want new dice," Babe said.

Stick Man reached for the horn and offered Babe a selection of ten dice. Babe studied them as if he were selecting two precious gems. He picked out one die from the top and chose the last die at the bottom. He placed them into his palm and rubbed his index finger over the two cool cubes, carefully, daintily, tapping them, caressing them. He softly blew on the dice.

"Do it, babies," Babe whispered to them. "Ride those boxcars. *Now.*"

He lobbed the dice high in the air.

Time shivered. Shimmied. Stopped. Then seemingly in slow motion, the dice arced, floated, and slowly dropped onto the felt. They somersaulted over each other, skidding toward the end of the craps table. The small white cubes banged off the back wall together, in tandem, but one die bounced back and lurched like a drunk, tripping, tumbling, falling, stopping on—

Six.

The other die shot past, a dancer, sliding, swaying, jitterbugging, dipping from one side to the next. Babe, his bottom lip trembling, followed the roll of this die, his face frozen, his eyes cinched, locked in on the cube as it began to slow. He clearly made out six black dots. Unmistakable. *Six black dots.* The die pulled up, landed—

And then the cube teetered and rose up, and—incredibly— began to turn over, to flip on its back, and Babe saw the six black dots turning into one—*one black dot*—a total of seven, which would be the end of it all—but no, the die started to tip again—or did it?— and then, *yes*, the die cozied up next to its twin, its brother with his six black dots and—

The die stopped.

The crowd exploded.

The Fat Man slammed his fists onto the table.

In the fog of smoke, of promise, of dread, Babe bent over the table to see the number that the two dice formed together.

There it was. In a flurry of black dots.

His past, his present, and his future.

Eleven.

The second die had come up five.

"That's eleven," **Stick Man confirmed.** *"Did not make twelve."*

He tapped the point of his wooden stick on the felt in front of the Fat Man. "Winner."

The Fat Man raised his arms as if he were signaling a touch-down.

"Winner!" he shouted.

Loser, Babe thought. *That's me. I've lost everything. I have—nothing.*

Then he whispered so low that only he could hear, "I lost her land."

Babe wrapped his arms around his midsection. He felt as if he'd been kicked in the gut. He gasped, a sound he'd made only once before, four years previously on Omaha Beach, when he came upon the rows of dead men in the sand and, sickened, fell to his knees.

Tonight—this morning—he moaned with the same sick feeling. He tightened his arms around his stomach. He felt himself teetering.

Then the room went dark.

LEGS

◆

A COMBINATION OF
TWO OR MORE BETS SET
UP IN ADVANCE, WHICH
TOGETHER MAKE A SINGLE
BET. IN ORDER TO WIN,
YOU MUST WIN EVERY
"LEG" OF THE BET. ALSO
KNOWN AS A PARLAY.

26

2:43 A.M.

Their voices floated at him in fragments, sailing by him, disconnected, pieces from a dream.

"We should call a doctor," Hootie said, adjusting his sling, lightly massaging his arm. "A real doctor. Not that senile eighty-year-old horse doctor quack you got me."

"Don't need a doctor," Karter said. "He had a panic attack. Nothing to worry about."

"How do you know?"

"My uncle Leon got them all the time. May he rest in peace."

"Sit him up," Hootie said.

Karter reached his arms behind Babe, cradled him like a baby, and lifted his head off the long satin pillow and up to a sitting position. Babe moaned. Hootie leaned over and pressed Babe's flask to his lips.

"You giving him whiskey?" Karter said.

"No. Medicine. Macallan."

Babe took a swallow, coughed, gagged, and flicked at his nose with his thumb. He surveyed the room, then blinked at the blurry faces of Karter and Hootie bending over him, their features gradually coming into focus. He gestured to Hootie for another sip. Babe took a second pull from the flask and exhaled powerfully enough to ruffle the drapes.

"What happened?"

"You passed out," Hootie said.

"Panic attack," Karter said.

"Where am I?"

"Honeymoon suite," Hootie said.

"Where's the bride and groom?" Babe said.

"Spontaneous two a.m. road trip," Hootie said. "We'll make it up to them."

Babe looked from Hootie to Karter. Hootie again offered him the flask. Babe reached for it, then withdrew his hand. "I got to stay sharp."

Hootie shrugged, took a sip himself, and placed the flask on the nightstand. "Eventful couple of nights."

"We're still alive," Babe said.

"That's a start," Hootie said.

"I'm going to take you home," Karter said.

Babe wagged his head slowly, concentrating his gaze on the floor. "Can't go home. Not until I fix this."

Karter folded his arms across his chest and heaved a massive sigh. Hootie glanced at the chandelier above the bed as he traced the stubble along his cheek. Neither wanted to speak.

Babe swiveled his head from one to the other. "That's what I do. I fix things. Now I have to fix my life. And Rosie's."

"We still got time before the meet," Karter said. "Twenty-four hours."

"I think it's less, but I'm not good with math," Hootie said, catching Karter glaring at him. "But yeah, sure, plenty of time."

"I got to get that deed back," Babe said.

"First you got to deal with Wojak and the whiskey and how you're going to pay him."

"I know," Babe said. "What day is this?"

"Sunday," Hootie said.

"July Fourth," Karter said.

"Shit," Babe said. He shuddered and his body writhed as if someone had attached jumper cables to his chest, sending electric shocks through him from head to toe. He kicked off the bedsheets.

"Run the shower," he said.

"Good idea," Hootie said as Karter charged into the bathroom, crossing the room in what seemed like one step. "Best to sober up."

"No, I got to *think*," Babe said, wriggling out of his shirt. "I do my best thinking in the shower."

Ten minutes later, Babe appeared at the bathroom door wrapped in a towel. Karter and Hootie, sitting in two armchairs separated by an ornate floor lamp, stood up in unison. Babe ran a second towel over his head. He appeared strangely calm.

"If I don't have the money, they won't give me the whiskey," he said.

"They'll kill you, too," Hootie said.

Karter cleared his throat, loudly.

"What?" Hootie said. "Trying to keep it real. Can't sugarcoat it now."

"But no money, no whiskey, right?" Babe said.

"Right," Karter and Hootie said together.

"What if you flip that around? No whiskey, no money. *Right?*"

Hootie paused. "Where you going with this?"

"They're coming out of Canada," Babe said.

"Toronto," Karter said.

"That's it," Babe said.

"That's what?" Hootie said.

"How I fix this," Babe said. "Now I can go home."

27

4:15 A.M.

abe took his shoes off outside his alley house. He eased the front door open and tiptoed into the living room. He backed up, shutting the front door as quietly as possible, grimacing at the click the door made when it shut. He turned around slowly.

Rosie, in her nightgown, stood in the hallway, framed in the shadows.

"Well?"

"Wasn't my night," Babe said.

"Oh?"

"I can't talk about it. Not yet."

"First Johnny G, then tonight. Where are you? Where are *we*?"

Babe stopped, swallowed, nodded at the floor, then found Rosie's eyes, and started again. "Everything's coming at me at once, Rosie."

"What does that mean? Give me a vague idea."

"I can't explain now. I have a serious time problem—"

"Sounds like you have a serious *problem*, period."

"Nothing I can't fix."

Rosie moved her hands to her face. She dabbed her cheek with her finger. He knew she had begun to cry.

"I don't know what you're into, Floyd, but you got a family."

Babe crossed the room and pulled her into his chest. Her body went limp in his arms.

"It's going to be all right," Babe said.

"Then why do I have this feeling?"

Babe locked his arms around her and rocked her gently.

"It's going to be all right, baby," he said again.

"There it is. Your tell. The sign of real trouble."

"I don't have a tell. What's my tell?"

"You repeat yourself," Rosie said.

They made love, slowly, deliberately, silently, not even whis-pering. Babe tabled the urgency he felt. He drifted away, losing himself in Rosie's arms, then casting off further, into dreams, memories, hopes, plans, an escape, the fix. Afterwards, despite feeling the agonizing weight of every passing minute, he allowed himself to lie with her, ignoring the passage of time, her head resting in her customary place, in the crook of his arm. She slept while he smoked and studied the ceiling. At one point, he looked at her, asleep, her mouth slightly open, her breath whistling softly onto his cheek, a sweet warm breeze, and he couldn't help wondering if they had made love for the last time.

An hour later, he snuck out of bed and creeped through the narrow house like a thief. He padded to the telephone in the hallway and dialed Karter. He spoke in a hush.

"Well?"

"I found him."

"Will he do it?"

"He'll do anything for you, Babe. He called you the son he never had."

Relief swamped Babe. "Monique?"

"Handled. But that will cost."

"I knew she had a network. What about the plane?"

"Noon."

"Okay. Now I have to go over the details."

"Stay on the line. I'll patch you through."

Babe waited, moving his hands in circles on the telephone stand, over and over and over. He clicked his tongue and then exhaled deeply. He craved a shot of Macallan. To take his mind off his thirst, he leaned into the silence on the phone. The quiet turned into a hum and then dissolved into static. Finally, Karter's voice, distant and sporadic, came back on the line. Babe heard him say, "Go ahead, sir."

"Hello," a different voice said, closer, clearer.

"Sergeant Ruggs," Babe said.

"Private Boyce. Been a while."

"Yes, sir. Four years."

"Time flies. How goes civilian life?"

"Trying to stay one step ahead of chaos."

"Heard chaos caught up to you a short time ago."

"Nipping at my heels. Karter tell you the whole story?"

"He filled me in. I already knew most of it."

"How?" Babe said.

"My business is to seek out, sift through, and digest information. And listen. Mainly that. *Listen.* In other words, I'm an investor."

"So, news travels."

"Information is power. I assume you've been keeping tabs on me."

"Yes, sir. You've done well. I'm not surprised."

"And I hear you've been doing better than holding your own."

"Like you said, until a short time ago."

Babe gripped the phone cord tightly, wound it around his fist. He sighed, trying to maintain his emotional ballast. But with time cruelly ticking by, he got to it. "I kept the business card you gave me. 'Rail King of the Midwest.' I hear they still call you that."

"They call me a lot of things. The good news is, they call me. Put it this way. I provide certain services. Supply and demand. Whatever the demand, I supply. Then I transport the particular items needed. At a cost."

Babe knew this. Since his honorable discharge four years ago, he had kept track of Henry Ruggs and the services he provided by rail—running booze, drugs, women, jewelry, expensive suits, guns, even exotic animals. Sidelines to his legal transportation business.

Accoutrements.

Babe clicked his tongue again. "I got a situation, sir. And a ticking clock. I need immediate access to a boxcar containing a shipment that is very personal to me. According to my information, this shipment is being transported by rail from Toronto to Windsor, continuing to an abandoned train station in Cuba, Missouri, an hour and a half from St. Louis. Pickup's tomorrow at midnight. Thing is, I don't know which train. Or which boxcar."

The phoneline crackled for a moment. Babe focused on the background noise he heard. A flow of traffic, a car horn, the grinding of gears, the rumble of a truck. He realized that Ruggs was speaking to him from a payphone near a highway.

Ruggs lowered his voice. He seemed to read Babe's mind. "You never know who might be listening, son. That's why I'm at a payphone. Let's leave it at this. You are correct. I am the railway *king*. If a certain shipment is being transported by rail anywhere between Toronto and Toledo, I have access to it. And I owe you for that."

"Me?"

"You provided the initial seed money. I invested in you."

"My ability in the ring."

"No. Your ability to win."

Babe allowed those words to land. He felt himself starting to pace.

"My investments in you paid off so much that I was able to form a successful conglomerate of business concerns, HRE," Ruggs said.

"Henry Ruggs Enterprises."

"Correct."

"Did Karter present the basics to you? And the time frame?"

"He did. I am apprised of the situation. He said you would provide the details. I'll listen and see if I can be of service."

Babe cupped his hand over the receiver, lowered his voice to a whisper, and laid out the four parts of his plan. At one point, Ruggs chuckled. At another, Ruggs murmured, "Damn, son." After hearing the most audacious and intricate part of the plan, Ruggs laughed loudly and said, "Shit."

When Babe finished, Ruggs said, "Well, well."

"So?"

"Creative. Ingenious. Dangerous."

"Doable?"

"I wouldn't still be on the line if it weren't."

Babe stopped pacing, pulled up, and leaned his free hand onto the telephone table. For the first time since the craps game, he felt himself breathe freely and not as if something had lodged in his throat.

"Okay," Babe said. "Okay."

"Got a lot to do on my end. How soon can you get here?"

"Leaving at noon."

"I look forward to our reunion."

"What about payment?"

"You're paid up in full. But if you're interested, in the future, as a sideline, I run a good, clean local cage match. Bunch of brawlers think they can fight. They can't. They're stiffs. But they have big stupid money backing them. This is low-hanging fruit. We could pluck it right off. I'm talking serious pocket change. Not one of these chumps would last a round."

"I'm retired."

"I respect that. Just thought I'd ask. Well, then, I've got work to do."

"Thank you, Sergeant Ruggs."

"War's over, son. Call me Henry."

"Not sure I can do that. How about Sarge?"

Sergeant Ruggs laughed as more trucks thundered by. "Safe flight."

"I'll see you soon, Sarge."

Babe clicked off the phone and moved to his dresser. He dug beneath his stack of underwear and socks and found his passport and a box of bullets. He eased the passport into his shirt pocket. Then he emptied the contents of the box into his hand and dumped all the bullets into his jacket pocket. He closed the dresser drawer with his hip. He took a step forward and stopped. A split second from his past appeared in front of him like a series of photographs. He saw himself in Paris four years ago. With Amelie. And then alone, walking the streets. Listening to music in a late-night jazz club, dancing, drinking with Karter. Shooting dice in shadowy casinos behind heavy doors down dark alleys. Winning. Always winning.

And he wondered—

What if?

What if he had settled in Paris?

What if he had never come home?

What would have happened?

What would he have become?

Useless to go there. Ridiculous.

But he wouldn't be here, at this precipice, at the verge of losing everything, desperately fighting to retrieve what had been his a few hours ago.

Fighting to get even.

Isn't that the way it is for us? Babe thought. *We have to fight like hell just to stay even.*

28

JULY 4, 1937
ELEVEN YEARS AGO

abe, on the brink of turning thirty, walked through the fairgrounds with a young woman, his date for the Fourth. He'd since forgotten her name. He recalled Lila or Lola or Lulu, something that began with an *L*. He remembered that she was tall, hyper, a nonstop talker, a loud and inappropriate laugher. A minute after they stepped onto the fairgrounds, he found himself plotting to get away from her. Unfortunately, no escape route came to mind, at least nothing that wouldn't be impolite or hurtful, so he stuck with her, wearing a phony, pasted-on smile, nodding dumbly at everything she said, listening to one-tenth of it. He bought her a cotton candy, and he sipped a soda as they drifted toward the booths where women he knew—moms, aunts, neighbors, store clerks, teachers—sat on lawn chairs hawking homemade casseroles, chili, biscuits, pies, cakes, and other more elaborate desserts they'd baked. Babe and his date passed the last booth and walked into a clearing where they stopped to watch the finals of the greased pole climbing contest. A first timer, a young guy named Sonny Agnew, had a five-body-length lead over his opponent. Sonny flew up the pole and reached the top in what seemed like one second flat. He held his clenched fist high as the crowd below roared.

Babe gaped. "Sonny's clinging to the top of the pole, one-handed. He's some kind of a freak."

"What a stupid competition, when you think about it," Lila or Lola or Lulu said. "All that grease? Or motor oil? Slathered all over him? Imagine how long it will take him to get *clean*. Hours. Maybe *days*. And for what? To win a greased pole climbing contest? It's insane. Who *cares*? Does he even win anything? He probably gets a trophy or something. Is there a cash prize? Do you win any money? Do you?"

Babe didn't answer. He had tuned her out right after "stupid competition." He chugged his soda and crushed the can.

As he tossed the flattened, empty can into a trash bin, he noticed *her*.

A figure pulsing in light. A vision.

Rosie Charles.

Walking with Freddy Davis, of all people. An unremarkable guy whom Babe had played craps with on occasion. A hard-luck gambler and poor craps shooter. He threw the dice too hard, often flinging them off the table, killing the momentum of a roll and pissing off the players. Freddy worked the loading dock at a warehouse. He was a thick-necked, muscular guy with a pencil-thin mustache who liked hot, sticky days like today so he could wear T-shirts and reveal his bulging biceps, which he would intermittently flex to impress women.

Babe stared at Rosie and Freddy walking close, their shoulders occasionally rubbing, mainly because he was so oafish. Freddy suddenly boomed out a laugh at something Rosie said, his laugh so loud and long it was obviously fake. Babe knew Rosie slightly, but he hadn't seen her in years, maybe close to ten years, when she was in her teens. It had to be that long ago because he would have been aware of her now. She had matured, magnificently.

"Unless you *do* win money, a lot of money," Lila or Lola or Lulu said. "Which I doubt, but then again, the greased pole climbing contest might be *the* big thing in this town. A cultural event. I wouldn't be surprised. How can we find out if the winner gets any money? You must know somebody who can tell us. You know a lot of people. You know practically everyone in town, Floyd. Don't you?"

Babe didn't answer. He had his eyes riveted on Rosie. He wanted her to feel his look, so he turned up the light inside his mind. He wanted her to feel the heat of his stare. He tried to *will* her to look at him. He felt he had that power. At least sometimes, with some women. Probably not with Rosie. But then she turned his way, as if she did feel his eyes on her. She looked surprised and started to smile, but then shut it down and turned away. Babe almost shouted something to her, but then Rosie turned back and lit him up with a brilliant, two-hundred-watt smile of her own. She gripped Freddy's massive biceps and guided him toward the arcade side of the fairgrounds.

"*Do* you?"

"Huh?" Babe said.

Lila or Lola or Lulu swatted his arm.

"You're not even listening to me."

"No, I am. I heard every word you said."

"So, will you?"

"Yes. Yes, I will." He squinted toward the sun for a second and turned back to Lila or Lola or Lulu. "Will I what?"

"I knew it." She sighed theatrically. "Find out if you get any money if you win the greased pole climbing contest."

Babe changed the subject. "Let's go to the arcade side. Maybe I can win you a prize."

He headed off without her. She froze, her mouth dropping open like a trapdoor.

"Did you want me to come *with* you?"

Babe stopped, backed up, and came back for his date. He flashed her an even broader, phonier smile.

Babe and Rosie nearly collided at the first booth. She stood to the side as Freddy aimed a toy popgun at a cardboard target of a cartoon outlaw.

"Pardon me," Babe mumbled.

"Sorry," Rosie said.

They maneuvered for position. Babe retreated a step, and Rosie sidled up to Freddy as he continued to waggle and aim the popgun.

"Hit the varmint in the center of his forehead and win your honey a big ole teddy bear," a fiftyish carny with liquor on his breath sang to Babe by rote.

Freddy steadied the popgun in the direction of the cartoon varmint, shut one eye, and squeezed the trigger. The gun popped and a cork dribbled out of the barrel, landing a few feet in front of the carny.

"Nice shot," the carny said.

"The thing jammed," Freddy said.

"Try it again, big guy. Ten cents a shot, three for a quarter."

"Here," Freddy said, flipping a quarter to the carny.

Freddy took aim again and fired three rapid shots—one cork

sailed to the right of the cardboard varmint, the second missed wide left, the third flew over the varmint's poorly drawn Stetson.

"I'd like a chance."

Babe looked directly at Rosie as he spoke.

"Oh, I bet you're a good shot," Lila or Lola or Lulu said.

Babe paid no attention to her. He handed the carny a dime and took the popgun from Freddy, who handed it over reluctantly. Babe didn't even glance at Lila or Lola or Lulu. Instead, he faced Rosie, keeping his eyes fixed on her, never breaking eye contact. He eyed the target in his peripheral vision and pointed the popgun over his shoulder. The popgun pinged and the cork shot out, whamming the cartoon villain in the forehead, dead center. The cardboard cutout flipped, the carny grunted, cursed, rang a cowbell, and limped toward Babe, his arms hugging an oversize teddy bear.

"Never saw that before," the carny said, thrusting the bear at Babe.

"Lucky shot," Babe said.

He clutched the bear and looked at his date, who beamed.

"I'm sorry," Babe said. He offered the bear to Rosie. "This is for you."

Freddy, incredibly, didn't seem to care. Instead, he peered at something in the distance.

"I keep thinking about that greased pole climbing contest," he said. He shook his head in reverence. "I never saw anything like that Sonny Agnew. He near flew up that greased pole. Like he was shot out of a cannon. *Boom*. A force of nature. What a talent."

Lila or Lola or Lulu rolled her eyes.

"Does he get any prize money for that?" Freddy asked. "He really should—"

Babe's date hollered, "I was thinking the same thing."

"I wonder how much," Freddy said.

She eyed Babe dismissively and linked her arm through Freddy's.

"I'm Freddy."

Lila or Lola or Lulu said her name and the two of them walked off, never looking back.

"I was going to say I couldn't take the bear," Rosie said. "But apparently circumstances have changed."

"It's all yours," Babe said.

"I think we should share it," Rosie said.

"Fair enough," Babe said. "At least until we have kids. Then we can pass it down."

Rosie laughed. "Oh, now we're having babies?"

"I'm pushing thirty," Babe said.

Rosie put her arm around Babe. "Then we should probably get started."

They wasted no time. They married four months later. Six months after that, Rosie gave birth to the twins. As time went on, Babe and Rosie discovered that they differed on a lot, argued more than they'd ever expected. But they never disagreed on one major tenet of life and marriage: when it's right, it's right, and you know it.

Babe and Rosie both knew that *it*—the two of them as a couple—was right. More than that. They were necessary. Babe knew from the first moment, from his trick shot shooting the cardboard varmint over his shoulder, nailing him in the forehead, and winning the stuffed bear they would call Blue, that more than anything, they fit.

I know her, Babe thought then. *I've known her forever.*

She is where I want to be, he thought now.

She is home.

29

SUNDAY, JULY 4, 1948

abe came into the living room and reached for the front door. Instantly, he withdrew his hand as if the doorknob had scorched his fingers. He felt his breath rushing into his diaphragm. He stood there, facing the door, his breath coming hard, and then he closed his eyes, exhaled slowly, and settled himself. It occurred to him that he had never before needed to calm himself this way. Never. Not before he fought. Not dealing with Johnny G or the aftermath of his death. Not before gambling. Never before gambling. He had always been a man in motion. But now. This. This . . . *plan*. This desperate last stand. This Hail Mary. Whatever this turned out to be—unsettled him.

He took another breath and absently patted his suit jacket. He wore his summer suit, a pale-blue linen, crisp white shirt, black tie, no vest, spit-shined brogue shoes. He tapped the inside pocket of the jacket. It felt shockingly empty. Panicked, he thrust his hand inside his jacket, feeling, searching, and then he remembered. The night came blazing back in a flood of images. The horror of the craps game. The dice coming up eleven. Losing, losing, *losing*. His money, his savings, his stake, all of it, gone. His fingers, perfectly manicured, dangled in front of his face as if in a fever dream. He saw his long, bony fingers encircling Rosie's deed. He saw himself pressing the creased document between his thumb and index finger and dropping the deed, watching it flutter and land in slow motion on the felt. He saw the grotesque image of a diamond pinky ring glistening, glaring, blinding him, and the deed being swept away, disappearing—Rosie's land, their future—clutched in the chubby fingers of a harumphing, fat stranger. The Fat Man pocketing the deed and lumbering out of the casino—the last thing Babe saw before his world went black.

"Daddy."

He exploded out of his trance. He whipped around and saw Rosetta standing in the doorway, in shadows, clutching Blue, the overstuffed teddy bear.

"Tulip. How long you been there?"

"Just now."

"You need to be in bed."

She ignored him and walked over to him. "Where you going?"

Babe knelt down to her. "I have to go out."

Rosetta yawned and rubbed her eyes. She leaned forward and practically fell into his arms. "Where?"

"Business."

"Take me with you. I'll be quiet. Let me get my book."

"No, Tulip. This is an all-day thing. You have to stay with Mama."

Rosetta nodded. For less than a second, her thumb shot into her mouth. On occasion, she still nuzzled her thumb in secret, usually when she got tired and no one was around. But she didn't really care if she took a pull or two on her thumb in front of Babe. When it came to illicit activities, like her clandestine thumb-sucking, she knew he could be trusted to keep her secret. They trusted each other. They were partners in crime. Outlaws.

Babe waited awhile and then started to gently remove Rosetta's thumb from her mouth, but she beat him to it, slapping her hand to her side.

"Today's the Fourth," she said.

A reminder. A test.

"I know."

"You climbing up that greased pole?"

She grinned when she asked this, her eyes practically twinkling.

"I've decided to decline this year. I don't want to embarrass Sonny Agnew."

"Next year then. I'm counting on it."

"Absolutely."

She giggled. He laughed and pulled her close. At this level, with him on his knees, their foreheads touched. She yawned again and rested her head on the shoulder of his linen suit. She circled her arms around him, clinging to him. She tightened her arms, knocking him slightly off balance.

"I've never missed a July Fourth before," Babe said. "Except for the war."

"Was I born?"

"You were two."

Then, to his surprise, Babe felt his eyes watering. He slammed them shut, feeling them sting. He cleared his throat.

"I'll be back by tomorrow," he said.

"Blue and I will wait for you."

"I'll be back," Babe said.

He'd repeated himself.

My tell, he thought.

Rosetta yawned a third time, this one louder and more emphatic. She lifted her head and kissed her father on the cheek.

"Good night, Daddy," she said.

Clutching Blue, Rosetta bounced out of the room, disappearing in the shadows of the hallway.

"*Au revoir*, Tulip," Babe said.

Until we meet again.

Babe climbed to his feet and pressed his palm into the front door. For a moment, he took in the sounds of the early morning—a truck rolling down Main Street, a rooster crowing, a bird crooning, a train whistle bleating in the distance. Babe exhaled again, heavily, slowly opened the front door, and walked into the dawn. He never looked back.

Hootie arranged for the plane. He knew somebody whose cousin's nephew flew a crop duster over his uncle's fields. For twenty dollars plus gas, the kid agreed to fly Babe in a Piper Cub. A two-seater. The pilot and Babe. Hootie decided to keep the details of the trip confidential until the last minute. Why worry the kid? Or upset Babe with the details? The less they both knew, the better. The trip was sort of a straight shot. Six hundred fifty miles one way. Two legs. The first leg—three hundred twenty-five miles, a stop to stretch, to refuel. The second leg—another three hundred twenty-five miles. Six hours plus to get to the destination. Babe would meet Ruggs in Detroit, pay off the pilot, the kid would refuel, and fly home.

Babe faced the Piper Cub and studied the contours of the plane. He considered its striking sun-yellow color and snub nose. Somehow the plane reminded him of a golden retriever puppy.

Friendly. Eager. Babe walked along the side, pressing his palm on the plane's sleek surface as he hunched below the wide single wing. Babe couldn't imagine how Hootie had arranged for this plane on such short notice. He really didn't want to know.

He finished circling the plane and walked over to the Commander parked fifty feet away. Hootie and Karter waited for him, both men leaning against the rear of the car. Hootie had abandoned the sling but kept his arm tight to his side. Babe lobbed his car keys to Karter. The big man snatched them and eased them into his suitcoat pocket.

"We all set?" Babe said.

"Everything's in place," Karter said.

"If all goes according to plan—and it will—you'll pick me up tomorrow," Babe said.

Karter bit down on his matchstick, then slid it across his mouth, corner to corner. "Boxcars."

"Boxcars," Babe said.

He nodded at a skinny, freckled-faced kid with a mop of red hair who continuously slapped a pair of smudged goggles against his pants leg. "Who's that?"

"The pilot," Hootie said.

"Does he even have a driver's license?"

"No," Hootie said. "He didn't pass the mental."

Babe grunted. With Hootie and Karter trailing, Babe walked over to the kid and extended his hand. "I'm your passenger. I'm Babe."

"Yes, sir, Mr. Babe. I know. I'm Billy Ray."

He shook Babe's hand weakly. Babe recoiled, mostly from the moisture puddled in Billy Ray's palms. He patted the side of the Piper Cub. "Ever fly one of these?"

"Not this nice. But yeah. Every day. I crop dust my uncle's fields."

"How far you fly?"

Billy Ray looked confused. "You mean, total?"

"Give or take."

"Let's see. I fly over two fields, about four hundred feet each, dust back and forth twice, so four times four hundred feet." His red face reddened deeper. "I failed math."

"Don't look at me," Hootie said.

"Why?" Billy Ray scratched his now pulsing maroon-tinged cheek. He looked from Babe to Karter to Hootie. "Where we going?"

"Nobody told you?" Babe said.

"I was about to," Hootie said.

"Detroit," Babe said.

"What?"

"That would be more than four times four hundred feet," Karter said. "Which is sixteen hundred feet."

"Detroit?" Billy Ray said.

"Karter will map it out for you."

"Already done," Karter said, reaching into his coat pocket and producing a neatly folded aeronautical map that he had marked up and redlined.

"We won't be refueling for about three and a half hours, so you might want to take a piss now," Babe said.

"Detroit, *Michigan*?"

"There another one?" Babe said.

"Let's go over the map," Karter said, escorting Billy Ray toward the plane. "It's a straight shot. You can't fuck up. Or you better not."

"Yes, sir." Billy Ray mumbled something else into his shirt, then tripped over himself as he walked next to Karter. Karter caught him before the kid hit the ground. Billy Ray coughed, then, disoriented, started walking in the wrong direction, away from the plane. Karter grabbed his arm and faced him back toward the plane.

"I got a good feeling about him," Hootie said to Babe.

Babe snorted.

"He'll be fine," Hootie said.

"You won't be in the plane. You'll be on the ground."

"With such short notice, he's the best we could do."

"Long as he stays above trees," Babe said.

Hootie grimaced and rubbed his arm. He cleared his throat and looked at Babe for a long time. He scratched the stubble on his cheek, started to speak, stopped. He clearly had something on his mind.

"Listen," Hootie said. "You tied up my daughter, gagged her, and locked her in a closet for eight hours."

"Didn't want her to witness anything," Babe said.

"Smart."

"How's the moron?"

"He hasn't changed, if that's what you mean. He's still dirt stupid and racist as shit. I'll handle him. My responsibility."

"Your burden," Babe said.

They toed the packed-down sod of the ground at the same time.

"How long will Huell stand down?" Babe said.

"How long will your truce last? Not long. But if your plan with Ruggs doesn't work, it won't matter. You'll be in a shallow grave somewhere between here and Toronto, and I'll be swinging from a tree in Klan country. If the plan works, we'll both say a prayer, settle ourselves, and deal with Huell once and for all. After tomorrow night."

"Plan's going to work," Babe said.

"You sound sure."

"I am sure," Babe said, then sniffed. "Pretty sure." He paused. "I'm thinking fifty-fifty."

"Same," Hootie said, rubbing his arm.

Babe squinted into the rising sun. "Have you suggested to your son-in-law that he might consider an alternative living arrangement?"

"I changed the locks," Hootie said. "Heard he's living in Cousin Huell's barn."

"What about your daughter?"

"Staying with us."

"Funny how a minor thing like attempting to murder her father put a dent in their relationship."

Hootie patted his sweating brow with his handkerchief. "We're hoping for a quick divorce."

"Can't be too quick." Babe stared at his brilliantly shined shoes. "I've never missed a Fourth."

"Extenuating circumstances," Hootie said. "Couldn't be helped."

"Keep an eye on Rosie and the kids."

"Always." Hootie pulled an envelope out of his pocket. "Babe."

He went quiet. Babe eyed the envelope. He knew what it was. A sour taste swam in his mouth.

"No," Babe said.

"What, this?" Hootie flicked the corner of the envelope. "It's your cut of the house's take from last night. Well, yours and fucking Clyde's, to be honest. Take it."

He pressed the envelope against Babe's chest.

"Hootie—?"

"You need it," Hootie said. "For the trip. For expenses. You need it."

"It's your savings. I'm not taking it."

"My *savings*?" Hootie dropped his mouth open, too wide, expressing an amateur actor's exaggerated outrage. "This is not my savings." He repeated the words slowly as if speaking to a child. "It's your cut of the house's take."

"I was a player, not the house." Babe shook his head and mumbled, "Hootie."

"Come on, Babe. When did I get to the bank?"

"What bank? You keep your savings in your shoe."

Hootie rested his hand over the envelope, fastening it against Babe's chest. Babe tried to shove the envelope back at Hootie, but Hootie stepped back, out of reach, dug his hands into his pockets, and croaked, "Take it. Please." He took a step farther away, but Babe charged him and wrapped both arms around him, pinning Hootie's arms, locking him in a bearhug, squeezing him. Hootie flinched, swallowed the pain emanating from his arm, then batting back tears, looked past Babe, blinking, nodding, and said, "Okay. Good."

"You all right?"

"Yeah." Hootie sniffed. "Just my arm."

"I know."

Babe released him. Hootie pulled away and started to stride quickly across the clearing. Fifty feet away, he turned, and shouted, "Travel safe!"

He headed toward his cruiser, his fast stride slowing to a walk. When he reached his car, he turned back again and shouted, a reminder, "Try not to get killed!"

At noon, Babe climbed into the passenger seat of the Piper Cub. Billy Ray, goggled up, his helmet on but too big, the straps flapping, handed Babe the second pair of smudged goggles.

"Thanks," Babe said. "How you doing?"

"Better after I threw up. Settled my stomach."

Babe nodded. "Did Karter give you the extra hundred?"

"No," Billy Ray said. "Two hundred. Plus, the original twenty."

"Not bad for a day's work."

"More than I make in six months." Billy Ray exhaled. "Never been to Detroit. I ain't been out of Caruthersville. Never been anywhere. Never dreamed I'd go anyplace like Detroit."

"It'll look good on your résumé." Babe slipped on the goggles and patted the side of the plane. "Clock's ticking."

Babe flipped a thumbs-up to Karter, who swatted the side of the plane, mirroring Babe. Billy Ray offered his own thumbs-up to Karter and then fired up the Piper Cub. The propellor whirred and Billy Ray taxied the plane past the clearing and onto a dirt airstrip. He revved the engine, pulled back on the throttle, floored the Piper Cub, and the two-seater took flight. Billy Ray whooped, shouting in exaltation, then made a loud *woo-woo-woo* sound as if he were a hound baying at the moon. Babe folded his hands, closed his eyes, and began to pray. But after whispering, "Dear Lord, please," he opened his eyes a crack and saw that they had risen flawlessly above a clump of trees. They were soaring. Billy Ray had pressed himself forward, his face lined in concentration and wonder, his fists tight and white on the wheel, piloting the plane intently. Babe unfolded his hands and leaned back. He decided to save his prayers for later, when he knew he would need them.

CRAP OUT

◆

**THROWING TWO,
THREE, OR TWELVE
ON THE FIRST ROLL
AND, THEREFORE,
LOSING**

30

Sometime later, not far from Toronto, on the Michigan Central line, a train whistle blew, echoing through a small coastal town. Thirty seconds later, the mixed freight train—two boxcars and five passenger cars, including a dining car and a sleeper—pulled lazily into the outdoor train station at Oakville, Ontario, and chugged to a stop. A moment passed and a handful of passengers from Toronto disembarked, men and women in their work clothes—uniforms and scrubs—working the U.S. holiday. Then ten passengers got on. A mom and her two elementary-school-age kids. An older couple. Four more people, including two businessmen, holding briefcases. Last, an attractive woman in a swirly, low-cut summer dress approached the stairs leading up to the train. Blond. Early thirties. Shapely. Strong perfume preceding her. The businessmen stopped in front of the steps and allowed her to go first. She smiled at them. She took the stairs and her skirt flew up, hiking up well past her knees, showing thigh, as she sashayed into the passenger car. She didn't seem to notice. But the businessmen did. One gawked, the other whistled. Inside the train, the woman veered right and began walking through the moderately populated passenger car. She took a window seat a row behind a baldheaded man in a suit who sat on the aisle—a heavyset man with a stumpy neck, thick, wild eyebrows, plump, purple lips, and a sinister five o'clock shadow, so dark he could easily shave morning, noon, and night and still show stubble. He didn't appear to be someone with a delightful sense of humor or who smiled often. The blond—Madeline—eyed him curiously and for a long time. She reached into her purse and eased out her makeup kit. She touched up her cheeks, her eyes, and applied a new coat of lipstick. She crossed her legs and settled in for the ride.

Up front, in the train's cab, the engineer ran his fingers through his hair like a comb and put on his striped cap. He slid out of the cab, exited the train, and allowed himself to stretch on the station's platform. He yawned mightily, tightened the straps on his coveralls, and looked back toward the train, his thirty-second break over. He found himself facing a man, another engineer, dressed in coveralls and a striped cap. This engineer removed an unlit pipe from his lips and stuck it in his pocket. He smiled.

"Dan Waters," the second engineer said, offering his hand, waiting for the first engineer to respond, but he just stared.

"Do I know you?"

"I thought you might know the name. I'm on now."

"Sorry. What?"

"Your shift's over. I'm coming on."

The first engineer looked at his watch. "I got the rest of the run to go. All the way to Windsor."

"Central changed it last night. They didn't radio you?"

"No."

Dan Waters shook his head. "Why am I not surprised?"

He laughed. The first engineer waited, confused, and then laughed along with him.

"Par for the course, right?" Dan Waters said. "I got the paperwork right here. The timesheet and revised schedule."

Waters fished a neatly folded, typed sheet of paper out of his coveralls. "At least you're getting golden time. I'm still working my way up."

"New guy, huh?" The first engineer looked at the paper Waters held out to him. "First I heard of the change."

"Consider this your lucky day. A real holiday. You get to go home early."

The first engineer kept studying the paper that Waters handed to him.

"Yeah," the first engineer said, still scanning the paper. "I got to call them."

Waters shrugged. "Sure."

Just then, the conductor's face appeared in the cab's window.

"All aboard!" he shouted.

A few other latecomers scrambled to get on the train. The first engineer hesitated, looked at the train about to leave, then folded the paper and handed it back to Waters. "Screw it. Have a good run."

"See you down the line," Waters said as he climbed onto the train and entered the cab.

"Who are you?" the conductor said when Waters stepped inside.

"Dan Waters. Replacement engineer. The other guy radioed in from Toronto. Said he wasn't feeling well."

"Seemed fine to me," the conductor said.

"What do you want from me? He called in sick."

"Lazy ass," the conductor said, and then yanked the train whistle.

The train pulled out of Oakville Station.

Fifteen minutes outside Caruthersville, Billy Ray found his flying groove. That's all it took. Billy Ray manned the Piper Cub so smoothly that Babe relaxed and allowed himself to take a minute and enjoy the breathtaking view of the lush green fields and plump brown hills of Missouri, and then he felt his eyes closing and he nodded off. Seeing Mr. Babe sound asleep next to him, his mouth open, snoring softly, the goggles rising and lowering slightly, Billy Ray felt a sudden rush of power and pride. *I'm Mr. Babe's private pilot*, he thought. *I'm flying royalty.*

Seven hours later, they touched down outside Detroit, Billy Ray negotiating a landing so expertly, with a minimum of hopping and bumping, that it shocked him and Babe both. After Billy Ray taxied and parked, Babe climbed down from the small plane, his entire body feeling exhausted and electrified at the same time. He looked around and spotted a hot-off-the-assembly-line, gleaming new 1948 Cadillac idling at the entrance to the airfield.

"Nice ride, kid," he told Billy Ray. "You got a future as a pilot."

Billy Ray blushed. "I'm just glad we didn't crash."

Babe reached into his trouser pocket, extricated a roll of cash, and peeled off a hundred-dollar bill. When they had stopped to refuel three hours into the trip, Babe had removed Hootie's money from the envelope and distributed the bills into various pockets and hiding places within his suit, pants, and shoes.

"Here," he said to Billy Ray, whose eyes seemed to be bugging out.

"You already paid me."

"It's a tip," Babe said. "For a job well done, a snack, some gas, and for your silence."

"Yes, sir, Mr. Babe. My lips are sealed. If anyone asks, I was with a girl all afternoon."

"Work on your alibi. You have a safe flight back. Stay above the trees. And, remember, keep quiet."

Billy Ray made a *zip-my-lips* gesture. Babe slapped Billy Ray on the shoulder and then trudged across the field, toward the Caddy.

An hour later, presenting their passports to a suspicious bor-der guard with a walrus mustache at the entrance of the Ambassador Bridge, a mile and a half stretch of concrete and steel girders spanning the Detroit River, Babe and Ruggs sat silently in the Caddy, Ruggs at the wheel. Ruggs chomped on an unlit cigar, saving it for later, he said, much later, a victory smoke. Despite the continuous whoosh of crisp cool air from the car's top-of-the-line air conditioning system, Ruggs kept his window open and hung his left arm outside, steering the Caddy with only his index finger.

"Power steering," he said, emphasizing the word *power*.

As they crossed the bridge and entered Canada, Babe took a longer look at Ruggs. Except for a two-inch scar that zigzagged down his right cheek, Sarge looked the same—shaved head, his body taut, hard, and lean, his movements agile, catlike, quicksilver even as he drove.

Babe found himself staring at Ruggs's scar. Ruggs caught him looking.

"Cut myself shaving," Ruggs said.

"Happens," Babe said. "Especially with a dull blade."

"This blade was sharp," Ruggs said.

Babe grunted, then turned and looked out the window. The neighborhood in Windsor they drove through reminded him of certain sections of downtown St. Louis. A hazy gray cloud curtain sat bunched over an industrial landscape as far you could see, city blocks lined with warehouses and factories. Babe's mind wandered and for a moment he swore he was dreaming, still in bed, spending a lazy Fourth of July morning under the covers, his body wound around Rosie, his mind crackling, on kid alert, waiting for his brood of four to pounce, Rosetta, the youngest, the most fearless, in the lead. He felt himself smile, then the smile faded as his mind plummeted back to reality and his eye fell back on Windsor, Ontario. Ruggs drove by another factory, another warehouse, and then the train station, which took up an entire block.

"Everything a go?" Babe said.

"Lot of moving parts on short notice," Ruggs said.

"I know you were up against it. I had no choice."

"But." Ruggs bit down on his cigar. "Done, done, and done."

Babe released a tiny whoosh of relief, causing a cloud circle to form briefly on his window.

"We're heading to Glencoe," Ruggs said. "About a three-hour drive. That's where we meet the train. Everything you need is in the trunk. You do your thing. Then I meet you back at Chatham-Kent."

"You got to beat the train."

"Piece of cake," Ruggs said.

"If you spent five minutes thinking this through, I'm sure you would find a dozen flaws, come to your senses, and abort the whole mission."

"Yeah," Ruggs said. "Good thing I don't have time to think this through."

31

Back in Caruthersville, while Babe drove across the border with Ruggs into Canada, the two sisters spent the Fourth of July, 1948, a Sunday, the same way they spent the holiday four years ago—together, without their husbands. Leaky, named a parade official this year, begged off being with Carla, citing a list of official duties and responsibilities. This year, after overseeing the parade, whatever that meant, and exaggerating his importance, he would head down to the riverboat and help prepare the fireworks for the evening.

"You? Help with the fireworks? I would keep you *away* from the fireworks," Carla said. "I'd be afraid you'd blow up the riverboat."

"Funny," Leaky said, his face blank. He stormed out the door past Carla, who stood at the kitchen sink, smoking a Lucky, tapping the ash into the drain.

Back in 1944, Leaky, a volunteer firefighter, rode shotgun on a hook-and-ladder in the parade down Main Street, waving maniacally to the crowd lining both sides of the street, feeling giddy, reveling in the attention, surely drunk. After the parade, he volunteered wherever parade officials needed him, which meant cleaning up the parade route with Carlyle. That year, Babe spent his Fourth of

July in France, courtesy of the United States Army, recovering from the Normandy Invasion.

Rosie felt similarities between that Fourth and now. She felt—a weight. A heaviness. A sickening sense of uncertainty. She kept herself occupied with the children, a welcome distraction, allowing time to pass without dwelling on the mess she'd cleaned up in the hotel room, or on Babe, his urgent, secretive, and possibly desperate situation, whatever it was, and his absence. She and Carla and the kids watched the parade and cheered the homemade floats, especially those driven by the Breakfast Club. Tony drove a flatbed truck draped with red-white-and-blue bunting, a cluster of politicians, civic leaders, and the guy who owned the auto repair shop where Tony worked, riding in the back, all of them dressed in spiffy white suits and straw hats, waving to the crowd, blowing kisses to the children. Ridiculously, at the end of the parade route, Carlyle drove a shiny garbage truck, grinning and waving from inside the truck's cab, the back of the trash truck emblazoned with a banner announcing, "The Finest in Caruthersville Sanitation."

Standing along Main Street, Carla and Rosie stood side by side with Rosie's kids. So far, after six years of marriage, Carla and Leaky had not been blessed with children, so Carla doted on her nephews and niece. She picked up Rosetta, and they both waved to Carlyle, who saluted them. After the garbage truck passed, Carla returned Tulip to the sidewalk where she started to run literal circles around her brothers, driving them crazy and making herself dizzy.

"This parade gets dumber every year," Carla said. "I mean, a garbage truck?"

"Small town, that's what it is," Rosie said. "I kind of like it."

"You would," Carla said.

"What does that mean?"

"Nothing. You're just more—accepting."

Rosie held her tongue. She knew that Carla had switched gears and was no longer talking about the parade.

"Sometimes I wonder," Carla said.

"About what?"

"Life," Carla said, fishing in her pocket for her cigarettes, pulling one out of the pack, popping it into her mouth. "Luck." She struck her lighter, leaned into the flame. "Destiny."

After the parade, Rosie and Carla went to the park by the river where booths had been set up, reminding the sisters of the carnival they had frequented as kids with their parents. They walked down the rows of booths, the same, familiar games offered every year, the same unfortunate-looking carnies returning every year, ogling the women, stinking of drink, while casually overseeing Skee-Ball, ring toss, balloon darts, Ping-Pong ball toss, bobbing for apples, fishing for prizes, and the most challenging game, shooting for prizes, the game at which Babe had won Blue. Rosie lingered at this booth, remembering. She smiled, clutching herself around her middle. The carny approached, presenting her a toy gun, but Rosie waved him away and left the booth.

"When does Babe come home?" Carla spoke casually, pretending to reposition her hat.

"He said he'll be late," Rosie said.

"You mean, late, like in time for the fireworks, or—?"

Rosie bit her tongue. She hated when Carla played these games. Goading her. Feeling somehow inferior—less than—but acting superior, as if she had privileged information that she may or may not share. *Oh, she wants to tell me. She's dying to tell me.* Rosie knew her sister had something more to say. But Rosie was not in the mood to hear it.

For dinner, Rosie and Carla laid out blankets by the seawall next to the river. After feeding the kids egg salad sandwiches, potato salad, and celery sticks—"Eat your greens," Rosie would say, invoking her mother—they allowed the four of them to join others their age in games of tag and hide-and-seek by the river. Rosie swept the remains of dinner off the blanket and deposited everything into a nearby trashcan. She looked at her sister getting comfortable on the blanket, resting on her elbows, crossing her legs at her ankles, staring at the river, inhaling yet another smoke. She definitely had something on her mind.

Rosie sat down on the blanket and folded her hands in her lap. "Carla, let it out. You'll feel better."

Carla pretended to be confused. "What?"

"Whatever it is you've been dying to tell me all day."

"Am I that obvious?"

"Little bit."

"Well, it's just—"

She exhaled and waved the smoke cloud away from in front of her face.

"I am going to be honest with you," Carla said. "This has been difficult for me."

Here we go.

Rosie knew what *this* was about.

This always pertained to their marriages, specifically to Babe and Leaky, to their husbands, to their men, and to their circumstances, mostly financial.

But somehow, Rosie could intuit that Carla was bursting to tell her something that went beyond the usual comparisons. Usually, Carla contrasted the two men with offhanded, cutting remarks along the lines of "Oh, I know, Montel got caught in that unfortunate predicament, and Babe would never allow himself to get involved in *that*; he's too *smart*," or "Babe has always been able to provide for you, but where does he get the money? What does he do for it? Who does he *owe*?" or "Babe has been blessed with the gift of gab, native intelligence, street smarts, and popularity, and Montel, well, Montel has never been blessed or *gifted*." Carla pointed out that even when it came to nicknames, Babe won—Floyd, known universally as Babe, versus Montel, known as *Leaky*?

Carla finished her cigarette, crushed the butt in a paper cup she used as an ashtray, and scooted closer to Rosie. She started to speak, then stopped, suddenly struggling to find the right words.

"Oh, Carla, just say it."

Carla reached over and gripped her sister's hand.

"I have to tell you something." She started again, looked at her sister with something resembling pity, and then said softly, dramatically, "Rosie, it's bad."

Rosie looked away. Her sister loved drawing things out. She lived for melodrama. She saw life as a soap opera with her as the star, the victim, the unfortunate, put-upon wife, the tragic older sister.

Carla stared again. "Babe always has things under control. He's the man. Everyone knows him, relies on him. Everybody *loves* him. Leaky is Leaky. He's an also-ran. The sidekick. I love him, but let's face it, he's the child I never had. So, I don't know how to tell you this."

"Carla! Tell me. You're driving me crazy."

Carla sighed. "They had a big dice game at the Hall last night."

"I know about it."

"You do?"

"Yes. Floyd tells me everything."

This derailed Carla for a moment.

"He does?"

"Yes. Well, okay, almost everything. On a need to know."

"I see." Carla adjusted herself on the blanket. She pulled her legs up and got into a sitting position. "Montel also informs me of everything. Because I make him tell me."

"I'm sure."

"Last night, he was Babe's second. Meaning he was by his side for the whole game. Naturally, Montel doesn't bet. I won't let him. And he knows better."

Carla began tapping her pack of cigarettes, and then she wedged her hands beneath her thighs. But when she spoke next, her tone had changed. Her voice grew darker, heavier.

"Montel told me what happened last night. He was there for all of it. He told me everything. He wasn't going to at first, but I got it out of him."

Rosie waited for Carla to finish, but her sister went uncharacteristically quiet.

"Well?" Rosie said.

"Did Babe tell you?"

"Tell me what?"

"That he lost."

"Carla, he doesn't lose. He never loses."

"Well, that was before. Last night, he lost."

Rosie hesitated. "What do you mean, lost?"

"Rosie, he *lost*."

A sudden chill ran through Rosie. She shuddered. She didn't

know what Carla was about to say, but she didn't want to hear it. Her hands started to tremble.

"I think," Rosie said, "you should stop talking now."

"I have to get this out."

"Carla, please."

"Rosie." Carla gagged and then she spit the words out. "He lost everything. He lost your money. He lost your land."

Rosie gasped. "The *land*—"

"Yes."

"He couldn't have. How could he—?"

"He bet the deed."

"He doesn't even have it. The deed's in the safe deposit box."

"Babe got it yesterday. Leaky bumped into him coming out of the bank. Rosie, he bet the deed. *He lost your land.*"

Rosie sprang to her feet. She looked down at her sister. Her entire body shook. She wanted to strike Carla, to slap her across the face. She wanted to pummel her, but then she saw tears gushing down her sister's cheeks, and her sister started sobbing, and for this one moment, this one instant only, she felt sorry for her, for having to be the one to tell her this horrifying, lifechanging, life-ending news.

"Rosie, I didn't know how to tell you—"

"No," Rosie said, not in disbelief but in belief. In somehow knowing. In maybe knowing all along that this could have happened. That this was how it would end.

Destiny.

I thought I knew him.

Maybe I don't know him at all.

Her eyes drifted toward the river. She saw Floyd and Lloyd, the twins, laughing, and Melvin chasing them, roaring, all of them delirious, oblivious to the upheaval that Rosie felt, and then she saw

Rosetta—Babe's Tulip—sitting against the seawall, her knees curled into her, reading a book, of course, in the center of all the chaos. She always found her own space, her own comfort. She would do so for the rest of her life. Rosie didn't worry about her.

Carla reached for Rosie's arm.

Rosie yanked her arm away.

"I can't."

"We don't have much," Carla said, "but Montel and I have saved a few dollars—"

Rosie whirled on her.

"Don't you dare."

Carla blinked, her eyes red and swelling now, filled with tears, the sobs shaking her. "I don't understand."

"This is what you've been waiting for, isn't it? You've been waiting for this day—this moment—for years. Leaky may be this, Leaky may be that, but he's not a loser, he's not a fool. Leaky would never lose everything we own in a *craps game*. Whose husband would you take right now? Who's got the better *man*? You happy, Carla? You won."

"I didn't say that. I would never say that."

"You don't have to."

"Rosie, please, I'm your sister. We're family. We have to stick together. Please. Listen to me—"

Rosie's rage drowned out the rest.

Rosie didn't know what she would do, where she would go.

But she knew she had to flee.

She had to get out of this place, while she could.

Rosie's rage knew that much.

32

Late that evening, well after the dinner rush, as the train barreled from Oakville to its next stop, the tiny town of Glencoe, the burly, bald-headed businessman sat alone in a booth, the only passenger in the dining car, demolishing a cheese sandwich and sipping a tall glass of beer he poured from a bottle on his table. He was on the job, true, and he was being paid handsomely to stay alert, to be Wojak's eyes and ears on the train. *Babysit the boxcar.* That's how Wojak described the job. But *one* beer? A single bottle poured into a frosty glass that he would nurse over the next hour? Come on. It was the Fourth of July. No fireworks on this train. He'd carefully scoped out all the passengers on the train. Everyone was either under twelve, half-asleep, or half-alive. *Yeah. I can allow myself to celebrate the holiday with one lousy beer. Who's gonna know?*

As he brought the glass to his lips, the train lurched, and someone walking down the aisle behind him slammed into his back. The beer sloshed over the lip of the glass, and the bottle flew off the small table and smashed on the floor.

A woman screamed and then gasped. "Oh, I'm so sorry."

Purely by instinct, Alfred Polansky, the businessman, swiveled, his right hand bunched in a fist, ready to strike. At the same time, his left hand slid down his side and gripped the gun in his holster.

He faced a young woman. He remembered that she'd come on the train at Oakville. She stood next to him, her cheeks flushed a hot pink, her hand covering her mouth.

"I can't believe it. The movement of the train—"

"Yeah."

"I'm so sorry," Madeline repeated.

She pulled the cloth napkin off the table across the aisle from Alfred and bent down to pick up the shards of glass. As she leaned over, her dress hiked up, and Alfred caught a lot of leg.

"Careful," he said. "Sharp."

"I'm not clumsy," Madeline said. "I'm really not."

"Yeah," Alfred said.

"I can't believe I did this."

"Happens," Alfred said, realizing he had almost no beer left in his glass.

"Shit!" Madeline said.

"What?"

"I cut myself."

"Tole you." Alfred got up—he moved surprisingly quickly for a big man—and knelt down next to Madeline. "Where?"

Madeline showed Alfred the cut at the bottom of her left palm. She started breathing heavily, panting almost.

"I can't look. I hate the sight of blood."

"I hear some people are like that," Alfred said.

"Not you?"

"No," Alfred said. "Gimme."

He pointed at Madeline's hand. She turned her head and extended her bleeding palm. Alfred gently wrapped her hand in his napkin.

"You got to wash it out," he said.

"I'm feeling a little faint," she said.

"Sit down."

Alfred helped Madeline to her feet and guided her to a chair at the table across from him. She seemed disoriented and instead sat in Alfred's spot. He hesitated and then banged on the table with his fist as if he were knocking on a door and then moved swiftly to the bathroom at the end of the dining car. He returned almost instantly, carrying two fistfuls of balled-up toilet paper, one wet, the other dry.

"Here," he said, offering the toilet paper to Madeline.

"I can't look." She looked deeply into Alfred's eyes. "Would you?"

"Sure."

Madeline moved, allowing Alfred room to sit down next to her. She turned away while Alfred dabbed her hand with the clump of soaked toilet paper. As he patted her hand, he felt something like a tiny lightning bolt streak through him. He felt his head go hot. He swallowed and kept attending to Madeline's wound.

"Can I look yet?" she said.

"Nah. Still bleeding."

Madeline whimpered. Alfred switched to the dry toilet paper now, keeping his large, hairy, paw-like palm on top of hers. They didn't speak for some time. Finally, Alfred said, "Bleeding stopped. Pretty much. Keep the toilet paper on it."

Madeline, still facing away, nodded.

"Can I look now?"

"Yeah."

Madeline turned to Alfred, looked into his eyes, then peeked at her palm wrapped in toilet paper. "Fancy bandage."

Alfred snorted.

A laugh, Madeline realized.

"Lemme see if I can get you a Band-Aid."

"I'm okay. But I wouldn't mind a glass of water. I'm afraid I might pass out. Feel my forehead."

Madeline grabbed Alfred's hand and pressed it against her forehead. She held his hand there for a slow count of ten.

"I'm so warm," Madeline said, her voice hushed.

"Oh, yeah, uh," Alfred stammered.

Alfred, too, felt uncharacteristically warm. Finally, reluctantly, Alfred withdrew his hand from Madeline's forehead.

"I'm so sorry," she said. "I've ruined your dinner."

"No big deal. Just a cheese sandwich and a beer."

"Let me at least buy you another beer."

"You don't have to."

"Please. I'll ring for the conductor."

Madeline raised her arm above her head to pull the cord that called the conductor. As she did, Alfred snuck a glance at her breasts. She moaned softly and shrugged, indicating that she couldn't reach the cord. She looked at Alfred and seemed to pout. He snorted again, his laugh, then reached over her head and pulled the cord.

"Thank you. I'm Madeline, by the way."

"Alfred," he said. "I'm Alfred. Call me Alfred."

Madeline smiled. The kind of smile that seemed to suggest something intimate, as if Alfred and Madeline had been let in on an important secret, something that only the two of them were allowed to know. She smiled again. That secret smile. Alfred felt his body burn.

"Alfred, where you headed?"

"St. Louis."

"Wow. Long trip."

Alfred shrugged. "Annual convention." And then he added quickly, "I'm in sales. Where you going?"

"I'm—" Madeline stopped. She contorted her top lip and looked off, as if she were trying to see something through the window on the other side of the train. She turned back to Alfred.

"Detroit," she said. "Yes. I'm going to Detroit."

"You don't seem too sure."

She tilted her head slightly and stared into Alfred's eyes.

"Actually, I'm not sure. You picked up on that, didn't you?"

Alfred shifted his weight. "Yeah. I mean, you know. Yeah."

"You're very perceptive."

Alfred's cheeks felt on fire.

"I don't know," he said.

"You want to know a secret?"

"Sure."

"I'm on the run."

Alfred perked up.

"From the cops?"

"From my husband. Ex. My ex-husband." She smiled again, that intimate smile. "I like the way that sounds."

"Um," Alfred said because that's the best he could do.

"The divorce was final yesterday." She gripped Alfred's biceps for support, for emphasis, for ballast. "I couldn't take it anymore. He—" She swallowed and turned away. She spoke then in a tiny, birdlike chirp. "He hit me."

"Huh," Alfred said.

"The son of a bitch." She turned back to him. "Pardon my French."

"I don't give a shit."

Madeline's eyes widened. Alfred realized what he'd said and snorted. Madeline cracked up and then composed herself.

"I never should've married him. I was attracted to him, but I didn't know him. As a person. I was young. I wanted sex. It was all about sex. It was a terrible mistake. Never marry for sex. Oh, I'm sorry. Are you married?"

"Nah."

On the repeated mentions of the word "sex," Alfred squirmed. He dropped his hands into his lap, felt foolish, self-conscious, then brought his hefty fists up and rested them on the tablecloth in front of him. His body started to tingle. He sat stock still. He feared if he moved, he would knock over the entire table.

"What's in Detroit?" he asked, his voice cracking.

"My sister. I left everything behind in Toronto. I don't care. He can have the house. I just had to get away."

"I'm, you know, uh, sorry," Alfred said, his large head bopping back and forth on his fire hydrant–size neck.

"You know what, Alfred? I'm not. I feel like celebrating."

"Your escape," Alfred said.

"Yes. Exactly. My escape."

"From that son of a bitch," they said together, and they cracked up again, Madeline, losing it, dropping her head on Alfred's shoulder, her hand still gripping his arm.

The door to the dining car opened then and the conductor, a short, pudgy Black man named Mosby, entered.

"Careful," Madeline said, stopping the conductor. "I had an accident. I broke a bottle."

"I'll mop it up," Mosby said, seeing the mess on the floor. "No problem. Did you want to order something?"

"Yes," Madeline said, again taking in Alfred, her look smoldering.

She licked her lips. Mosby shifted his weight, waited for their order.

"Two beers," Alfred said.

"Actually," Madeline said, "make it two glasses of champagne."

Alfred looked at her.

"We're celebrating," Madeline told the conductor. "It's the Fourth of July, and we're celebrating our freedom."

"Yes, ma'am," Mosby said.

"You sure?" Alfred said to Madeline.

"Absolutely," Madeline said, fumbling in her purse, then slapping a twenty on the table.

"We'll be pulling into Glencoe shortly," Mosby said. "I'll clean this up, then get you your drinks."

"Thank you," Madeline said.

"Oh," Alfred said. "Bring a Band-Aid."

"Yes, sir," Mosby said.

Madeline sheepishly raised the clump of toilet paper wrapped around her hand. She looked at Alfred, smiled, and pressed his arm. Alfred's face flushed crimson.

"Next stop—Glencoe!"

The conductor's voice boomed through the train. Previously, he had swept up the pieces of the broken bottle into a dustpan and mopped up the spilt beer, but Madeline and Alfred were so deep in conversation that they hardly noticed when he came in. Led by Madeline, a probing questioner and eager listener, she and Alfred had covered a range of topics—the war (Alfred had not served because of a mangled and deformed toe; he offered to take off his shoe and show her, but she politely declined); the high prices of everything from groceries to gas and, in particular, booze; favorite singers (she loved Doris Day and Peggy Lee; he preferred Spike Jones and Gene Autry); favorite foods (she, seafood and salads; he, kielbasa). Intertwined through all these subjects, they revealed their most intimate relationships. In graphic detail, she described losing her virginity to an older man, possibly a relative, when she was fifteen; he related his first time, a boring event, really, going with a friend to a local house of ill repute on the South Side of Chicago. Finally, they discussed marriage. She shared more detail about her failed alliance to her abusive husband; he admitted that he'd never married because "I guess I ain't found the right one." He spoke pointedly, sharper than he intended, shining a long, lingering look at Madeline, causing her to blush, her cheeks pulsing hot pink again.

They aborted the conversation when the conductor's voice boomed again, "Glencoe! Arriving Glencoe!" The train rumbled into the tiny station with a jolt and a screech of brakes and came to a halt. They heard the whoosh of air hoses blasting beneath them, followed by the *woo-woo-woo* of the train whistle. They settled back, silent for the first time in hours, gathering themselves, catching their collective breath, or in Alfred's case, asking himself, *Is this right? Is this real?* He realized, in fact, that he didn't care.

It had gotten late, nearly 11:30 p.m., but neither Alfred nor Madeline made a move to leave the dining car that still only the two of them occupied. Their private sanctuary.

"Never got our champagne," Alfred said.

"I know," Madeline said. "Rather poor service on this train. Considering what you pay."

"Yeah."

"I'm sure the conductor will come by with it once we leave Glencoe. Unless you want to cancel it and call it a night."

"No," Alfred said, faster than he meant to.

"Good," Madeline said. "Me, either."

33

To Ruggs, the tiny train station at Glencoe looked like something out of a fairy tale. The gingerbread-shaped building sat at the far edge of a wide lawn behind a tall green hedge. The station sported a shingled roof, poking up at odd, misshapen angles, the farthest a tall peak with a weathervane. Instead of an open, inviting entrance, the station's front appeared dark, cold, sinister. It reminded Ruggs of a witch's cabin.

He parked the Caddy around the corner, out of sight, but close enough for him to have eyes on who came and went into the station. After a moment, two people exited the train and came through the station, and one person, lugging a small suitcase, ran inside, breathless, obviously late for his train. Ruggs checked his watch and announced the time.

"Eleven thirty-six," he said.

"Check," Babe said, standing next to the Caddy's open trunk, making sure his watch was in sync.

"You're in motion," Ruggs said. "I'm on the move."

"Copy that," Babe said, stepping back, running his hands down both sides of his new outfit.

He exhaled and eased the trunk lid shut.

It closed neatly, clicking in place.

It would be unseemly to slam down a luxury car's trunk.

He walked past the Caddy and headed into the station.

At 11:45 p.m., Mosby, the conductor, shouted his final "All aboard," the train whistle screeched, and the mixed freight train bound for the U.S. steamed out of Glencoe station. In the dining car, Madeline and Alfred rested against the vinyl back of their booth. Madeline checked her watch. She seemed antsy.

"The train on time?" Alfred asked, noticing her looking at her watch. Madeline absently circled two fingers around her wrist.

"Yes. I think so." She looked at the door to the dining car. "Should I ring for the conductor again?"

"Give him a few minutes."

"You're right. We just left the station. Guess I'm tired."

Madeline dropped her head onto Alfred's shoulder and nuzzled her chin into his substantial neck. Her sudden move threw him off, but then he caught a deep whiff of her perfume. The scent nearly knocked him over. He closed his eyes and took it in. Strong. Exotic. Sexy.

Madeline, he thought. *Don't even know her last name.*

Nobody had ever made him feel quite this way. Nobody. It felt intoxicating. And—strange. He opened his eyes and studied Madeline's face. He peered at the sharp lines of her face, her thin, vulnerable neck, her blond hair flying all over, bunched up and brushing his cheek. She had her eyes closed now, too, and a soft, purring sound slipped out of her slightly open mouth. She looked so peaceful. So perfect. He wondered—

Too perfect?

"Here we go. Two glasses of champagne."

The conductor.

Striding into the dining car, his voice cheery.

A tall, wiry Black man.

Moving with power and purpose and grace, like a dancer.

Or a fighter.

Not Mosby.

Babe.

Babe's crisp conductor's uniform swished as he came toward them, carrying the champagne flutes aloft on a tray. He wore white gloves and had his conductor's cap cocked forward, covering most of his face.

"Dom Perignon. The best."

He brought two fingers to his lips and kissed them. He smiled and placed one of the flutes in front of Madeline, the other next to Alfred's thick right hand, which he'd balled into a fist. Between the two flutes sat the twenty-dollar bill Madeline had put on the table more than an hour ago.

"May I punch your tickets, please?" Babe said.

"Of course," Madeline said, fishing her ticket out of her purse.

Alfred grunted. He pulled his crumpled ticket out of his jacket pocket. He held on to it while he stared at the conductor.

"You do this at every stop?"

"Yes, sir. Rule of the railroad."

Alfred grunted again and slowly handed over his ticket. Babe punched both tickets and handed them back. He pressed the empty tray against his chest and took two steps back. "Let me know if you need anything else."

"Don't forget your payment," Madeline said, fanning a long finger over the twenty.

"Thank you. I'll get your change."

"No need. It's all for you."

Babe bowed and swept up the bill. "Much obliged. Enjoy the champagne."

He backed up again.

That's when he noticed Alfred's eyes were boring into him like high beams. Alfred shifted his position, the vinyl of the booth crinkling as he moved. Then Alfred leaned forward, as if preparing to launch himself out of the booth.

Babe dropped his hand inside his conductor's jacket, steadied his fingers an inch away from Pearl, his barber's blade.

Alfred grunted.

Babe grinned.

"If you need anything else—"

He backed up another two steps, his eyes locked on Alfred.

Alfred shifted again. Babe knew that Alfred sensed trouble or at least had something on his mind.

Babe turned, his gloved hand reaching for the dining car door.

"Hey. Conductor."

Alfred's voice cut through the dining car.

"Boy."

Babe flinched.

He spun around, moving his hand deeper inside his jacket, resting his fingers on his barber's blade.

"You forgot something," Alfred said.

Babe froze.

"The Band-Aid," Alfred said. "Where's the Band-Aid I asked you for?"

Band-Aid.

Babe had no idea what he meant.

Then Babe realized—

He's talking about the other conductor. Mosby. Short, fat, and sixty, and he can't tell us apart. So fucking predictable.

"My mistake," Babe said. "Slipped my mind. I'll bring it right to you."

"Not for me," Alfred said, gazing at Madeline. "For my friend."

"Yes, sir."

Babe turned again, put his shoulder into the door, and left the dining car.

"These people are so stupid," Alfred said.

"I don't really need it, thanks to you," Madeline said.

Alfred grunted. He reached for his champagne.

"A toast," he said.

"Indeed," Madeline said. "To us."

"Yeah."

"And to the future."

Madeline extended her pinkie and took a dainty sip of the champagne. "Oh, my. That is delicious. So elegant."

"Chug," Alfred said, with a goofy grin.

"I don't think we should chug Dom Perignon," Madeline said.

"You're right," Alfred said. Then, mimicking Madeline, he stuck out his pinkie finger and guzzled the champagne in one gulp.

Madeline laughed, wiped her mouth with the back of her hand, and took another dainty sip.

Ten minutes later, Babe returned with an assortment of Band-Aids and the bottle of Dom Perignon.

"Another glass?" he said.

Madeline giggled. "I'm feeling a little tipsy."

"On one glass of bubbly?" Alfred said. "Lightweight."

"I know. Okay, sure, one more glass."

Babe tucked one arm behind his back and filled the champagne flutes.

"I got this one," Alfred said, reaching for his wallet.

"It's on me," Babe said.

Alfred glowered.

"For forgetting the Band-Aid," Babe said.

"Thank you," Madeline said. "Very kind of you."

"Leave the bottle," Alfred said.

"Yes, sir."

Babe placed the nearly empty champagne bottle on the table and left the dining car.

"Another toast," Madeline said, raising her glass to Alfred.

He snorted and raised his glass.

"To friends on a train," she said, clinking his glass.

"Yeah," Alfred said.

As she sipped, she rested her hand on his thigh.

He coughed.

Madeline tilted her head toward him and smiled her secret smile.

Twenty minutes later, in the middle of a story Madeline was telling Alfred about her childhood and her horny cousin who chased her around the woodshed when she was twelve, Alfred felt queasy, and then nauseous, and then drowsy.

"I'm really tired," he said.

"It's one in the morning," Madeline said without looking at her watch.

Alfred yawned, an earsplitting howl causing Madeline to

shudder. He shook his thick neck and shoulders and yawned again. Madeline poked her hand under the table and began tracing her fingers along Alfred's thigh.

"You know, Alfie, I have a sleeper car."

"Alfred. Call me Alfred."

"Would you like me to tuck you in? Then we can take it from there."

Alfred yawned a third time. His eyes started to close. Alfred forced them open and looked at Madeline. She smiled.

"Yeah," Alfred said. "Tuck me."

He started to stand. Madeline scooted out of the booth. Alfred made it to his feet, took a step, teetered, and gripped the side of the table to steady himself.

"Dizzy," he said.

"Now who's the lightweight?" Madeline said.

Alfred sniffed, swiped at his nose, took another couple of steps, and wrapped his arms around his midsection.

"I don't feel so good."

Madeline put an arm around his shoulders. "Lean on me. It's not far."

"Fuckin' room's spinning."

"You can make it, Alfred. One step at a time. You're okay."

"Gonna puke."

"I got you," Madeline said, but this time her voice seemed huskier, harsher, impatient. She sounded like a working woman coming to the end of her shift.

Guided by Madeline, Alfred staggered and lurched out of the dining car, somehow making it to the first compartment in the sleeper car where he collapsed, unconscious, onto a lower bed. The bed had been made up for the night by the conductor—Babe—who looked over Madeline's shoulder as she pulled the covers up to Alfred's chin. She placed an envelope on his chest, addressed to *Alfred* in her own florid cursive handwriting, and stepped out of the compartment. Alfred stirred and opened his mouth. His lips fluttered and he began snoring like a racehorse with a sinus condition.

"Sweet dreams, Alfred," Babe said.

He closed the door.

BOXCARS

◆

TWELVE THE HARD WAY,
TWO SIXES

34

MONDAY, JULY 5, 1948

At precisely 1:17 a.m., the train pulled into the Chatham-Kent station, a weathered hump of a building resembling a barn. In the parking lot next to the station, which served two tiny villages and the surrounding farmland, two cars waited, idling—a tan, late-model Chevrolet with the trunk open and Ruggs's unmistakable Cadillac. The train jerked to a stop, the locomotive nosing to the far edge of the platform. The lights inside the station flickered, either sending a signal or signaling shoddy electricity. The train's air hoses hissed, the brakes screeched and locked, and the boxcars and passenger cars rocked in unison. After a moment, two people hurried off the train and rushed toward the Cadillac.

Madeline and Babe.

Babe flung open the passenger door and stepped aside as Mosby, the conductor from Glencoe, the short, pudgy, sixty-year-old Black man, exited the car. He tipped his cap to Babe, hustled onto the train platform, checked his pocket watch, and began pacing from one end of the platform to the other. In the parking lot, Babe popped the Caddy's trunk and wriggled out of his conductor's uniform while Madeline walked directly to Ruggs on the driver's side. He dangled his arm out the open window.

"Well?" he asked.

"Easy," she said.

Ruggs reached across the passenger seat, grabbed an envelope, and handed it to her.

"What we agreed. Plus."

"Thanks."

"Now disappear."

Madeline saluted him with two fingers. She came around to the trunk where Babe, now nearly dressed in his suit, presented her his conductor's uniform and cap. She balled up the clothes and speed-walked toward the tan Chevy. She tossed the conductor's clothes into the trunk, brought the hatch down, and slid into the backseat.

Tucking in his shirt and beginning to knot his tie, Babe closed the Caddy's trunk, walked to the passenger side of the car, and got in. Ruggs flicked his headlights toward the train. On the platform, Mosby stopped in mid-pace, acknowledged Ruggs's signal by taking off his cap and putting it back on. Mosby checked his watch again, walked toward the front of the train, and leaned against a pole near the locomotive. He sighed and murmured, "Fifteen minutes. Gonna be tight."

In the Caddy, Babe rolled down his window to get a clearer view of the train parked at the platform. He poked his head out the window and looked behind him at a second track crisscrossing the main track. A *frog*. That's what Dan Waters, the engineer, said railroad linemen call the point where two tracks cross. A *railroad frog*, to be precise, a junction, which at this moment was empty.

Babe brought his head back inside the Caddy. "He's late."

"Give him two minutes," Ruggs said.

"*Lot* of moving parts," Babe said.

Ruggs reached into his shirt pocket and retrieved a cigar. He bit off the tip. "Be cool."

"Worse comes to worst, I'll drive the train."

"Yeah. That'll work."

"How hard can it be?"

A rumble from beyond the railroad frog caused them both to jump. Babe looked behind him again while Ruggs checked the rearview mirror.

"He's here," Ruggs said.

A mini train, just two cars, a locomotive and a boxcar, roared up to the junction below the platform and stopped. Moonlight bounced off the locomotive's steel roof, giving off a slanted, dusty glow. Ruggs flicked his high beams on and off. On the platform, Mosby walked to the cab of the waiting Michigan Central Line and shouted something.

Dan Waters, the engineer, exited the locomotive of the original seven-car train. Waters moved quickly—not quite running, but close—and took the stairs at the end of the platform down to the tracks. He arrived at the two boxcars connected to each other and stepped into the narrow space between them. He kept one foot on the track, the other on the ground. A practiced, proper move. If the boxcars moved unexpectedly, Waters gave himself a split second to leap to safety and avoid getting crushed between the two railway cars.

"Feel like we should oversee this," Babe said.

Ruggs rested his hand on Babe's forearm. "We'll only be in the way."

Babe reluctantly nodded. Ruggs removed his hand. Babe leaned forward and concentrated all his attention on Waters. The engineer stood on the track between the two boxcars, a man at work, a flurry of motion. Waters twisted a metal lever at the rear of the first boxcar—the one attached to the locomotive—and then moved off the track. He counted to five. He stepped back onto the track and began unhooking the air hoses and turning two more levers, including one that opened the angle cock. The boxcar suddenly bucked like a massive metal bull, and Waters hopped out of the way. With a whoosh of steam and a groan of metal, the two boxcars banged briefly and then uncoupled, leaving only the first one connected to the locomotive. Waters had created a second two-car train—the locomotive and the boxcar. *The* boxcar. The boxcar that contained Wojak's three thousand cases of primo whiskey bound for Cuba, Missouri. Dan Waters raced to the locomotive and climbed into the cab.

"Go!" he shouted, and then he jumped down from the cab.

The locomotive sat motionless for less than five seconds and then the driver of that two-car train—a trusted Ruggs employee—fired up the engine. The locomotive with the boxcar attached nudged forward and began to move, veering up the second track, gathering speed, moving farther and farther from the rest of the train as it chugged away from Chatham-Kent station.

"There goes our liquor," Ruggs said to Babe, and he grinned. "Partner."

"I'll be right back," Babe said.

He flew out of the Caddy, ran to the end of the parking lot, and dropped down to the railroad tracks. He sprinted toward the waiting two-car train, the second locomotive and boxcar. Waters stood on the tracks ahead of him, in the space recently vacated by the first locomotive and Wojak's boxcar. He waved his arms as Babe climbed aboard the locomotive. Babe didn't go inside the cab. He held on as the engineer drove the mini train up to the frog, stopped, and then backed into the space where Waters had stood a few moments ago. Waving his arms in a forward motion, Waters directed the engineer, then held his hand up, telling the engineer to stop. The locomotive grumbled, hissed, and halted. Babe jumped down and approached Waters.

"Everything alright?" Waters said.

"I had to see for myself," Babe said.

"Just don't get caught between the boxcars. That's for idiots like me."

Waters maneuvered himself behind the newly arrived boxcar and the remaining boxcar attached to the locomotive of the Michigan Central Line. Again, he stood astride the tracks, one foot behind the boxcar, the other on the ground. He grunted, put his shoulder into the lever on the new boxcar, twisted it, huffed, and moved off the track. He stood next to Babe as the boxcar lurched and rocked. When it settled, he stepped between the boxcars again. He spun two more levers and tightened them. This time, he coupled the boxcar on the train to the new arrival. He attached the air hoses, turned a lever, making certain that this boxcar and locomotive were properly and securely aligned and attached to the other cars on the Michigan Central Line. Babe checked his watch. It had taken Waters twelve minutes to switch the two boxcars. Waters stepped off the track and clapped Babe on the back.

"Almost there," Waters said.

He removed a flashlight from the pocket of his coveralls and turned it on and off twice. Ruggs returned the signal with his headlights. Without a word, Waters and Babe walked back to the parking lot. Waters got into the backseat of the tan Chevy. He acknowledged Madeline with a nod as Babe got back into the front seat of the Caddy.

Thirty seconds later, an engineer wearing coveralls and a striped cap rushed onto the platform, breathless. Mosby, the conductor, extended his hand.

"Collingwood?" Mosby said.

"That's me. Talk about short notice. What happened?"

"Food poisoning," Mosby said.

"What about you?"

"I never eat train food."

"So, it's us the rest of the way?"

"My shift ends at Windsor, the next stop." Mosby consulted his watch. "We got to make up the time. We're about fifteen minutes late."

"Let's do it," Collingwood said.

He climbed inside the cab.

Mosby started to follow but stopped before he climbed aboard the train. He glanced at the new boxcar attached to the locomotive. Then he looked back into the parking lot just in time to see the tan Chevy and the Cadillac driving away, in opposite directions.

On the two-hour drive to Windsor, Ruggs shadowed the train as much as possible, sticking to backroads that ran parallel to the train tracks. He and Babe spoke little, except to review the details of what would be happening in the next day and in the near future.

"I'll pay you back, with interest," Babe said.

"Don't worry about that. I'll take a bigger cut of the profits until we're even, then we'll go fifty-fifty."

"That'll work."

"And remember, I can arrange a cage match or two. That'll catch you up quicker."

"I'm still retired."

"Fair enough," Ruggs said.

Suddenly, gunshots blasted over and behind them. Ruggs gripped the wheel and lowered his head. Babe removed his gun from his holster, ducked down, and peered over the seat, trying to get a glimpse of the shooter.

Wojak, Babe thought. *He's on to us.*

The gunshots rang out again.

"Where they coming from?" Babe said.

Ruggs kept his head low. He scanned the street for a safe place to pull over, a side street, an alley, behind a building, someplace where they could take cover.

The shots came again, a staccato burst lasting fifteen, twenty seconds, *ka-ping-ka-ping-ka-ping-ka-ping-ping-ping.*

"What kind of gun is that?" Babe asked.

Ruggs leaned back and started to laugh.

"That's not gunshots," he said. "It's fireworks."

"At this hour?"

"Expats. They shoot them off all night to annoy the residents. Their little patriotic joke."

"Funny," Babe said, sliding his pistol back into his holster. "Scared the shit out of me."

"Happy Fourth of July, brother."

"Right," Babe said. He felt a tremor in his hand. He held his fingers straight in front of him and saw that he was shaking.

This whole night—

Running on fumes.

Running on empty.

Putting everything on the line.

Everything I've earned, everything I am.

This is it.

The end. The beginning.

The shaking slowed. Babe lowered his hand, leaned his fingers onto the dashboard.

"If I survive this, Sarge, after I pay you back, I'm going to build a new house for Rosie and the kids, and then I'm going to retire."

"If you say so."

"I do," Babe said. "I do."

In Windsor, across the river from Detroit, Mosby, the conduc-tor, ended his shift by handing his timesheet to the new conductor who would take the train all the way to its last stop, Cuba, Missouri. From their vantage point inside the Cadillac, Ruggs and Babe watched Mosby cross the platform and disappear inside the train station. Thirty seconds later, the man named Mosby got into the backseat of the Caddy.

"Good work," Ruggs said. "How's Alfred?"

"Out cold. I'd say he was sleeping like a baby, but most babies get up every two hours."

Just before noon on Monday, July 5, at the edge of a private airfield outside Windsor, Babe shook hands with Mosby, and then he and Ruggs got out of the Caddy. Ruggs handed Babe a business card.

"I wrote my private number on the back," Ruggs said. "Call me twenty-four, seven."

"The whiskey?"

"I'll start selling it when you give me the word."

"If you don't hear from me—"

Ruggs cut him off. "I will."

Babe extended his hand. Ruggs took it and then pulled Babe into his chest for a sudden, surprising hug. To Babe, it didn't feel like two old friends embracing. It felt like a father hugging a son. After a solid twenty seconds, Ruggs pulled away, smiled, leaned forward, and squeezed Babe's shoulders. Babe clicked his heels and saluted—he couldn't help himself—and Ruggs laughed and returned the salute. Babe jogged toward the runway and boarded a small cargo plane designed for fifteen passengers and three crew members. Today, the plane carried only the pilot and Babe.

35

Babe managed a few restless hours of sleep on the flight from Windsor to St. Louis. He woke up as the pilot began the plane's descent. He yawned and checked his watch—5:05 p.m.

The plane touched down with a thump and a clatter. Babe squinted through the window. On the ground, he saw what he needed to see.

A massive figure in an ill-fitting suit, rolling his neck, trying to get comfortable in the late afternoon heat.

Karter.

His shadow blotting out the top of the Commander.

Waiting.

On time.

Always on time.

"You're alive," Karter said as he drove toward Wydown/ Skinker, the most expensive neighborhood in St. Louis. "That's a good sign."

"So far. The tricky part's coming up. We all set for the meet?"

"Everything's a go."

Karter slowed the Commander and took the scenic route,

through Forest Park, massive and lush, acres of countryside plunked into the heart of downtown. Karter kept the Commander at a crawl, passing ponds dotted with rowboats paddled by couples, then up a road, driving by a concert shell, a zoo, bridal paths with couples on horseback, then through a maze of wide-open grassy fields where kids played pickup baseball, couples and families picnicked, and younger kids arced on swings, swarmed play structures, and ran through fountains. Fourth of July aftermath. Crowds of people not wanting to let go of the holiday, or each other.

Families, Babe thought.

He pictured his kids, playing in such a park, screaming in joy.

In his mind, he saw Rosie, watching them. Her face lit up.

Rosie.

He wanted to say something to Karter, to ask if he'd spoken to her, if he'd seen her. But he couldn't formulate the question.

Or he was too afraid to hear the answer.

Family.

So many words flying through his head, colliding, exploding, dissolving, and that's the only word that stuck. The only word that mattered.

They exited the park and pulled onto Forsyth Boulevard, the ritziest address in the city. They crept by whole blocks of mansions and mansions taking up whole blocks. They came to a corner. A four-story brick mansion took over nearly two blocks. The mansion wore a mansard roof like a huge, drooping stone beret. Karter stopped the car.

"You sure he's home?" Babe asked.

"Positive."

"His house is bigger than downtown Caruthersville."

"You want me to go in with you?"

"No. Stay close, though. In case he needs a little more convincing."

Babe took the walk slowly, a surprisingly short distance from the corner. The sidewalk to the front door betrayed nothing. A trimmed lawn spread out on either side. Rosebushes. A fruit tree. Nothing fancy or ostentatious. An ordinary walkway from the street. At the front door, Babe banged a cast iron door knocker three times. He pressed his ear to the door and waited. After a moment, he heard soft footsteps. Bedroom slippers swooshing across a polished hardwood floor. A pause, an intake of breath, a series of clangs, clicks, rattling chains, and Hanford, The Fat Man, opened the front door himself. No security. No first line of defense. He was so vulnerable. Or arrogant. He wore a silk bathrobe and leather slippers. His round cheeks pulsed when he saw Babe. His pudgy face broke into a wide smile.

"I've been expecting you," Hanford said. "Come in."

"I can't stay," Babe said.

"You sure? I just decanted a ten-year-old Cognac."

"Enjoy it."

Hanford kept his smile wide and locked in place as he scanned the street behind Babe. He saw Karter standing at the Commander. Even from here, Hanford could feel the heat of Karter's stare.

"Your driver?"

"My business manager."

"He looks concerned," Hanford said.

"He's not. You don't want to see him when he's concerned."

"Let's get to it. Why you're here. The deed."

"I want it back," Babe said. "I'll pay you for it."

He reached into his suit pocket and pulled out a stack of cash, the stash Hootie gave him.

"It's worth twenty thousand," Babe said.

"More if I build on it and flip it," Hanford said.

"I'll pay you thirty."

"That's a nice return."

"Fifty percent in twenty-four hours. You're not going to beat that. Whether you flip it or not."

"Very tempting," Hanford said. "But no. I'm going to hold on to it."

Babe looked at the Fat Man. He felt his rage rising. This piece of human excrement enjoyed torturing him, playing his sick cat-and-mouse game. More than that, Babe felt furious with himself. How could he have bet the deed? It was foolish. Desperate. Worse. It was hubris. His hubris could cost him his marriage. Babe glared at the Fat Man.

I'm not going to beg him, Babe thought. *I'll kill him first.*

"Thirty-five," Babe said.

Hanford hissed. "I'm not enjoying this."

"I'm enjoying it less."

Hanford took a step toward Babe—a massive, threatening step. His size obliterated the space between Babe and the doorframe.

"I know you," Hanford said.

Babe wouldn't back down. He stepped into Hanford's space. The two stood head to head, gut to gut, heart to heart.

"Is that right?" Babe said. "Who am I?"

"Me," Hanford said. "You're me."

The words hit Babe like a slap.

"I'm so far from you," Babe said.

"You're exactly me. That's how I beat you. I read you like a map."

"Forty," Babe said.

"There is no number," The Fat Man said. "There's only the game. There's always the game."

Babe blinked, confused. "The game?"

"You can't pay me for the deed," Hanford said. "But you can play me for it."

Babe sensed movement and menace behind him. He didn't have to look. He could feel Karter on the move, starting to stride up Hanford's walk, closing the gap between Babe and the Fat Man. Babe held his hand up, and Karter froze in place.

"When?" Babe asked Hanford.

"Saturday night. My game. My people. Twenty-thousand-dollar buy-in."

"Time and place?"

"I'll be in touch."

"I won't lose twice."

"You know how many times I've heard that? Hundreds."

"Not from me. I've never said it before. I'll never say it again."

"It's a cash-only game. No paper this time."

"See you Saturday night."

Hanford closed the door in Babe's face.

Babe turned and practically crashed into Karter.

"Don't say it," Babe said.

"Not saying a thing." Karter swiveled his shoulders inside his too-tight suit jacket, reached into his pocket, cupped a fresh matchstick, and flipped it into the corner of his mouth. He allowed Babe to pass him on the sidewalk leading back to the Commander before he spoke.

"Starting off ahead this time," Karter said. "We got almost a whole week to come up with the money."

36

11:27 P.M.

*T*ommy Wojak came prepared. Three tricked-out black Cadillacs retrofitted with retractable sunroofs, bullet-proof exteriors, and impenetrable metal grilles kicked up a funnel of dust as they roared up the dirt road leading to the small, boxy, abandoned Cuba, Missouri, train station. The three Caddies skidded, nearly plowing into each other, then corrected and formed a horseshoe, blocking the loading area at the far end of the station platform. A show of force.

Wojak didn't like it.

He charged out of the backseat of the third Cadillac and screamed at the drivers of the other two cars.

"What the fuck is this, the Indy fucking 500? *Fuuck!*"

He plowed his hand through his heavily lacquered hair and kicked at the ground.

"Sorry, boss," Gregor, his driver, said.

"Get out of the cars!" Wojak screamed into the night.

The doors to the Cadillacs swung open, nearly simultaneously, resembling a synchronized circus routine. Six heavyset men built like wrestlers, wearing black pinstriped zoot suits that couldn't conceal the bulge of their guns, rolled out of the cars. Wojak's muscle. Tommy had hired them for double duty—unloading the boxcar and protecting him from anything that might go wrong. *Probably overkill*, Wojak thought. But he wasn't taking any chances. He had recently climbed a consequential rung up the ladder of The Outfit's Polish hierarchy, run by Hymie Weiss, and had been bequeathed this territory. He hadn't met Babe Boyce until four days ago, Thursday night, but he'd heard stories. Most people—even the people in Chicago—liked Babe. He was a man of his word. He got things done. He knew the right people. He could provide you with liquor, gambling, women. The Caruthersville connection. For now. The Outfit respected him, even relied on him. Of course, they didn't trust him. Tommy Wojak certainly didn't trust him, but he didn't trust anybody. He lived his life with his head on a swivel, watching his back, his front, his sides, all day, all night. By his calculation, he hadn't slept in fourteen years.

Wojak scoped out the area next to the train station. Across from the station was a building, a beat-up garage that had been used to store and repair railroad cars. A shambles now, its roof partially caved in, the walls cratering, the paint peeling, the building sat boarded up, empty. Wojak felt strangely uncomfortable standing between this abandoned building and the empty, boxy train station. For one thing, very little light fell on either building. He looked at the station's platform, mostly cloaked in shadow. The only light came from a sliver of moonlight and the spillover from a streetlight fifty feet away. The dim lights outside the train station flickered, threatening to go out. The bulb in the rickety streetlamp designed to illuminate the station's platform had been removed.

"This station don't operate no more," Gregor said.

"That's why we're using it," Tommy said, annoyed. "Deserted. Quiet. Out of the way. Hey!"

He started to run toward his men. They were standing in a line, their suit pants bunched around their ankles, urinating into some bushes.

"What the *fuck*!"

"Long trip, boss," one of them said.

"Hurry it up," Tommy said, raking his hand through his hair again. "Then go check this place out. We got here early for a reason."

"Nobody here but us," Gregor said.

At that instant, the door to the boarded-up storage garage rose up and a twenty-foot box truck, the size of a small moving van, roared out of the building. The truck's headlights and the bright lights from four high-powered flashlights hit Tommy and his men in the eyes, temporarily blinding them. The truck kept coming, and then the driver, Carlyle, abruptly shifted into neutral. Karter, Tony, and Babe kept their flashlights trained on Wojak's men. Babe lowered his flashlight and stepped forward, walking in front of the truck.

"Good evening, Tommy," Babe said. He nodded at Tommy's enforcers who stood at the bushes, frantically pulling up their pants. "Gentlemen."

"Train's not due for a half hour," Wojak said.

"I know. I thought we'd all wait together. Bond. Share some quality time."

He grinned at Wojak.

Tommy stared back at Babe, unhappy. He recoiled at a noise. He looked back at his men and saw one of them tripping over his pants, falling headfirst into a hedge.

Riding the Michigan Central Line, Alfred Polansky woke up
somewhere between St. Louis and Cuba, Missouri. He sat up suddenly, bleary-eyed, lost. At first, he couldn't identify his surround-
ings. Then it hit him. *Sleeper car. Madeline.* His mouth felt dry and
his head pounded. He took a moment to gather himself, the tiny
bed much too small for his girth, the flesh from his ample waist
flopping over the sides of the mattress. He started to remove the
blanket over him and a paper crinkled on his chest. He reached
down and found Madeline's letter. The events of the evening came
rushing back at him. Meeting her, sharing the champagne, making
time with her, nearly passing out in the dining car. He remembered
how she draped her arms around him and guided him to the
sleeper car. But after that? Nothing. It felt as if eight full hours had
been sliced out of his life.

He groaned and looked down at himself. Fully clothed. Even
his shoes. He had imagined getting into bed with Madeline—
dreamed about it—but then his world went dark, as if someone
had temporarily turned out the lights on his every waking moment. He groaned again and stared at the envelope. He hesitated,
then ripped it open and fished out a letter. Before he read it, he
smelled it. He couldn't identify the strong scent—something flowery, definitely perfumed, and extremely sexy. His nostrils flared
and his eyes watered. He gripped her letter between his thick index fingers and stumpy thumbs and he read:

Dearest Alfred,
I'm so sorry we couldn't continue our evening. Too much bubbly.
Ha. Anyway, I decided to get off the train at Glencoe. I wish you

could have come with me. I know. Crazy. Well, if you're ever in Glencoe, look me up and we can pick up where we left off. Here's my number.

Alfred read her number aloud, slowly, as if trying to memorize it.

Then he whispered her two last words:

"Love, Madeline."

He folded the letter, slipped it back into the envelope, and fit the envelope snugly into his jacket pocket. He stood up, swayed, his head still spinning a little. He started to push his way out of the sleeping compartment but stopped at the door. He pulled Madeline's letter out of his pocket, closed his eyes, and gave the envelope another whiff.

MECHANIC

♦

**A CRAPS PLAYER
WHO CONTROLS
THE DICE EXPERTLY,
PERHAPS BY USING
SLEIGHT OF HAND**

37

shock of thunder.

The ground shaking.

A series of piercing whistles.

Three bleats in the distance.

"Train's coming," Wojak said.

He stood on the platform of the rundown, deserted Cuba train station, buffeted by a phalanx of his six men—bodyguards, protectors, mob soldiers—positioned behind him in a semicircle, casting sinister shadows in the moonlight. Babe had embarrassed them, caught them literally with their pants down. They looked pissed off, eager to engage, bent on revenge.

"Late," Babe said.

He stood between Karter and Tony. The box truck, with Carlyle at the wheel, idled behind them, exhaust fumes fanning toward them, fouling and stinking up the air.

"Three minutes," Wojak said. "All the way from Canada. Come on. Give them a break."

"Still late," Babe said, tapping his watch. "I don't like late."

"Stickler," Wojak said.

Babe stared at Wojak, making him turn away.

"And I don't like surprises," Babe said.

The train shrieked and careened around a corner. The wheels tore into the steel tracks and kicked up sparks. A few flew at the men on the platform. They ducked, flicked at the tiny dots of fire. The seven-car mixed freight train from the Michigan Central Line, originating in Toronto thirty-six hours ago, slowed to a crawl, lurched into the deserted Cuba Station, and jerked to a stop. The seven cars of the train seemed to pulsate before steadying. The conductor pulled the whistle again, the sound jolting Wojak.

"Yeah, you're here. We see that," Wojak said. "Fucking guy."

The conductor and the engineer hopped down from the locomotive's cab. They smoothed their uniforms as they walked. A moment later, a single passenger disembarked from the passenger car.

Alfred Polansky.

He waddled toward Wojak, grinned, and extended his stumpy hand.

"Boss."

Wojak ignored Alfred's offer of a handshake.

"Anything?"

Alfred shrugged his thick shoulders. "Uneventful."

"My favorite word," Wojak said.

He made his way through his enforcers and headed over to the boxcar coupled to the locomotive. "Let's unload this thing." He waved at Babe and his men. "Bring your truck over."

Carlyle hung his arms over the steering wheel, waiting for Babe's signal. Babe held up a finger, as if testing for wind. The signal to hold up. Babe stepped into a pool of light, purposely making eye contact with Alfred. Babe had to know right now if Alfred recognized him. He had to call this bet. If Alfred knew him from the train, the night would go bloody in a blink. Babe felt Karter slide next to him. Karter would eliminate Alfred first, not allowing him to escape, to bring word to Chicago. Then he would take out Wojak, no matter how many men formed a wall around him. No wall, no fortress, no number of men would be enough to stop Karter. Babe knew that. Babe didn't want that.

"Evening," Babe said to Alfred with a tip of his hat.

From across the platform, Alfred squinted at Babe.

Alfred stood stock still as if posing for a portrait.

"He recognize you?" Karter mumbled.

"Nah." Babe grinned at Alfred. "Predictable."

Babe smiled wider and waved at Alfred. Alfred's lips undulated into an insincere, half-assed return smile and then he backed up and disappeared into the night shadow.

"RAF," Babe muttered to Karter.

Babe raised his finger again, lowered it quickly, Carlyle's go signal. Carlyle shifted into first gear, brought the truck beyond the locomotive, hit reverse, and backed the box truck in front of the boxcar. He jumped down from the truck's cab and walked toward Karter and Tony, keeping the truck running. Babe spoke to his guys, never taking his eyes off Wojak.

"Kindly help these young men unload the boxcar. Once we get an assembly line started, Karter and I will pitch in. Shouldn't take us long, right, Tommy?"

"Depends how fast your men work. My men are motivated. They want to get back to Chicago. They want to go home."

Babe nodded at the burly, scowling, armed men in their zoot suits.

"Family men," he said.

Karter snickered.

"Open the boxcar," Wojak said.

The engineer crossed to the boxcar, tapped the numbers of a combination into a lock, unclicked the lock, and shoved open the boxcar door with a *clang*. Babe peered inside and saw the neatly piled pallets filled with cases of whiskey. He made a move toward the boxcar.

"Uh-uh," Wojak said.

Tommy rubbed the tips of his fingers.

"Money first, then the whiskey."

To accentuate his point, Wojak's men moved toward Babe. Karter cut in front of Babe and took a step toward the men. That's all it took. One step. All six of the men backed up.

Babe reached into his jacket pocket and produced a stack of bills. He slapped the stack against his thigh. "I've got the money right here. As we agreed. Fifty-four large. But what's in there? I see a boxcar full of wooden crates. I want to make sure that's my whiskey. All of it. Every bottle. High-grade, brown whiskey. As we agreed."

Wojak started to speak. Babe cut him off.

"Not that I don't trust you. It's like you said. I'm a stickler."

Wojak patted his lacquered hairdo. "So, what do you want to do? What are we talking about?"

"I want to sample the whiskey."

Wojak sniffed and hiked up his pants.

"Happy to have you join me," Babe said.

Wojak swiveled his head from the line of men who flanked him, to the boxcar, to Alfred, to Karter, who kept his eyes on all of them without moving a muscle, then back to Babe. Finally, Wojak spoke over his shoulder.

"Open a case," he said.

"Boss," Gregor said, backing up toward the boxcar.

"I got it," Carlyle said.

He stepped onto the boxcar, revealing a crowbar he'd taken from the truck. He and Gregor entered the boxcar together. They kept their eyes on one another as they each took an end of the first crate and carried it off the train. They dropped the crate on the ground between Wojak and Babe. Babe nodded at Carlyle. He swung the crowbar and splintered the case open. Carlyle reached in, grabbed a bottle, and handed it to Babe. Babe offered the bottle to Wojak. "You sure you won't join me?"

Wojak held up his hand.

Babe took his time removing the wrapping around the cork stopper. He eased the cork out of the bottle with a soft *pop*. He tilted his head back and took a swig from the bottle. He sloshed the whiskey in his mouth, swallowed, then took a second pull, this one longer. He looked at Wojak, his eyes opening wide in astonishment.

"Good?" Wojak said. "I know it's not Macallan, but close, right?"

"Taste it," Babe said.

"I'm not much of a drinker. I take your word."

Babe shoved the bottle into Tommy's chest. *"Taste it."*

Babe's tone made Tommy's men step toward them again. Karter drew himself up. The men stopped but held their ground. Several squirmed. One man shook his wrists. Another cracked his knuckles. A third scratched his stomach, his fingers tap-tap-tapping near the long pocket of his zoot suit, two inches from his gun.

Wojak took the bottle from Babe.

He wiped the lip of the glass with his sleeve and took a sip.

He grimaced.

He took another sip.

He spit the contents onto the ground.

"I know Macallan," Babe said. "That's not Macallan. That's not even whiskey. It's Lipton."

"Tea?" Wojak said.

"Yeah," Babe said. "Tea."

Babe pulled another bottle out of the case. He opened it, took a long sip, and swallowed.

"Tea," he said.

"Open another case!" Wojak shouted.

Two men scrambled into the boxcar and hauled out another case of the whiskey. Carlyle tore into the wood with his crowbar, took out two bottles, passed one to Babe, the other to Wojak. Babe and Tommy opened their bottles at the same time, mirroring each other, each taking long gulps. Babe sloshed the liquid in his mouth while Wojak gargled his. They spit them out together, the liquid arcing and splashing on the ground.

"It's *tea*," Babe said.

"Fuck," Wojak said.

Wojak walked in a circle, frantically thrusting his hand through his hair, back and forth. He huffed, making a guttural sound.

Babe lowered his voice.

"What is this, Tommy?" he said.

"Open all the crates!" Wojak screamed. "Every one of them!"

Carlyle, Tony, and four of Tommy's men descended on the pallets in the boxcar. They hauled out case after case, placing them on the ground, stepping aside as Carlyle tore each case open with his crowbar.

"Someone else taste it," Babe said.

Wojak pointed to Gregor and another man. They opened two bottles and started drinking.

"Lipton, definitely," Gregor said.

"I think it's Salada," the other man said.

"Who gives a *fuck*?" Wojak screamed. "It's fucking *tea*!"

Out of the shadows, Karter suddenly appeared in front of Wojak, towering over him. He lowered his hand onto Wojak's shoulder and squeezed. His fingers, sharp as pincers, pressed hard enough to shatter bone. Wojak squealed. Wojak's men moved forward. Karter drew his gun and placed the barrel against Wojak's forehead. The men halted.

"This is your move?" Babe said. "You're trying to sell me tea instead of whiskey? No wonder you wanted the money first."

Tommy swallowed, started to speak, then choked when he heard the click of the hammer of Karter's gun.

"Who's trying to fuck me, Tommy?" Babe said. "The Outfit? Hymie Weiss? Jake Guzik? With all I do for them? Or is it you? Just you. On your own. You going rogue? The new guy, trying to make an impression. Is that it?"

Tommy gagged. "I—no—I don't know how—"

"Shut up," Babe said.

A hush fell across the station platform.

Nobody dared speak that way to a ranking officer in The Outfit.

Nobody.

In particular, a Black man.

"Babe, listen. We can't lose our heads. None of us. Let's all cool off. Give me a chance to figure out what happened."

"You're not doing anything, Tommy. I will. I'm going to contact Chicago myself. I'm calling your boss. I'm calling Hymie Weiss himself. I'll get to the bottom of this. But this exchange isn't happening tonight. The deal's off."

Wojak groaned, a sour sound that rose from his stomach and fired into his throat.

"I doubt we'll be seeing each other again," Babe said. "Actually, after tonight, you may not be seeing anybody again."

"Babe," Wojak said, his voice cracking. "I'm asking you for a favor. This is on me. Let me figure it out. Let me make it right. Please."

"Somebody's trying to fuck you, Tommy. Somebody on the inside."

Babe held for a count of ten before he spoke again.

"Tell your men to back up to the end of platform and stay there in a line until we leave."

Wojak nodded at his men.

The six of them retreated into the dim light of the station platform. They stopped in front of the empty passenger cars.

"Stay there," Wojak said.

Karter lowered his gun.

He and Tony climbed into the open back of the box truck, Karter keeping his gun aimed at Wojak. Carlyle and Babe climbed into the truck's cab. Carlyle hit the accelerator. The truck drove off.

Carlyle drove the truck down a dark side road two miles away and stopped. Babe and Karter vaulted out of the back of the truck and jogged over to the Commander, parked in shadow, barely visible against some high shrubbery. Babe took the wheel.

"I should drive," Karter said.

"Want to keep my mind occupied," Babe said.

The red tip of a matchstick emerged in the corner of Karter's mouth.

"Whew," he said.

"Exactly. We're still in action. Saturday night. The game. The deed."

They drove in silence for a long, slow minute.

"I will win it back," Babe said.

Karter stared into the night. "I know you will."

Back at the desolate train platform in Cuba, Wojak bent over and gripped his knees. He violently rose up, stood tall, arched his back, and screamed a guttural, prehistoric wail that echoed through the night for a solid ten seconds. Then he turned toward his men and screamed again.

"FUCK!"

That's when he saw Alfred.

Trying to hide.

Alfred had slinked away to the far end of the platform. He stood with his back against a telephone booth, almost obscured in darkness.

Almost.

Wojak stared at him. He started walking toward him, taking quick, deliberate steps. Alfred froze. As Wojak came upon him, Alfred reached behind him and felt the cool glass of the phonebooth. He began shaking his head.

"You making a call?" Wojak said.

Wojak and his men surrounded Alfred and the phonebooth.

"No, no, no," Alfred said.

"What are you doing?"

Alfred's voice raised an octave. "I was just—"

"What?"

"Nothing."

"You did this," Wojak said.

"NO."

"You were our man on the train. You were supposed to babysit the boxcar. What did you do?"

Alfred's voice squeaked. "Nothing. I swear. I didn't do nothing. I don't know how it happened. But I had nothing to do with it."

Wojak frowned, his forehead narrowing as he tried to put the pieces together. He nodded at Gregor, who reached inside Alfred's jacket and removed Alfred's gun.

"Did you see anything on the train?" Wojak said.

"No."

"Right. Sure. So, okay, I'm going to start breaking your fingers, one by one."

"I didn't see nothing. I swear on my mother's life."

"Did you talk to anyone on the train?"

Alfred turned white.

Wojak spoke evenly, his voice ice.

"Who did you talk to, Alfred?"

"Nobody. I mean, you know—"

Then, by sheer reflex, Alfred patted his jacket pocket.

An insignificant gesture.

A touch. A tap.

A caress.

Tommy saw it.

"What's in your pocket?"

"Nothing. You know."

Three men blew by Tommy and slammed Alfred into the side of the phonebooth. They opened his jacket, reached inside the pocket, and found Madeline's letter. The first guy handed it to Tommy. Wojak tore open the envelope and read the letter.

"'I'm so sorry we couldn't continue our evening. Too much bubbly. Ha.'"

Wojak looked up and blew the last two words of the letter into Alfred's face.

"'Love, Madeline.'"

"She's someone I met on the train," Alfred said. "We talked."

"And?"

"That was it."

Wojak slapped Alfred across the face.

"*And?*"

"We had a drink. That was *it*. I swear."

"What did she look like?"

"I don't know. Sort of tall. Good looking."

"White or Black?"

"White. What do you think I am?"

"Call the number," Wojak said to Gregor who, letter in hand, had already folded himself inside the phonebooth.

"You had one drink?" Wojak said to Alfred.

"Maybe two," Alfred said miserably.

Wojak slapped him again.

Alfred rubbed his reddening cheek.

"Okay. Three drinks. Four. I don't know. We didn't do nothing."

"Thank you, Operator," Gregor said into the phone.

He hung up and came out of the phonebooth.

"That number is no longer in service," Gregor said.

"Can't be," Alfred said. "You dialed wrong."

"Take care of him," Wojak said to his men.

"Wait, wait, wait, Tommy. I swear—"

The three men came up behind Alfred, lifted him by his armpits, and started pulling him toward the abandoned garage. Alfred fought them at first. Then Gregor belted him in the stomach. Alfred's knees buckled and his chest caved in, the wind and spirit knocked out of him. The men dragged him inside the boarded-up building, Alfred offering no resistance. He started rambling. "Me, Madeline. We talked. We laughed. We had—something."

Wojak's men shut the door.

38

DAWN

abe gunned the Commander, practically standing up
as he drove. He rode the gas pedal like a jockey driving his horse to the finish line. The sudden accelera-
tion slammed Karter back into the passenger's seat, causing the
matchstick to fly out of his mouth. Karter caught the matchstick in
the palm of his hand and popped it back into his mouth.

Babe careened around the corner and pulled in front of his alley
house just in time to see Rosie herding the boys through the front
door. They three of them struggled with a large suitcase.

"No," Babe said.

Babe kicked the car door open and sprinted toward his family.
His sons hesitated, trapped now between their parents. The boys
broke away from Rosie and threw their arms around their father,
circling him, clinging onto his waist and legs. Babe closed his eyes
and caressed each of their heads, one at a time.

"Get in the car with Uncle Montel," Rosie said after a while, her
voice thin but firm. Heads down, the three of them unlocked themselves from Babe and ducked down the alley and into Leaky's
idling Buick.

"Rosie," Babe said.

She stood straight as a soldier, her hands gripping her own bulging suitcase.

Only then did Babe see Rosetta, his Tulip, standing behind her mother. She held her small rose-colored suitcase with one hand. With the other she held Blue, her ragged teddy bear. She squeezed Blue, strangling him. She looked away from Babe. He could tell she had been crying.

"Rosie," Babe said. "Please. I'm taking care of everything. I'm fixing it."

"You gambled the deed. You lost our land."

"Temporarily."

Rosie snarled at him. "Do you have the deed? In your possession?"

"Not yet. I'm working on it. I'll have it by the weekend. That's a promise."

"That's a no."

Babe looked at the ground.

"Oh, I get it," Rosie said. "You're going to win it back in another craps game. Right? Is that your plan?"

Babe couldn't look at her. He couldn't speak. He had turned to stone.

Rosie slowly shook her head. A head shake that meant years. Too many years. Too many indiscretions she'd turned away from, pretended not to see, too many lapses she'd forgiven, too many losses she'd endured. For what? For nothing. Literally.

Nothing.

She'd given him every chance, and she'd waited for him. But she'd waited too long.

She looked into his eyes. She could read his thoughts. Always could.

Forgive me.

No.

I've had to forgive you so many times. I've had to clean up after you too many times.

I can't do it anymore.

I am—exhausted.

And I am finished.

But she only said, "Babe."

The word hit him harder than a punch.

Babe.

She had never called him "Babe" before, not once. Only Floyd. He was Floyd to her. His given name was her pet name, her term of endearment, her special name.

Babe stammered. "You never—never—call me that."

"I do now. You are now Babe. Larger than life. Con man. Rogue. Gambler. Fixer. Legend. *Babe.*"

Rosie came right up into him, her nose brushing his.

"Babe isn't real. Babe is a figment of this town's imagination," she said. "I didn't fall in love with Babe. I didn't marry Babe. I married Floyd. He's real. He's a man. Just a man. He was *my* man." She pulled back. A tear trickled down her cheek. "Everybody in this county calls you Babe. But I never could. I didn't want Babe. I wanted Floyd."

She spun and started to move past him. Babe stepped in front of her, blocking her way. He held up his hand, but his hand trembled.

"Rosie, don't do this," he whispered.

"You gave away our future. For what?"

She drew herself up taller. She seemed to tower over Babe.

That can't happen.

"Please," Babe said.

She shook off his plea.

"This is where we are," Rosie said.

Now he shook his head, struggling to speak.

"We have each other," Babe said. "The two of us. Us, Rosie, *us*."

"There've been others," she said. "I've shut my eyes."

"One-nighters. They don't matter. Never mattered. I've made mistakes. Bad decisions. No more. I'll get the land back, I swear." He swallowed. His throat felt so tight he thought he might strangle.

"I have to start over," Rosie said.

"I do, too. I'm *going* to start over. We'll both start over."

"Without you," Rosie said. "I'm starting over *without you*."

She whispered that, but it came out a scream.

That was it. All she had, all she had to say.

She stepped past Babe, leaving Rosetta standing in the doorway.

"Tulip," Babe said.

Rosetta hesitated. Then she handed him Blue.

"Take him," she said, her eyes filling up. "I don't need him anymore."

39

riving back to Chicago, the three Cadillacs followed
one another in a line, moving with the pace and
gravity of a funeral procession. Gregor drove the
middle car. Wojak sat in the backseat. For hours, Wojak had said
nothing. He knew the soldiers in the other two cars would be
grumbling, bellyaching about how slowly Tommy had them driving. Miles below the speed limit. He didn't give a shit. All he cared
about was coming up with the answer to two simple questions.

Who?

And—

How?

Who switched all the cases?

How did they do it?

Wojak went over each moment in his mind, again and again,
looking for a clue, searching for a flaw, a loophole, trying to un-
scramble the puzzle.

He came up with nothing.

He couldn't see it.

He closed his eyes and felt a pain like a needle drilling into his
head.

"Fuck!" he shouted.

Gregor craned his neck, caught Wojak's eye in the rearview mirror. Wojak turned away, stared out the window.

He chewed his knuckles.

He closed his eyes tighter, tried to drown out every sound on the road, in the car.

Think.

No.

Remember.

No.

Listen.

Then, like a tiny bolt of lightning, he saw it. He heard it. It crackled through him. The slightest flicker. A tell.

He sat forward in his seat.

The truck.

"They kept the truck running," Wojak said. "They wanted to get out quick."

"I don't follow, boss," Gregor said.

"Boyce knew," Wojak said. "He was behind the switch. I don't know how he did it, but I'm going to find out."

Wojak slapped the leather seat next to him.

He leaned forward and barked, "Turn the car around."

TUESDAY, JULY 6, 1948
8:13 P.M.

Floyd "Babe" Boyce sat at the counter of the empty café in the Sportsman Hall. On the stool next to him, he'd placed Blue, Tulip's teddy bear. His head slumped, Babe faced the neon sign—BabyLou's Kitchen—that he had specially made in Paris for Rosie. The red and blue lights doused him. But he didn't notice. He sat in the café, but he felt somewhere else, as if he were lost in his recurring nightmare of running into the infinite wall.

"Looks like it's just me and you, Blue," he said.

He stared into his coffee cup, rotating the cup, watching the liquid swirl. He raised the cup to his mouth and drained the contents. He swallowed and felt his eyes water. He reached into his suit jacket pocket and pulled out his flask. He poured a shot from the flask into the cup. Macallan. His drink. He rubbed his finger over the bullet hole in the flask.

Suddenly, something curled inside his gut. A jolt of heat. A tremor of determination.

"This cannot *be*," he said, violently. "We got to fix this."

He heard a *pop*. Then the red and blue neon lights forming "BabyLou's Kitchen" flashed and sizzled and went out.

"Perfect," Babe said.

Then he laughed.

He actually laughed.

The sign had lasted four years, much longer than he'd anticipated. Talk about timing. The neon sign picked this moment to die.

Even the lights have gone out on me, he thought.

Babe shook his head and stared into Blue's button eyes.

"Wait," he said.

He hopped off his stool and moved behind the counter. He unscrewed the blue neon bulb in the sign, then reached under the counter, fished around, and brought out a lightbulb that he'd purchased some time ago, for this very purpose, in case the light went out. He slowly screwed in the new bulb and stepped back as the blue light came back on.

"There," he said, looking back at Blue. "The sign ain't broken. Just needs new bulbs. I'll pick up the red one tomorrow at the hardware store."

He sighed and peered into the pale blue light that fell down the length of the counter. In that instant, he saw something. The light seemed to form a shimmery blue path. A way out. A neon blue exit ramp. With a sudden certainty, he shoved his hand beneath the counter again and poked his fingers along the shelf below, digging around among silverware rolled up in napkins, second-string salt and pepper shakers, small bottles of Tabasco, and even hotter sauce for those customers who demanded *heat*. His fingers tapping, probing, reaching, poking, and then at last he came upon the objects of his search, what he knew he would find hidden away—

A pair of dice.

His backups.

His emergency pair.

"Bones," he said.

He brought them out from under the counter and dropped them into his palm. He rubbed his thumb over the two tiny cubes—gently, lovingly—as if he'd discovered two long-lost gems. He tilted his head, gawking at them with familiarity, with reverence, with trust, and then with confidence, bordering on cockiness.

"Let's see," he said.

He bent his face directly over the dice, eye to eye with snake eyes, one dot per die, and then he looked up and followed the sparkly blue hue that fell over the laminated surface of the counter. He looked back at the dice in his hand. He began turning them over slowly, staring at the black dots, counting them, until he created the combination he wanted.

"Two fours," Babe said, as if instructing the dice. "Four and four. You hear me? Hard eight. That's what I want, dice. No. That's what I'm telling you. Demanding of you, dice. The hard *eight*."

Then, almost casually, with a sidearm motion, he flung the dice across his body and lobbed them onto the counter. They hit and tumbled and bounced and clattered and slid and came to a shockingly abrupt stop six inches before toppling off the end of the counter, stopping decisively—obediently—each die showing four black dots.

"That's what I'm talking about," Babe said. "Hard *eight*."

He sniffed, brought himself to his full height, then thrust his shoulders back military straight, as if standing at attention. He looked at the neon blue in "BabyLou's Kitchen" and then glanced at Blue perched on the stool at the counter.

"Nah," Babe said. "This ain't over."

♠

AUTHOR'S NOTE

I really hope you enjoyed *Flipping Boxcars*.

A note about the book. It's a work of fiction. I made it all up.

Except for the main character.

Floyd "Babe" Boyce.

He was my grandfather.

Babe was a legend in our family. He was handsome, dapper, suave; a fighter, a gambler, an entrepreneur; and always in *charge*. Babe impacted me in so many ways—how I dress, the way I think, the way I conduct business, how I see the world.

Except . . .

I never met him.

I've only seen one photograph of him, in his army uniform. But that photograph spoke to me. I felt connected to him. It was almost as if he were speaking directly to me. I could imagine his confidence, his style, his gift of gab. Family lore filled in some of the blanks about Babe—his sense of humor, his charm, his sophistication, his business acumen, and his love of gambling, especially craps, which was his passion, his obsession.

Rosie, Babe's wife, my grandmother, was real, too. She was a woman ahead of her time. She was smart, entrepreneurial, tough, a midwife, a teacher, a fantastic cook, and a doting, strong, and loving mom, Babe's better half. Carl Holt, the town's sheriff, was also a real person. And Caruthersville, where the book takes place, is an actual town. The Sportsman Hall, the riverboat, all the stores and streets I mention, and the legendary Fourth of July festivities, including the greased pole climbing contest and its perennial winner Sonny Agnew—all real. I should know. I grew up in Caruthersville.

Babe and Rosie had four children—three sons and a daughter. Floyd and Lloyd, the twins, and Melvin were my uncles. Rosetta, whom Babe called Tulip, six years old in the book, brilliant, funny, and wise beyond her years—was my mother.

All the rest of it, the story—the events of those five days that occurred over Fourth of July weekend in 1948—all made up.

I would never let facts get in the way of a good story.

I'll holla,

Cedric

ACKNOWLEDGMENTS

God bless our elders! We live in a time where true extended family connection is getting lost. As a boy, I and many of my generation were surrounded by uncles, aunts, and cousins. Now its rare families even talk with members beyond those they live with, let alone see each other outside of holidays. The family unit has been severed by a number of causes: the passing of the baby boomer generation, the rise of single parent households in the '70s and '80s, the mass incarceration of fathers throughout the '80s and '90s, and much more; however, if you are fortunate enough to have one or two older relatives who qualify as the griots of your family, you are lucky.

Appreciate them. Talk to them.

You remain connected to your linage through those wonderful storytellers. It's even, in part, how this book came together.

The story of my grandfather Babe Boyce (whom I have never met) was first told to me by my loving mother, uncles, and relatives. The bits and pieces of his life opened up my imagination to a man that at times I could see so clearly I could smell his cologne. The collection of those moments shared with me throughout my life inspired me to write this novel. This tale is about a man with whom I share a bloodline, an entrepreneurial spirit, dogmatic drive and determination, charisma, hustle, and wit blended with a willingness to take great risks in order to live the life you imagine. I inherited all of that DNA, so the first person I must thank is my grandfather and my extended family all the way up the family tree. We are FAMILY.

This is my second book, but first novel. Any writer will tell you that you're rarely the same person from the start of your journey to your finished product. Writing asks a lot of you; you must dig and discover stuff about yourself and others, and engage in deep and trivial conversations about dates, past events, language, and who has proof. Its challenging, stressful, and rewarding all at once. I'd like to also thank the following people who were a part of this journey with me. You are all important contributors.

Though this book is a fictional tale of my grandfather, it's really an ode to the resiliency of my wonderful grandmother Rosie Boyce, whose dedication to her family and her dreams taught us all to push forward.

To my loving and dynamic mother, Rosetta Boyce Kyles (deceased). Thank you, Mommy, for sharing your stories, thirst for higher learning, spirit, and laughter.

My uncle Melvin Boyce, I could not have captured this world without you!

Sharita, my sister, you are my guiding star, always there shining a light that will lead me home.

Yasmine Coleman, my cousin and assistant, thank you for your research digging into the family history and always being available to me.

My aunt Peggye Jackson, the family historian, your stories helped to shape my fictional world.

Alan Eisenstock! You are the man! From our earliest meetings,

ACKNOWLEDGMENTS

your enthusiasm about helping me shape this idea was exactly what I needed to bring this train into the station. Thank you!

Patrik Bass, from the day you came on board your passion and professionalism have been just what the author ordered (LOL).

I am surrounded by very capable professionals who help to make my many dreams come true.

The top of that list is "Swanny"—my longtime friend, manager, and business partner—Eric C. Rhone.

My agents at CAA: Anthony Mattero for shepherding this project, and my day one guy, "Mr. Makes Things Happen," Steve Smooke. My attorney, Gordon Bobb; my PR team of Arnold Robinson and Lucine Chammas; and big shout-out to my uncle Erick "Big E" Hubbard.

A special thank you to the people and memories of my hometown, Caruthersville, Missouri.

I am grateful for the love and support of my beautiful wife, Lorna Kyles. You are my muse. I love you.

My children: Tiara, Croix, and Lucky, and my grandcookie, Kylo. To my sister-in-law, Angie Wells, you rock always.

Thank you all for your love and support. I'll holla!

Cedric

GLOSSARY

Big Red—seven

bones—dice

boxcars—twelve the hard way, two sixes

collar a nod—take a nap

crap out—throwing two, three, or twelve on the first roll and, therefore, losing

easy way—rolling four, six, eight, or ten with any combination, except for doubles

first thing smoking—a train

front line—a bet placed before the shooter rolls the dice to start a game; bettors win on seven or eleven, lose on two, three, or twelve

gate—any man, in a greeting

gum beater—blowhard, braggart

hi-lo—a bet on two or twelve

hummer—exceptionally good

jelly or jelly roll—sex

legs—a combination of two or more bets set up in advance, which together make a single bet. In order to win, you must win every "leg" of the bet. Also known as a "parlay."

mechanic—a craps player who controls the dice expertly, perhaps by using sleight of hand

midnight—twelve

press it up—raise the bet

♠

GLOSSARY

square pair—two fours, also called "hard eight"

stroker—a player who makes overly complicated bets and causes dealers to work harder, unnecessarily, usually pissing them off

take down—removing your bets

woofing—aimless talk

wrong way—betting against the dice

♠